THE RIVER K

The *Maple Leaf C* making the turn on its big set.

ILLUSTRATION BY REBEKAH PARLEE

The River KILLERS

BRUCE Burrows

TouchWood
Editions

TouchWood Editions
www.touchwoodeditions.com

LIBRARY AND ARCHIVES CANADA CATALOGUING IN PUBLICATION
Burrows, Bruce, 1946–
The river killers / Bruce Burrows.

Issued also in electronic formats.
ISBN 978-1-926971-56-8

I. Title.

PS8603.U7474R57 2011   C813'.6   C2011-904175-8

Editor: Linda Richards
Proofreader: Lenore Hietkamp
Design: Pete Kohut
Cover image: Kayak Bill

We gratefully acknowledge the financial support for our publishing activities
from the Government of Canada through the Canada Book Fund, Canada
Council for the Arts, and the province of British Columbia through the
British Columbia Arts Council and the Book Publishing Tax Credit.

The interior pages of this book have been printed on 100% post-consumer
recycled paper, processed chlorine free, and printed with vegetable-based inks.

This is a work of fiction and all the characters are made up,
including the boats. Only the *Maple Leaf C*, *Ryu II*, *W 10*, *Jessie Isle*,
James Sinclair, and *W.E. Ricker* are, or once were, real boat names.

1 2 3 4 5 15 14 13 12 11

PRINTED IN CANADA

This book is intended as a salute to all the people who venture onto the ocean to try and make a living, and an extended middle digit to the people who try and prevent them from doing so.

To the hardworking, dedicated people at DFO who do not deserve the disparagement expressed in this book, both of you have my deepest sympathy.

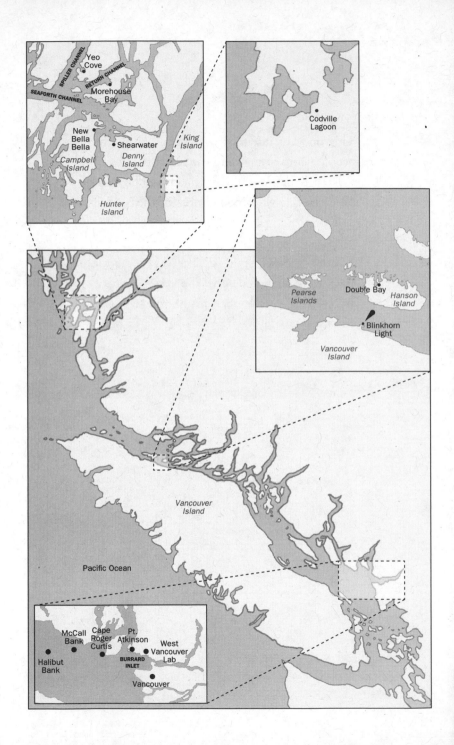

One

Four seine boats surged out of the narrow pass like killer whales on the hunt. There had been no salmon in Double Bay, so now the boats were on the move, hungry for prey. The three aluminum boats, sleek and fast, turned south and headed down Johnstone Strait. The old wooden boat, lower and slower in the water, wallowed heavily across the strait toward the Blinkhorn light.

That was us then, the old *Maple Leaf C* and her crew of five hard-working but still poor fishermen. Flash forward to now: imprisoned in an Ottawa office, I surrendered to the flood of memories, the feel of the sun hot on my neck, the glare that dazzled across the water and the five of us on the bridge of the old *Maple Leaf*. We were desperately looking for fish in hope of making some money before the end of salmon season. It had been a tough year for us, relatively fishless but definitely not painless. More breakdowns than fish and more times in the wrong spot than the hot spot. However, hope springs eternal for fishermen as well as Leafs fans, and we were blessed in addition with the mindless optimism of the young.

Who am I? Daniel Edward "Danny" Swanson. My clan inhabits coastal BC like ubiquitous hobbits, humanoid but genetically distinct enough to form our own subspecies. We mostly log, some of us fish, mine a little, but always in a symbiotic relationship with the big machines that are the other dominant species in our habitat. We work with them, we work on them, and, some would say, work for them.

The females of our clan, as well as the males, could go on at length about the relative merits of hoe-chuckers versus grapple yarders. Our young could identify D-8 cats and articulated skidders before they learned Mother Goose. The relationship was intimate, although it had not yet led to actual interbreeding, even if we did wonder about Uncle Zeke.

When one of my young nephews asked why Daddy's loader wasn't eating supper with us, it was pointed out that the machine wouldn't fit through the door. And my aunt muttered that that was the only damn reason.

So there I was, one of the five humans who functioned as replaceable components in the complex hunting machine that is a West Coast seine boat. It was a mid-August afternoon, 1996. The whole crew was operating on caffeine consciousness after fishing for thirty straight hours, fighting to remain alert, straining tired eyes and burnt out synapses in the effort to spot a sockeye jumping.

As we approached Blinkhorn light we could see seven boats already there, so we turned slightly, looking for open water where we could make a set. Skipper Mark spotted the jumper, the distinctive anxious lunge of a sockeye close in to the beach. "Get ready, guys! Beach set."

Fergie and I scrambled into the skiff, which was being towed bow up off the stern of the *Maple Leaf C*. Billy and Christine took up their stations by the drum and the winch. Mark guided the big boat dangerously close to the cliff that rose almost vertically from the water. We scanned the rock face intently, looking first for a place where we could land the skiff, and then something to tie to. Mark yelled and pointed from the bridge and we could see the spot, a narrow shelf of rock just above the waterline, a crevice scarring the clean rock face, and thirty feet above, a finger of rock that could serve as a natural bollard. He swung the boat hard over and we circled for another pass. This time we'd be going for the tie-up and my stomach knotted hard. The tide was running like a river and I knew it would be tricky. There were lots of ways to screw up, but only one acceptable result: get the goddamn end of the net tied to the goddamn beach. Fergie and I might not have been the best skiff crew on the coast, but we'd never missed a tie-up and sometimes we were too proud of that. Occasionally we'd taken chances that other guys hadn't gotten away with. There were enough ways to get hurt doing this job without pushing your luck. No time now to ponder risk factors and safety rules. Just pretend that neither existed.

We bore down on the tie-up spot. Mark blew the horn and lots of different things started to happen all at once. Billy hit the pelican hook with a hammer, causing it to release the skiff line. The bow of the skiff dropped sharply. Maintaining my balance, I threw the sea anchor into the boiling wake and started feeding slack from the coiled beach line into the water. The sea anchor dug into the water and started to pull the net off the drum. I prayed it would come off clean and not backlash as the drum turned faster and faster. I knew Billy would be peering around the corner of the drum stand, watching the net intently for embryonic screwups while dodging bights of heavy lead line that threatened to break his neck. Fergie, standing in the stern of the skiff, was leaning hard on the oars, driving us toward the rock shelf where we would land. I continued to feed slack into the water, just enough so that the skiff was free to move forward but not enough to loop back and tangle Fergie's oars. The bow of the skiff hit the rock and I jumped, beach line in hand and strap over my shoulder.

Now came the hard part. I had to shimmy up the crevice, dragging the inch-and-seven-eighths beach line and heavy strap with me. I had to get up to the rock finger and tie the beach line to it, and do it quickly. Grunting and cursing, I started the climb. The skin on my knees and back was not standing up at all well to the abrasive rock. But urgency trumped pain. The net, with one end of the beach line attached to it, was drifting downstream with the fast-moving tide. The beach line was only twenty fathoms long and in about one minute it would start to pull away from me.

Adrenaline is a very good painkiller, so I ignored the skin I was shedding and dragged the beach line upwards. Sweat threatened to blind me as I gasped for breath. The net was almost all off the drum, the corks forming a long "C" in the water, a full quarter mile from end to end. Our end of the net, which had been upstream of the tie-up spot, had drifted down to a spot directly below and was starting to pull away from me. I was running out of time.

I reached the top of the crevice, level with the rock finger. I threw the rope strap over it like tossing a hoop over a peg. It settled down to the base of the finger with just enough slack that I could tie the beach line to it. With the last of my strength, I pulled on the beach line, getting out all the slack. I started tying the beach knot, quickly, like a cowboy wrapping the legs of a roped calf. Taking a bight of beach line, I passed it under and around the strap. The tide was running hard, so I did a wrap and a half, then two wraps back around the beach line itself. I'd calculated the length of the bight perfectly so that there was just enough of a loop left to pull a bight of slack through it and begin the chain. The beach line was coming tight now as the tide applied tons of force to the net. That force was transferred to the beach line and along it to the knot that I was attempting to tie. As the line tightened up, the knot would slip, so I had to make sure my hand wasn't caught in a loop as I pulled through the last bights of the chain.

And then it was done. The line strained tightly from the end of the net to the strap around the rock. Water dripped from the line, wrung out as the rope stretched and shrank under the strain. With a sudden shock, the knot slipped and scrunched up tight, smoking from the friction. I cringed momentarily before remembering how brave I was. Fergie was standing in the skiff, lounging over his oars. He shook his head. "Couldn't have done it better myself."

"You couldn't have done it, period," I gasped. "This was a job for a highly tuned physical machine. Got a light?"

Fergie laughed and threw me his lighter, then turned and rowed out to the end of the net to untie the sea anchor. I carefully coiled the bitter end of the beach line on the upstream side of the rock. There was a bit of a ledge I could stand on when the time came to release the knot.

My breathing was almost back to normal, so I lit a cigarette. I leaned back against the cliff, enjoying once again the feeling of having done it, pulled off a tough one. The set looked good. Our end of the net had pulled out of the water a little as the beach line tightened up. I followed the line of white corks as they traced a shallow arc through the green waters of Johnstone Strait. Almost a quarter mile away, the *Maple Leaf C* held the other end of the net against the tide so the fish would be pushed into it. That was the advantage of a beach set as opposed to an open set, where the net just drifted in the water.

From my vantage point on the cliff, I saw them first: schools of sockeye, heading right for the middle of the net. I yelled and pointed. "Going in! Going in!"

Mark saw them too. Black smoke belched from the stack of the *Maple Leaf C* as Mark pushed the throttle ahead. He wasn't just holding the end of the net now, but pulling it upstream to a point where he could turn and tow it back toward the beach. As the boat pulled on the outside end of the net the strain was transferred to our end. The beach line creaked and stretched even more. It had shrunk under the strain to less than half of its normal diameter. I cowered away expecting it to snap. "Look out, Fergie. She's gettin' tight."

Fergie was concentrating on the sockeye. They were no longer swimming like tame little piggies toward the middle of the net. They'd turned and were coming our way, threatening to escape around the end of the net. Fergie started banging on the skiff and I found some rocks and hurled them into the water. The banging and splashing had an effect and the fish turned again toward the middle of the net.

The *Maple Leaf C* had started the turn. Heeled hard over, she shuddered and strained as she towed her end of the net around in the beginnings of a circle. Soon she was pulling straight toward us, and I could see Billy standing by the drum, frantically popping the plunger in and out of the water to scare the fish from swimming out his end. The winch was screaming as Christine wound in the slack in the running line. I watched Mark on the bridge. He was motionless, almost rigid at the wheel. He knew what we all knew. This was a big one, maybe a whole season's worth of fish in one set.

As the big old seine boat slowly pulled closer to us, dragging one end of the net with her, we all felt the tension build. There was the realization that a valuable catch was almost, but not quite, within our grasp. For me, there was the additional tension of hoping but not knowing if the beach knot would release when it was supposed to. Because if it didn't, I would have to cut the strap, and I was hoping not to have to get anywhere near a rope straining that close to the breaking point. It was quivering with a pent up force that could kill when unleashed. And it was my job to unleash it.

As a small boy, I'd taken immense pleasure in hunting flies with an elastic band. As they bumbled and buzzed against the windowpane, I'd pull the elastic tight, aim, and then let it snap. The result was almost always a messily squashed fly. It was too much fun to feel guilty about then, but now I was subject to an occasional foreboding of karmic justice. I was now the fly, the beach line was the elastic band, and I half feared some malign insect spirit seeking retribution.

There had been too many beach men snapped into oblivion by beach lines breaking, beach lines whip-lashing free of a hang-up, or beach lines coming tight at the wrong time. And whenever that happened, another green kid squashed like a fly, the big fishing companies that owned most of the seine boats would send to town for another box of beach men. Expendability was an unfortunate fact of our profession. But what the hell. Me? I was nineteen years old and bulletproof. Occasional intimations of mortality were brushed aside as signs of weakness. Not me. Not me.

I shrugged involuntarily as I dismissed these unpleasant musings. Only the immediate reality was important. And that reality was that we were on the verge of completing a really big set. The big boat was only one hundred feet from us now and my mind emptied, focusing only on Mark, waiting for the signal to release the beach line.

Two years earlier, we'd had an incident that was laughable (after the fact) as a result of mixed-up signals. At the time, the signal to release had been a simple wave of the hand. But on one occasion, Mark had been beset by a wasp. As he frantically tried to brush it away, I'd mistaken his gesticulations for *the signal*, and I'd let the beach line go prematurely. Ejaculations ensued. And so it was that *the signal* was changed to a wave of the hat.

So when I noticed that Mark wasn't wearing his hat, I felt a pang of unease. But seine boat skippers are nothing if not cool and resourceful. As I watched, Mark carefully and slowly reached down to the shelf under the controls, grabbed his hat, and put it on his head. Then he immediately pulled it off and began waving it frantically. I picked up the end of the beach line, braced myself carefully, and gave a sharp pull. The knot was supposed to unravel and come undone. It didn't.

I felt a sinking sensation in my stomach, but I set my feet farther apart, took a firmer grip on the rope, and pulled for all I was worth. There was a loud crack and the line simply disappeared. When it reappeared, it was floating flaccidly in the water, one end still attached to the net.

My specific job, the role of the beach man, had now been successfully completed. Relief energized me as I scrambled down the cliff and leapt into the skiff. "Giv'er," I yelled and Fergie rowed hard, not to where the big boat was but to where we knew she would be as she closed the circle of net.

As the skiff surged through the water, I grabbed the free end of the beach line and pulled the slack into the skiff. When all the slack was out of the rope, I kept pulling, which served to aid Fergie's rowing. Speed was important as we were needed back on deck. In about one minute and thirty seconds, the combination of the *Maple Leaf* towing on one end of the net and the deck winch pulling on the end that we had just released would result in closure of the circle trap.

The skiff bounced off the bow of the big boat, and I grabbed the line that had been rigged from bow to midships. As Fergie stowed his oars and pulled the oarlocks, I held on as the big boat continued to move ahead and the skiff slid back. When we reached the center cleat, I swung aboard and secured the skiff. Fergie was right behind me and went immediately to the port-side davit. I leapt back into the skiff and began coiling the beach line in readiness for the next set. Another hard-won safety lesson came into play here. Even though the skiff was rocking in the swell of boats roaring by, I was careful not to grab the side of the skiff for balance. Fingers caught between the skiff and the big boat would be squished like bananas between bulldozers.

While I was coiling the line, Christine and Fergie were completing a crucial segment of the set. Ever since we'd released our end of the net by undoing the beach line, Christine had been pulling it in toward the boat via the running line and the deck winch. She was good at this and always managed to pull hard enough to get the end in quickly without pulling too hard and breaking the running line. Fishing is ever so much the fine balance between "as hard as possible" and not "too hard."

As the end of the net was pulled up to the boat, Christine slowed and then stopped the winch. Fergie leaned over the railing, grabbed the safety strap, and, careful to get it on the right side of the running line, draped it over the purpose-built cleat. He yelled, "Down!" and Christine reversed the winch. As the running line came slack, Fergie pulled the blondie, releasing the metal link that attached running line to pursing line.

Christine then popped the winch into neutral and began pulling slack off the winch, so that Fergie could pull the line sternward about fifteen feet and feed it into the pursing block. He closed the block, yelled an okay, and Christine put the winch into forward so we could begin pursing up. We'd enclosed the fish by pulling the net into a circle, but they could still swim out the bottom. When the pursing process was completed, we would have closed that hole like closing a drawstring purse and the fish would have nowhere to escape.

Meanwhile, Billy had started to wind the net onto the drum. As the drum pulled in the rope that led to the end of the net, the wire cable that had served as the tow cable for the net came slack. While the net continued to wrap onto the drum, Billy carefully disengaged the big steel hook on the end of the tow cable and threw it free. He had to do it in such a way that neither he nor the cable became caught up in the net and wound onto the drum. This was another potential screwup that could not only ruin the set but ruin a drum man too. And we didn't want to see Billy wrapped onto the drum because, humanitarian considerations aside, he was the most important guy on the boat now. It was his skill at winding the net properly onto the drum, picking up the right amount of lead line, and making the corner after the rings came up that was now crucial for the success of the set.

As Billy wound in the net, using the spoolers to pile the net evenly, with the wraps tight to one another and no lead line rolling over the cork line, the circle of net shrank inexorably. Simultaneously, Christine wound in the purse line/drawstring at just the right speed. Fergie strained to pull the slack out of the end line, which gathered up the bunt end of the net, and I ran over to help him. Taking up my station by the drum, I saw a sockeye jump along the cork line, then another. "Inside!" I yelled. Mark had come down off the bridge and was trying hard not to look anxious. "Maybe we got 'em this time," he said.

With over half the net wound onto the drum, the purse line was tight and vibrating. As we peered over the side, watching for the shiny brass rings of our big drawstring purse to be pulled up to the surface, we saw bubbles forming in the water. "Holy shit," said Mark. "We might have to braille this one."

The bubbles told us there were a hell of a lot of fish in the net, their collective exhalations forming bubbles of carbon dioxide. We didn't have a stern ramp, so if there were too many fish to pull over the stern, anything over about fifteen hundred, we'd have to dip them out with individual scoops of the brailler, a dip net that could pick up a hundred or so fish at a time.

We saw the brass purse rings appearing out of the depths. "Coming up," I yelled, picking up the hairpin. Billy stopped the drum and ran the spoolers all the way over to our side. Christine slowed the pursing winch. The purse line had formed a "V" down into the water. But as the last of the slack was pulled out of it, the "V" was stretched into a straight line with the purse rings pulled neatly into a bunch. At this point, I yelled, "Whoa!" and Christine stopped the winch. I rammed the hairpin through the rings, threading them like rings on a crooked finger.

"Going up," I yelled and Christine activated the boom winch, which wound in the cable attached to the hairpin. We lifted it so that the hairpin and rings were suspended about two feet above the cap rail.

"By Christ, we've got 'em now," Mark yelled. And we did. Barring accidents such as tears in the net or the cork line sinking, the fish were trapped. And it looked like there were lots of them.

"Drum slow," ordered Mark. "Get the skiff around and pull some corks."

Fergie and I jumped back into the skiff and pulled it around to the other side of the *Maple Leaf*. We started pulling corks into the skiff, so the net wouldn't drift around the bow of the big boat, which would make impossible drumming in more net. As Billy continued to drum slowly, the circle of net drew ever smaller. The fish were concentrated in a smaller and smaller bag. They began to boil in the net like a single writhing creature. I'd never before seen a set this big.

The weight of the fish was threatening to sink the net so we tied the corkline to the skiff. The fabric of the net was rigid with strain. The tons of fish in the net were threatening to rip the mesh. "Hold 'er!" Mark yelled. "We'll never pull this over. Let's braille 'em."

Fergie and I leapt back out of the skiff again and onto the deck of the *Maple Leaf*. I was beginning to feel like a sand flea, leaping from one warm body to another. But I might have become a very rich sand flea. Getting a set so big that you had to braille was rare. And getting that big a set of sockeye, the money fish, was like winning the lottery. There were only a couple more moves to complete and then we could start hauling them aboard.

There were still six rings suspended on the hairpin. We needed to use that winch line, so we dropped the hairpin and tied off the six rings to the cleat by the drum. Then, after detaching the hairpin, we strapped the net and, with Billy using the spoolers to pull slack off the drum, we pulled one end of the bag high into the air.

God, that felt good. The net pulled up to the boom was like a flag signal to the rest of the fleet: "We've got a big one. Eee hah!!" And we began drying up.

Drying up entailed pulling up all the slack web in the net so as to concentrate the fish into a brailleable mass. And concentrate us as well, for visions of sugarplums were threatening to disrupt our careful moves. But by God, there wasn't much slack. Our net formed a bag almost one hundred feet deep. And the only reason we couldn't pull up slack web was because there wasn't any. The whole damn bag was solid with fish. This was so good it was scary.

So we strapped the bight of the net we'd pulled up with the single fall, secured it to a cleat, and then dropped the line. And attached that line to the brailler. "Okay, guys. Let's start dipping them."

And we did. Using the brailler, a dip net raised and lowered by the single fall, we repeatedly scooped into the bag of fish we'd gathered by the side of the boat. Again and again, we lifted braillers quivering with sockeye out of the water and into our hatch. There they fell into an ice and water slush that would keep them fresh and palatable and occasionally alive until the point of delivery. And we counted the scoops. We were, after all, mercenaries.

Each brailler held, conservatively, seventy-five fish at a six-pound average. In those days, we were getting a buck eighty a pound for sockeye. So by the time we'd dumped fifty braillers into our hatch, we'd reached a gross value of forty thousand five hundred dollars. The standard crew share, a union agreement from fifty years before, was seven/elevenths of the value of the catch after fuel and grub were deducted. There were five of us so our individual split worked out to almost thirteen percent of the gross. Already I'd made over five grand and there were still lots of fish in the net. I'd be able to pay my entire tuition at Simon Fraser University in the fall and maybe not have to work in the campus cafeteria.

Not bad for what was now approaching two hours of work. But it was this conception of huge amounts of money for short periods of work that underlay much of the animosity that the public held for commercial fishermen. Never mind that we'd already fished for almost three months and had made next to nothing. And there were the previous months of network and boat work in preparation for the season. Theoretically that should have been paid work, but the reality was that it often became a condition of keeping your job. So I didn't feel guilty in the least that we'd finally, finally cashed a winning lotto ticket. In fact, I felt pretty damn good.

By this time, we were all sweating from the effort of pulling the brailler through the bag of fish, lifting and swinging it over the hatch, dumping the fish, and then dragging the brailler back to dip it one more time into the writhing mass of trapped fish. We were starting to shed our hot and smelly rain gear, settling into a rhythm, and abandoning ourselves to the wet and slime. It was probably by about the seventy-fifth brailler that we noticed the strange fish. It was actually Christine who saw it, and it was purely by chance. Every once in a while when we dumped a bag of fish, some would miss the hatch and spill onto the deck. And one of those semi-escapees was the weird one. It was twice the size of a normal sockeye, and misshapen. The head and forward body looked like a deck bucket. The nether parts tapered to a serpent-like tail. The color was a dull, sickly green rather than the vibrant, healthy green of a normal sockeye. Despite the deformities, it somehow demanded recognition as a sockeye in the same way that a six-legged cow fetus is still unmistakably bovine.

When Christine pointed it out, we all stared at it and gave our heads a collective shake. There were a few attempts at identification; most centering around improbable crosses between salmon species, or even hybrids between salmon and other fish such as wolf eels. But we quickly laid it aside to ponder over later, and went back to work.

By the time we'd brailled all the salmon out of the net, it was ten at night, four hours after the closure of the fishery, and we were exhausted but euphoric. The *Maple Leaf C* was lower in the water than I'd ever seen her. Water was coming in through the scuppers rather than draining out. The other seine boats steaming by had all saluted us with congratulatory blasts on their whistles and thumbs-up from their crews, but their wakes were beginning to present a hint of danger. As low as we were in the water, it wouldn't take much to heel us over past the point of recovery. We guessed we had more than seventeen thousand fish aboard, over one hundred thousand pounds, almost all of it from that one amazing set.

It's a bit strange to me now, thinking back on how tired and delirious we all were as we de-rigged and Mark slowly turned the boat toward Alert Bay, that anyone even noticed the Frankenfish, stuck in the scuppers and in danger of being washed overboard. Billy grabbed it, ran a string through its gills and tied it to the deck winch. Just so, he explained, he could show it to the other crews on the weekend. It dangled there, one bulging eye staring at us reproachfully as we took off the rest of our rain gear and crowded into the galley. As I gave it a final glance before closing the galley door, I noticed the tag. A red plastic strip was threaded through the anal fin. I looked closer and at one end of the tag I made out the characters "PC-102." Strange. What the hell was a fish like that doing wearing a tag? I grabbed a pair of Vise-Grips off the tool shelf and clamped them onto the tag. I started to pull the tag out, then thought better of it. In this case, the tag should stay with the fish. I released the Vise-Grips and idly noted the grid of indentations they'd left on the plastic tag.

Mark slammed a forty pounder of vodka onto the galley table and went back to the wheelhouse. The rest of us sloshed healthy amounts into coffee mugs and grinned at each other in a wordless toast. We slumped on the bench around the table and began the traditional bantering about how many fish we had. Normally we all guessed an amount and whoever was closest would get ten or twenty bucks from the losers. This week, feeling stakey, we increased the bet to fifty dollars a head.

When we'd all stated our guesses, we began to speculate in earnest about the weird fish, quickly named Igor, which for some reason was more prominent in our minds than the seventeen thousand sockeye in our hatch. By the time we were on our second or third vodka, the theories had crossed the line between orthodox and quasi science and had plunged deep into the twilight zone. Billy pulled us back to reality. "Hey, you know what? It must be one of those Expo fish."

It made sense. As part of the international exposition held in Vancouver in 1986, a whole bunch of salmon, mostly coho, had been raised and released. They were tagged and when caught by sports fishermen would win him a large cash prize. Commercial fishermen weren't supposed to be part of the picture, but no one had told the fish. This one, probably second- or third-generation, had strayed out of the sportsfishing preserve that was the Strait of Georgia, and had ventured into our territory, Johnstone Strait.

"Jeez," Fergie said. "I know they were trying to breed them especially big but they must have produced some mutants. I wonder if our ugly little bastard will still qualify for a prize."

"Bonus!" said Billy. "I'll take it down to Vancouver and tell 'em I caught it using sport tackle. If they ask me what kind of gear, I'll tell 'em a number two black wall of death. Wait'll the papers get photos of it. Maybe it'll win the ugly fish award. When I come back, we'll split the cash."

He was burbling like a happy kid. He could hardly wait to get to Vancouver and return triumphantly with the prize.

But he never came back. He left for Vancouver after network the next day, and fell off the face of the earth. Christine, who was cat-sitting for him, had tried to phone Billy a few hours after he left but couldn't get him. Presumably he was in the wireless dead zone between Port McNeill and Campbell River. The unfortunate message she was forced to leave was that Billy's cat had died, suddenly and strangely, of convulsions. As time passed, and it became evident that we wouldn't have the chance to commiserate with him, the minor detail of his cat's death faded from memory.

When the cops suggested Billy had taken the prize money and run, we just stared at them. Not possible. Billy was our crewmate. More likely he'd been in full party mode and had fallen in with some bad people. And, as we found out, there'd been no prize money. Billy had been seen on the Vancouver ferry by other fishermen, and presumably his first stop would have been the Department of Fisheries and Oceans lab in West Vancouver, where they'd produced the Expo fish. But there was no record at the DFO lab of either Billy or Igor. And besides, they claimed they'd never produced any mutant sockeye, just ordinary everyday coho.

Billy disappeared eight years ago, and there had been absolutely no trace of him since.

Until now.

Two

The money from our big set financed another year at university for me. That was the last decent money I ever earned fishing. Although we didn't know it at the time, the salmon fleet had been targeted for "rationalization," also known as "downsizing" or "reducing capacity," or just "getting rid of the fuckers." To this day, I don't see anything "rational" about it, but the result was that within three years all the participants that had gloried in that big set, including the *Maple Leaf C*, were no longer fishing salmon. Sometimes I felt sadder for her than for us.

I loved that big old boat. She was the best seaboat I ever worked on. She was spacious and *wooden;* none of the clanging noisiness of steel, none of the cork-on-the-wave bounciness of aluminum, and none of the interior coldness of fiberglass. Years later, I met a guy who had deckhanded on her after I did, and he was a little more equivocal. "A comfortable ride, but the good news was that she had an excellent pumping system. The bad news was that she needed it." A tale of neglect that bothered me more than was sensible. Because she'd never betrayed our trust, had delivered us from the worst attacks of Hecate Strait. And we'd abandoned her to the ravages of time. Just one more quantum of guilt to add to my overall total, one more specific sin added to my generic Homo sapiens rap sheet of omission, commission, and submission.

For I had landed on my feet, after all. A degree in marine biology had led me to my present exalted station, working for the Department of Fisheries and Oceans in Ottawa. Current project: health, salmonids—an overview. What do we know and how reliable is our information? Not bloody much and very bloody little.

I felt like a bit of a turncoat, working for *The* Department of

Fisheries and Oceans. Fishermen called it DFO, dropping the definite article because the department defined indefiniteness. But amid the fuzz and haze of bureaucracy, the Wizard of Oz façade, and Mad Hatter twaddle, there lurked the odd rare soul who cared about fish and their environment. I hoped to find them and establish communication.

Mark had gotten into the one really stable fishery on the BC coast: halibut. Fergie was pounding nails instead of shooters and actually had a couple of guys working for him. Christine had run her own gillnetter for a few years but had finally acquiesced to the inevitable and sold it. Not wanting to leave the water, she had joined the Coast Guard and had managed to survive the cutbacks there.

It felt strange to relive those memories now. I was so far away from the where of it and the when of it, and even the *who* of it. The nineteen-year-old kid who had lived that one glorious day in an orgasm of sweat and blood was now me, an adult bureaucrat, not so much living as surviving, dreary day after distinctly unorgasmic day.

Even stranger was that in this of all places, I should come across any connection to those long ago events. It stared at me from my computer screen, as ugly as ever, with bulging baleful eyes. It was a harsh flat-light mug shot of Igor the Frankenfish, of whom DFO had denied any knowledge. Yet here it was in a DFO data bank. The high-resolution jpeg format permitted a detailed view of the fish. It was somewhat mutilated, looking like something had chewed a chunk off the tail. But I could make out the red tag, marked PC-102, and the pattern of indentations left by the Vise-Grips I'd wielded eight years earlier.

Memories segued into thoughts. We had been told the fish was never delivered to the DFO lab. So who took its picture and entered it into a DFO data bank? Why was there no record of the delivery of the fish, or Billy, the person who had delivered it?

Billy, Billy, what happened to you? You left Sointula on Wednesday morning. I know you were hungover. By the time you got on the ferry at Nanaimo, you'd probably had a few beers at the pub next to the terminal. Smug and Snuffy off the *Island Gale* told me that you sat in their van and had a few more beers on the voyage to Vancouver. And had lied seriously about our catch. Like all commercial fishermen, you downgraded our catch so the competitors wouldn't find out we had loaded up at spot X. As if they didn't know.

But Billy, pal, you couldn't have been seriously drunk when you drove your almost-new-but-badly-battered Camaro off the ferry at Horseshoe Bay. And there's not much trouble you could have gotten into between there and the DFO lab in West Vancouver. So it looks like you got to the lab, otherwise no picture of the fish. But why no records, and where the hell did you go afterwards?

I stared at the computer screen and then began banging on the keys. DFO search engine. Google. Every customized academic search engine I knew. Nothing.

Christ! This is supposed to be the most sophisticated fisheries database in the world. This is the Department of Fisheries and Oceans. Of bloody Canada. And I'm doing a simple project on salmonid health and when I find a certain entry I can't source it? What the fuck?

The dull Ottawa sky was dimming into dusk. A metaphor for the entire soulless city and my life in it. I pushed my chair back and thought. Hard. If there was any chance of tracing the source of that jpeg entry, I would have to talk to the data lords, the geeks and trolls who controlled the information that was the foundation, according to them, of everything the department did.

I was irritated by the prospect of that. The internal politics of DFO had increasingly come to favor the keepers of the data. Information is power. And the lower-order beings who now found themselves in possession of that power tended to gibber and posture like monkeys with a shiny stone. Or so I thought. But there was one who had crossed over, left the data kingdom, and ascended to the transcendental plane of "Policy." The problem was, she didn't owe me any favors and I had nothing on her. She was just a co-worker with whom I'd been friendly when we were both DFO rookies, doing lobster surveys in the Bay of Fundy. And in the power-centered interactions that typified most relationships within DFO, I didn't know if simple friendship would count for anything. But maybe she'd be at the staff party scheduled for that afternoon. Bette Connelly. She'd been out east, with most of her department, trying to smooth over "The Cod Problem."

That was a misnomer, in my opinion; the cod weren't the problem. People were. And the people who had caused the problem weren't the people suffering from it. Maybe this should be number one on my list of "Reasons Our Bureaucracy Keeps Screwing Things Up."

But I'd heard Bette was back. The party—reception, actually, according to the embossed invitations that were scattered about the building—was something we'd both normally skip; an announcement of cutbacks and layoffs spun as "gains in efficiency." But there was usually decent food, drinkable wine, and the odd old friend you could BS with.

Even though it was only three, I shut down my computer and glared at nothing while I attempted to marshal the forces of logic and deploy them against the mystery. After several painful minutes, I conceded defeat in the attempt at thought, but scored a decisive victory in the exercise of mindless impulse. I grabbed my coat and headed for "Tears" over on St. Laurent Avenue. The real name of the bar was the Duke of Connaught Arms, but because it was patronized by civil servants from all departments of government, it had quickly acquired the sardonic nickname.

I ordered the cheapest vodka they had, drank it, and ordered another. Gazing around the bar, I didn't see anyone I knew. So I had a peanut. Then another drink. By this time, my thoughts were much less chaotic, and more focused on the primary imperative: another drink.

Realizing my stomach had received no solid food for quite some time, I consumed the entire bowl of peanuts, then looked at my watch. Five-thirty. Perfect. The staff-party-slash-reception would be starting, and, with any luck, I could get some smoked salmon. Smoked salmon was pretty well guaranteed to be wild salmon. Damned if I was going to eat any of that farmed shit. I left the bar and headed back to the DFO building at 200 Kent Street.

Unfortunately, Bette wasn't there. Even more unfortunately, Fleming Griffith was. And still more unfortunately, I decided to talk to him. Griffith seldom mixed with the hoi polloi. God knows why he was there. He was a consummate DFO bureaucrat who had climbed to the top over a pile of bodies that were nothing more to him than convenient footholds. He had now attained the penultimate rung of assistant deputy minister and I could almost feel his foot on my face as he strove for the highest rung of all: deputy minister. He'd trampled as well on all my old friends, everyone who had once earned a living in the fishing industry and those still struggling to make a go of it, using them as stepping stones along the road to power and a hundred and eighty grand per annum.

They were featuring West Coast seafood, so I was able to grab a BC prawn, wrap it in a sliver of BC smoked salmon, and complement it with what may have been a glass of BC merlot. Feeling provincially patriotic, I beat a reasonably straight course for the almost and possibly yet-to-be deputy minister.

My entry through his circle of sycophants was less suave than I would have liked. A couple of them staggered back as if I'd elbowed them. As I squared up to him, I realized once again how pale he was, corpselike but animate in a Harry Rosen charcoal suit. It reminded me of the days when I was on the other side, a lowly fisherman, and my buddies and I had attended "advisory group" meetings with Griffith and his cohorts. The fishermen were tanned to the point of health concerns and the DFO types could have been cast in *Night of the Living Dead*. Two separate species, then, now, and, I was starting to realize, always.

Griffith was deigning to listen to some junior economist from Strategic Planning. When the guy was just getting to his point, which was probably as non-pointy as most economic thought, I flashed a charming smile and said a little too forcefully, "Fleming, how's she goin', eh?" The exaggerated vernacular was not so much a product of my drunkenness but of a desire to draw the line; tell him exactly who

I was and where I stood. That was stupid, of course. No bobbing or weaving or even an attempt at self-defense. He picked me off like the smooth professional he was.

First the faint smile, then the eyes narrowed slightly to let everyone know he was making a sincere attempt to identify me. He made sure the whole group was aware of his chummy attempt at democratic sociability as he grasped my elbow and turned me slightly. "Bar's over there, friend. Why don't you get yourself another one?" About half of his acolytes, the ones graced with the stuff of managerial capability, smiled at his subtle emphasis on "*another* one."

I'd been hit and staggered slightly. Figuratively, of course. But as my old skipper used to say, "We may not always go full speed ahead but we never back up."

I shrugged his hand off my arm. "Danny Swanson. Fish health. Question for you." A momentary flicker of annoyance on his face, and then the standard impassiveness.

I forged ahead. "Fleming, you used to run the West Van lab back in the eighties. I know you never actually did any science." That was my best attempt at a dig at him. "But were you aware of any unconventional research going on: genetic manipulation, unusual crossbreeds, that sort of thing?"

I was shocked to see that I'd scored a hit on him. He blinked and frowned momentarily before regaining control. Then he dismissed me. "You West Coast boys have great imaginations. You should try to drag yourselves into reality."

His eyes fluttered and avoided my gaze before he turned and oozed from the room. I knew there would be repercussions and I felt out of my element, as if I was wading into a swamp to do battle with the thing that lived there.

The next morning, I was not at all surprised to receive a summons from my supervisor. I walked into Bob Oldstream's office knowing I was in shit but not knowing how deep. The only thing I was certain of was that no matter how much Bob liked me, and I was pretty sure he did, there wasn't much chance that he would go out on a limb to defend me. DFO lifers like Bob may have managed to retain some semblance of human values after thirty years in the "civil" service, but only if not pushed too often to express them. I sat down and looked across the desk at Bob, but he refused to look at me.

"What the hell were you up to last night? Were you drunk? You upset Griffith and now he's pulled funding from the disease-transfer study. He can't fire you because you're a member of the union, but five contract employees are going to lose their jobs."

I felt guilty and then angry. Trust Griffith to make innocent people pay. It was his stock in trade. I searched my memory for the five unlucky ones, too junior to have any protection. "Maryanne and Cindy are going back to school anyway. I'll call in some favors and try to get the others reassigned."

"Already done." I looked at Bob in surprise. He must be closer to retirement than I thought. Still, he'd stuck his neck out, a little at least. "I'm tired of seeing people treated like shit. Plus, that's an important study. I need to be able to show those aquaculture idiots that their fish are making my fish sick."

By "my fish," he meant wild fish. I moved him up another two notches on my decent person scale. "So what's my penance?"

"You, my friend, are being kicked out of this nice warm office and going back into the field. Central Area Herring Manager. They start testing next week so you better get out there in a hurry."

Bob was actually doing me a favor. He probably assumed that, like most bureaucrats, I would hate having to leave my cosy office, especially for the central coast of BC in the middle of April. The truth was I would love it. And being back in BC would allow me to snoop around the West Vancouver lab. It was at the center of a couple of mysteries, not the least of which was, what had happened there that made Fleming Griffith feel vulnerable?

Three days later, I was sipping vodka and grapefruit juice at my sort of going-away party. I was definitely going away but it was only sort of a party. Mind you, it was early. There were maybe a dozen of us at a big table in Patsy's, Ottawa's only jazz bar. We were not quite succeeding at avoiding shoptalk, and I kept one eye on the door, hoping Bette Connelly would show up. I'd had several conversations with her voicemail, and in Ottawa an electronic surrogate is often preferable to its owner. But not in this case. I desperately wanted to talk to her before I left. When she walked in the door at about nine o'clock, my mood elevated to a point somewhat below rapturous bliss, but much higher than the muddy depression I'd been mired in. I stood up to shepherd her toward the bar where we could have a few words in private.

She was dressed in office clothes, dark skirt and light top, rather than the jeans and T-shirt I'd last seen her in. Her glasses were more stylish as well, and I would have said they made her look even more intelligent, except that would have been gilding the lily. She greeted me with a wry smile. "Danny Swanson. Tamer of small hamlets and slayer of evil ADMs. I knew you'd get in trouble the minute I turned my back."

The thought flickered quickly, *I'm kind of sorry you turned your back.* Out loud, "Sorry, Mom. I lost my head. Let me get you a drink and then pick your brain."

"You West Coast boys are such charmers. But it's your party. You still drinking vodka and grapefruit juice?"

"It's a health thing."

The easy banter reminded me of how well we'd gotten along when we were chasing lobster around the Bay of Fundy. While Bette got our drinks, I ruminated on how such a simple relationship could be so pleasurable. My train of thought was going in the direction of "simple relationships for simple people." Fortunately she handed me a drink before the train reached its destination. "What's on your mind?"

I sipped carefully as I pondered the best way to approach it. I didn't want to presume her loyalty, and I didn't want her to become collateral damage in my dirty war with Griffith.

"Couple of things," I said eventually. "When you and the data group were setting up the Fourth Reich, you spent a lot of time figuring out data-tracking and verification protocols. You probably understand that process better than anyone. So why is it that when I'm mining the database for my project on fish health, I can stumble across an anomalous file that has zero cross-referencing, nothing to show where it came from, nothing about the author, and nothing how the data entered the system? And when I repeat the links that got me there, the file has disappeared?"

She sipped her drink. "System deficiencies, also known as fuck-ups. There was a whole bunch of data, lots of different files, that had come out of a project at the West Vancouver lab, and they wanted to get rid of it. Mostly I did it without even opening the files. The only tricky part was that the database hadn't been debugged at that point, and sometimes their information wasn't 'filed properly.' Lost, in other words. I had a hard time tracking everything down so I could erase it. I assume that whatever you saw was just some lost file that escaped the purge. It's just floating around in there and you stumbled across it."

I hesitated about the next part. I didn't want to reveal too much because I didn't think it would be good for either of us. "When you guys were liaising with Science to get all their stuff into a usable format, there were reams of data coming out of the West Vancouver lab. They had all kinds of projects going on. Did you ever come across anything, or even hear about anything to do with hybrid or transgenic fish?"

There. I'd said it, and she looked at me appraisingly. "Transgenic?" The naughty word not usually pronounced in polite company. Canada was bound by international convention not to mess around with that stuff, but half the science types in DFO slobbered with adolescent lust over the possibilities.

"I don't know how you got onto this, Danny. We've had to kill three people to keep it quiet. At least I got a memo about studying the feasibility of killing three people. But seriously, I heard all the rumors, just like you, but I never actually saw anything scary. Mind you, I wasn't allowed to open some of the files. I was brought in because I was the queen geek, and they needed me to delete—and I mean deeply delete—a whole bunch of files that had become 'corrupted.' I didn't really buy that, but I knew I wasn't going to get any answers so I didn't ask any questions." She looked at me speculatively. "The project name was kind was kind of interesting, though. Chimera. Project Chimera."

I nodded, carefully avoiding her eyes. I knew I was being uncharacteristically intense, and she was aware of it. But she wasn't going to pry. "I guess that explains it. So, how's life in Policy Central? I'm jealous of all the exciting things you must be involved in."

"Yeah right. I just finished a two-week symposium on enumeration methodology, and tomorrow I have to write a briefing note on consultation requirements of the new Oceans Act. Still jealous?"

"I think I can overcome it." We clinked glasses and sat for a while in comfortable silence.

When we joined the others at the table, I could see that the mood had loosened up considerably. Even federal civil servants are susceptible to the effects of flaming shooters. Yes, the party had gotten to that stage. The conversation was loud and earnest and gossipy. Evidently there was to be a cabinet shuffle, which would give us a new Fisheries Minister. Interest was natural, not because we would have a new boss—we all knew the Minister of Fisheries did not run the Department of Fisheries. Interest centered around the power struggle. This was, after all, Ottawa, where politics pre-empted professions, families, sports, and even sex as the topic of conversation. For many, politics *was* sex.

We wanted to know whose interests would be served by the appointment. Would it be processors, large fleet owners, or independent fishermen? We all laughed at the last option, a definite non-starter. Most of the betting was on aquaculture, specifically fish aquaculture. The fish farmers had been in ascendancy lately and the reasons were obvious. Penned fish are easier to manage than wild fish, and fish farmers are definitely easier to manage than traditional fishermen. Or maybe they were just more palatable to the bureaucrats than a bunch of smelly people in rain gear.

Once the obvious ministerial candidates had been discussed and tossed aside, we started nominating "alternative" candidates. Someone mentioned Bruce Cockburn and we all agreed that if a tree fell in the ocean it would be louder than a fish falling in the forest. Conrad Black? You couldn't have a bug-eyed guppy as Fisheries Minister. Conflict of interest. Bette chipped in with Tie Domi, because he would defend fish with the same determination he did the Leafs.

"Leaves, that should be leaves," someone said.

"He's not going anywhere," I said. Bada bing, bada boom.

The waitress brought another round and the suggestions and responses became shouts and the laughter became louder.

Historical figures who displayed ministerial qualities: Alexander the Great. A step up from Fred the Not So Good. The Sultan of Oman's eunuch. Because he had no balls. Helen Keller. Deaf, blind, and dumb. Overqualified. The three stooges. One at a time, thank you.

"What about Whoopi Goldberg?"

"Better than a whoopee cushion, which is what we've got now."

"It's simple," someone said. "What we need is a single entity that combines all the best qualities of the last few ministers in one package."

"Only problem is," I said, "the Ebola virus can't get a Canadian passport and the bubonic plague is past retirement age."

"How about Saddam Hussein? I hear he's at loose ends, or soon might have a few loose ends."

"Yeah, but he got bombed."

"So did Fred whasisname. Regularly."

"Attila the Hun."

"Make that Attila the Hen. A bird in the hand is worth both of the Bushes."

"Margaret Thatcher?"

"We already said Attila the Hen!"

I waved my credit card at the waiter while the bantering went on.

When he took it, I told him the rest of the evening was on me. Hadn't done that since a big fishing week. When I had my next drink safely in my hand, I interrupted.

"Jesus Christ! No, I didn't spill my drink. I'm nominating Jesus Christ. Instead of multiplying the fishes, he could divide the fishermen, which is what you need to do before you subtract them."

"Right on! That would make life simpler. Get rid of the fishermen."

This from a stubble-headed guy in the corner. He was flushed and his glasses were slightly askew. I didn't know if he was serious or not but that opinion was held by the majority in DFO. The "fishermen are the problem" premise underlay all of their recent policy.

I whispered to Bette, "Who is that guy?"

She rolled her eyes. "Reginald Sanderson. Fleming's protégé. Dedicated to wallowing in his master's murk. Handle with kid gloves: for sanitary reasons, if nothing else."

"So, you don't really like the guy?" Another roll of the eyes, two in less than a minute. Extraordinary.

Last call. The waiters were scurrying around as everyone frantically ordered doubles. I glanced at Bette and saw her grinning at me. I felt a surge of bonhomie as I considered what a good friend she was.

Suddenly we were all leaving, and Bette and I found ourselves in a cab together.

"You should come visit me out West. I'll show you around. It's a different world out there."

"Maybe I will. God knows I'm tired of this place." Instinctively, I put my arm around her shoulder and indulged in an ambiguous snuggle. She shrugged it off. I looked wounded. "Danny, I need a boyfriend, not a straight man." "Why?" I asked as the cab pulled over in front of her apartment. "I heard your last boyfriend wasn't straight enough, and that's why you dumped him." She exited quickly and slammed the door without even inviting me up.

Three

The next morning, April 13, Air Canada flight 227 transported a very large headache from Ottawa to Vancouver. Unfortunately, the headache was mine. Some twit had given me a hangover, so I was coping with that rather than celebrating the fact that I was about to start a new life, or return to an old one, or start having one. Or something.

I spent a day moping around the huge DFO building where every phone number started with six six six. The apocalyptical significance of the prefix had been noted by every fisherman on the coast each time a new sacrifice was demanded. On that grey April day, I knew, I would swear, that the Beast was real and that I was trapped in its bowels. I prayed for release. If that meant being excreted, well, I felt like shit anyway.

But before relief, penance. I reported to regional director general Paul Desroche and was greeted with enthusiasm. "Danny, you're just in time to sit in on the Strategic Policy Working Group session. We're looking at licenses."

"Mine's in my wallet."

He stared at me for just a second. "I mean we're examining licensing policy. We may need to rationalize."

Good luck, I thought. Still, I'd never been present at the birth of an actual policy before, so I followed him with less of a lack of enthusiasm than was perhaps warranted.

We entered a small lecture room where about thirty people gazed rapturously at a man in a mismatched jacket and pants who was waving around a laser pointer. I was about to duck when Paul nudged me. "He's our economics guru."

The word "oxymoron" flashed through my mind but my lips did not move. Years of discipline.

The man was in full flight. Capturing maximum rents and facilitating market corrections followed by freeing the exchange mechanism. Hallejuah! He finished with a rousing chorus of growth through deregulation and, glory be, the discipline of the marketplace. I expected a few Amens and Praise the Lords, but there was only applause, worshipful though it may have been.

Paul strode to the front of the room. "Thank you so much, Dr. Solomon. We're always fascinated to witness the power of economic thought unleashed on the problems of fisheries management. And now gentlemen—and ladies, welcome Rebecca—reasoning from the general to the particular, what can we say about abalone licenses?"

Not much, I thought. *They're worthless pieces of paper because the fishery was managed into oblivion. The Minister giveth and the Minister taketh away.*

Nevertheless, an earnest debate broke out, in a room full of highly educated people whose collective salary almost equalled Conrad Black's annual bonus, about a fishery that hadn't existed for ten years. There was a policy void, and out of the void must come, what? Enlightenment? I don't know. But it was fascinating to watch.

Three overhead projectors were in play and transparencies were being flashed onto every available surface. The focusing knobs, as per DFO rules, were fused into fuzziness, so tables and lecterns were being screeched backwards and forwards in the quest for focus. Vague curves were superimposed over text that just might have been readable if the transparency had been the right way up. Numbers were flashing on Dr. Solomon's back as he waved at the X axis of a Laffer curve. It wasn't even mildly amusing. A new graph showed up, undulating on his shiny once-fashionable jacket. The curve started high and then plunged off his right hip. I leaned over to Paul. "Got a plane to catch. But this has been great. Keep me posted."

"It's all on the Web page. You can follow the whole debate and even post your comments. You don't have to be a member of the group."

"Super. I'll follow it closely. See ya."

Sometimes prayers are answered. At three that afternoon, a kind woman handed me a plane ticket to Shearwater. Somewhat off the beaten path, in fact so far off as to escape even minor bruising, Shearwater was my waypoint to joining the mighty *James Sinclair*, flagship of Western Command and floating HQ for the herring fishery.

The *Jimmy Sinc*, one hundred and thirty seven feet of recycled pop cans, was anchored in Shearwater Bay. One of the boat's inflatable runabouts, a Zodiac, picked me up and zipped me out to the mother ship. Standing on deck to greet me was Peter Van Allen. Pete had been attached to the herring fishery for almost fifteen years and knew just about everything there was to know about the fish, the fishermen, and the fishery. So naturally he was not in charge; I was. As I shook his hand I said, "I'm here pretty much as an observer and just another pretty face."

"You can have it if you want it," he said. "My stomach is way too old for this stuff."

Ah yes, the herring fishery. The biggest, fastest, wealthiest fishery in the world. The entire fleet lived on its nerves. The tension was such that fishermen and fishery managers alike gobbled antacid pills like candy.

Here's how the crapshoot works. Herring are fished for the roe, the eggs, of the females. When the fish school up for their massive spawning events during March and April, the roe content matures rapidly. The roe sacs are measured as a percentage of body weight. Starting at about five percent, the roe content will grow over a two- or three-week period to as high as twenty percent. The idea is to wait as long as possible to allow the roe sacs to get as big as possible. But if you wait too long, the fish spawn and then everything is lost. Or you might wait until the optimum moment to open the fishery, and then a storm will blow in, making it impossible to fish for two or three days. When the storm is over, the fish have spawned and the fishery is lost. And it's not just the lost revenue from the price of the roe. The fishermen have rented licenses worth millions of dollars. If the fishery is blown, they have to eat those costs.

The pressure on the manager to get it right is enormous. But the pressure on the fishermen to perform is even greater. The seine boats participating in the fishery are the biggest and fastest with the most aggressive skippers. Different company fleets have their own spotter planes to perform aerial surveillance. Subsea surveillance is undertaken by sophisticated sonars and sounders that would be the envy of many navies. Messages are transmitted from boat to boat using verbal codes or electronically scrambled ciphers.

The planes circle overhead. The big steel boats circle over the fish, jockeying for position. It's a game of high-stakes, high-speed chess and the boat with the inside position wins. And then the opening announcement over VHF radio. "This is the *James Sinclair*. Roe herring fishing by purse seine net is now declared open in areas seven-dash-one-three and seven-dash-one-four."

Before the message has even been completed, smoke belches from fifty smokestacks as fifty throttles are rammed forward. Nets start to peel off drums, not dragged off by the resistance of a sea anchor, but hauled off by power skiffs that pull in the opposite direction of the big boat. Many boats set on the same school of fish. Rammings are threatened and occasionally occur; guns are brandished and sometimes fired as the boats attempt to close their circles. It's a game of chicken won by the most aggressive. Diesel fuel and testosterone are the order of the day. It's big machines and big egos doing battle in a small arena for huge prizes. It's symbolic. It's excessive. It's exciting as hell. I was looking forward to it.

The first opening, in the Gulf of Georgia, had not gone well. Scattered fish and bad weather had meant the seine fishery was pretty much a bust, although the gillnetters had moved down to Yellow Point and gotten their quota. So now, here in the central area, there were lots of seine boats that were already half a million in the hole and looking to make up their losses. I prayed we could make it work for them.

Preliminary soundings showed some large bodies of fish in the area, although they would appear and disappear randomly. The roe content had gone from five percent to eight percent in a week. Things were looking not too bad. When the percentage got to about fifteen, and if there was sufficient fish in the area, we'd let 'er go. In the meantime, we would do constant sounding to keep tabs on how many fish was in the area, and two chartered seine boats would do test sets and sample the fish to measure the roe content. It meant twelve-hour days at a minimum but, by God, they would seem shorter than my usual Ottawa seven-hour shifts.

That evening, Pete and I convened in the wheelhouse at eight for the daily fleet update. We'd broadcast on VHF channel 78A to let the fleet know our latest findings, and listen to their concerns, and generally just have a gabfest. Sometimes it was a focused problem-solving sort of workshop and sometimes it was more of a bitch session. After the problems with the Gulf fishery, I was expecting more of the latter.

Pete led off. He gave the sounding reports, which showed a school estimated at two thousand tons in upper Spiller Channel, a couple of schools totaling maybe three thousand in lower Spiller, and scattered schools of around fifteen hundred tons even lower down in Seaforth Channel.

He then opened it up to the fleet for comments, and I was mildly surprised by the constructive nature of the dialogue. Guys were talking about trigger points and hail procedures and fallback plans as though they hadn't a care in the world. The only participants who hinted at aggressiveness were the processing representatives. These guys represented large companies that had to satisfy shareholders. To them, fish were nothing more than a commodity to be converted into shareholder dividends. In all the debates I'd heard over the years about how much to fish, where, and how, and who should catch them, the processors were predictably consistent in their voice: as much as possible, as soon as possible, for our fleet, as cheaply as possible. When fishermen expressed concerns about overfishing or sustainability, they were pressured to fish like hell this year and forget about next year. And they paid the price for that.

When the debate had been going on for twenty minutes or so, focused on arcane stuff like male/female/juvenile percentage, I was thrilled to hear a familiar voice. He followed the standard protocol of calling our boat name first, followed by his. "*James Sinclair, Coastal Provider.*" It was my old skipper, Mark, who had somehow managed to acquire a coveted herring command. "I was just wondering about our basic strategy here. Are we going to try and get the quota in one shot or have a short opening and then reassess the situation?"

It was a deceptively simple question. The answer would dictate every fisherman's strategy. Should he go for the one big set or be patient, knowing he'd get a least one more chance the next day? I motioned to Pete and he handed me the mike. "*Coastal Provider, James Sinclair*. Evening, skipper. Nothing's written in stone but we'd like to have a quick one, shut 'er down to get a good count, and then get the remainder of the quota possibly the next day." I didn't know if he'd recognize my voice after eight years so I threw in a reference that only he would understand. "We'd like to pull this off so everyone gets their share without going over quota. Everyone's got mouths to feed and the biggest mouth is the banker's."

That's what Christine used to say to us every week as we were trying to calculate our crew shares. And Mark would laugh and say, "The only bank I care about is Goose Bank where you get the big halibut."

There were a few more questions and then none, from which I deduced that the conference had ended. Everyone knew the fishery was a ways off so no one was panicking yet. I descended from the wheel-house and went out on deck. I could see the *Coastal Provider* about a quarter mile off our stern. As I watched, there was a scurry of activity as they launched their power skiff. It started up with a roar and headed straight for us, in contrast to most of the other power skiffs, which were heading toward the Shearwater Pub. As it got closer, I could see Mark at the wheel, and when he came alongside, I grabbed his tie-up line.

He was still clean-cut, dressed well for a working fisherman, and exuded mature responsibility. Occasionally, he had allowed us to drag him out of that grown-up persona, but it was still his default character. He grinned at me. "I knew they'd kick you out of Ottawa. Swansons aren't allowed there. No logs to haul or fish to catch."

"But you meet such interesting people. Just a few days ago, I was having cocktails with Fleming Griffith."

"I hope they pay you extra for that. Hey, jump in. We'll go for a beer."

"I don't know if I should be seen with a lowly fisherman." I was joking, but many in DFO were serious about what they saw as fraternization with the enemy.

"I'm the one who's got to worry about his reputation. Drinking with a DFO guy. What would my mother say?"

I climbed into the open aluminum skiff, powered by a diesel engine only slightly smaller than an icebreaker's, and we headed for the famed Shearwater Pub. The place was packed with noisy fishermen reliving their biggest sets. The older guys were using mugs of beer to illustrate the positioning of various boats they'd outsmarted to get their nets around a disputed school of fish. The younger guys were already on to shooters. *No sign of poverty here*, I thought, and then remembered that everybody was spending their grub money.

Grub money, enough to last the season, is advanced by the processors. But no one seemed worried about having to pay it back. After all, there's no way in hell, everyone thought, that we won't make enough money to cover expenses. Unfortunately, the cold math showed quite plainly that if everyone caught the area average (the total quota divided by the number of boats), everyone would lose money. To make money you had to get your share of fish plus someone else's. Thus the feeding frenzy that was herring season.

I saw a few familiar faces and nodded greetings. My cousin Ollie sat at a table under the TV. He'd spent years on a seine boat and suffered a crushed foot en route to earning enough money for a shrimp boat and license. I waved at him and he saluted me with his mug. There were no free tables, or even empty chairs, so Mark and I leaned against the bar.

"You know who else might show up here?" he said. "Christine. She's on the *Racer* and they're on their way up from the Gulf. We'll have a real reunion."

The *Racer* was the Coast Guard ship that Christine served on. They usually stood by during major fisheries to help patrol and rescue anyone who needed rescuing. And there were always a few rescuees, even in calm weather. Fishing was an intense industrial activity that took place on slippery decks on bouncing boats in a highly competitive situation. Somebody always got hurt. We just all hoped no one would get killed.

Unfortunately, there was already one missing in action. Les Jameson had left Port Hardy two days previously, headed for Shearwater in his super punt, but never arrived. They'd found the high-speed punt drifting in Fitz Hugh Sound, but no sign of him. I'd never much cared for Les. He was a scab and a DFO pet rock. But still, he deserved to live. I guess.

"I even heard that Fergie might be here on a gillnetter," Mark said. There was a moment's silence as memories sparked between us and we both thought of the one who wouldn't be here: Billy. I was tempted to tell Mark about how our Igor had made a mystery appearance in the DFO database, and that I was sure Billy had delivered it to the West Van lab before he went missing. But something made me hold back. Instead, I gestured to the waitress for a couple of pints and steered the conversation in a safer direction. "So, who'd you have to kill to get the herring job? Don't tell me you bought your own license." Anyone with enough money to buy a herring license would never waste the former by buying the latter.

Mark shrugged. "You know how the game works. I've got a pretty big halibut quota. So I hire as deckhands two guys who fish salmon for Jimmy Patterson. So I suggest to them they should tell Jimmy I'll deliver to him if he lets me run one of his herring boats. And they do and he does. So here I am."

"Nice one. But I don't know if I could take the pressure."

"Yeah, that's the toughest part of the game. But I'll try it for a couple of seasons, and if I don't like it, I'll stick to fishing the flat ones. At least I've got a fallback position."

I nodded. That made things easier all right. "How's your love life? I hear you split up with Shirley."

"Aw Christ, I've taken a vow of celibacy."

"That's a bit extreme. You never used to go more than half a day without drooling over some young lovely."

"That was the old days, Danny. What I've learned is that sex leads to relationships and relationships lead to problems and problems lead to a guy having to sleep on the boat and that leads to smelling like stale diesel, which means you don't have a hope of getting laid, so why bother in the first place?"

Jeez, I thought, *the breakup with Shirley must've been tough.* My journey through the nineties had left me, in my humble opinion, a caring and sensitive guy. But it's easier to be sensitive with casual acquaintances than with real friends. So in a sensitive but cowardly manner, I declined to ask about it or to commiserate. And Mark declined to query my single state, which was an embarrassment to my mother and a puzzlement to me. I told myself I was in that awkward stage of being beyond casual pickup dating, but not ready for serious relationship-type dating. An image of Bette flashed through my mind, and her closeness to me in the back of an Ottawa cab.

Thankfully, Mark interrupted my musings by changing the subject. "Hey, you must know Alistair Crowley. He lives in a float house just around the corner in Yeo Cove and fishes prawns. But he used to be a top-notch biologist in the West Van lab. Left or got fired. Rumor has it, he was messing around with superfish, doing gene splicing and shit like that. He's a strange guy but I sometimes trade him halibut for prawns. You know who I'm talking about?"

Crowley was the stuff of legend. He haunted the annals of DFO lore like Marley's Ghost. He had done brilliant work, first on acid rain and then on Pacific Ocean regime shifts. After those peer-acclaimed works, he had retreated deeper into the basement of the West Van lab and had begun experiments that few understood and even fewer approved of. And then he was gone. Fired? Quit? Medical leave? The rumors were numerous and unresolved. But he'd still been there in 1996 when Smiling Billy had, presumably, turned up on the doorstep with a large mutant fish.

"Yeah, Mark." I tried not to appear too eager. "I'd love to talk to him. Let me know when you're headed his way."

The raucous noise of the bar suddenly increased by a factor of, by God, the Kairikula brothers. They burst through the door like a Force 8 storm, yelling and insulting all and sundry in a generically malign fashion.

"Shearwater is the asshole of the world and the whole goddamn herring fleet is five fathoms up it." This from Hari.

The punch line from Jari. "So that makes everyone here a hemorrhoid."

Gleeful laughter as they swaggered toward the bar. The Kairikula brothers were, in their eyes, the pride of Sointula, and the product of a century of Finnish lineage. Some would say they were the product of a restricted gene pool. But I'd fished with and around them for years, and my many painful attempts to match their capacity for vodka had resulted in a typically shipmate-fisher-guy sort of bond.

I both cringed and delighted when Hari fastened his eyes on me. Hari to Jari, "Look who's here. It's Swede Swanson, the wannabe Finn. Hey Danny, you're a good guy. Gimme fifty bucks and I'll get you a Finnish passport."

Jari to Hari, "No fucking way. He's good for a Swede but not good enough to be a Finn." He elbowed through the crowd and threw his arm around me. "But he's good enough to buy me a drink."

Mark smiled to himself and leaned against the bar. It was starting to feel like old times. "Okay, guys," I said. "What can I get you? Virgin Chi Chi?"

Jari waved at the waitress, and she responded amazingly quickly with two double vodkas. The brothers and their tastes were well known from Steveston to Prince Rupert. Vodka and water on normal occasions. Vodka and Carolans for special occasions.

Hari downed his drink and looked at me sternly. "Haven't seen you around for a while, Danny. Someone said you came out of the closet."

"That's right," Jari said. "He joined DFO."

"Ohmigod, if there's one thing worse than sucking cocks, it's just sucking period." They guffawed and gasped for at least three minutes over that one. They recovered their breath and gazed reverently as the waitress removed her sweater to reveal a "Spawn Till You Die" T-shirt.

Mark interjected calmly. "I was just telling Danny we should run over to Yeo Cove and get some prawns off Alistair."

Hari looked at him. "You guys didn't hear? Sonofabitch blew his head off this morning. Crazy prawn fisherman, they're all the same. Traps, all they do is set traps, and fight over turf until they start goin' squirrelly."

I looked at Mark and saw shock deaden his face. "I saw him yesterday. He was as happy as I've ever seen him. Talking about getting a bigger boat." He paused. "Jeez, I've still got a box of his stuff. He lent me all his journals and records so I could study the local herring movements. There's no monetary value to it, but I should return it. It's part of his estate, I guess."

I was curious. "Let me look at it and I'll see it gets into the proper hands. It could be DFO property, or at least they might want it for their database."

The noise of the bar now seemed intrusive rather than welcoming. I looked at Mark. "C'mon," he said. "Let's get back."

Outside the bar, it was chilly and still. As we walked down the dock, I looked up at the cloudless sky. Unaffected by urban haze, the stars were clear and bright and compelling. They posed a question I didn't understand and twinkled an answer I was afraid I did.

Mark steered the power skiff for the *Coastal Provider* where he jumped aboard and quickly returned with a cardboard box full of journals. "This is Alistair's stuff." Then he roared me over to the *James Sinclair* and nodded goodnight as I climbed aboard.

I took the box to my stateroom and started going through it. There were seventeen lined journals, each one evidently covering a year of observations. They started in June of 1987, when I assumed Alistair had arrived in Yeo Cove. The last one had entries up to April 12, the day before Mark had borrowed them. But, as I continued putting them all in order, I came across one that didn't fit the sequence. It was undated and I opened it with curiosity.

It was unlike the others, which consisted of daily entries of environmental conditions correlated to fish counts and movements, the mundane observations of a working scientist. But this journal was full of pasted-in printouts from various databases and programs. I couldn't make heads nor tails of it. Bette crossed my mind again. She was the only person I knew who might be able to make sense of this stuff. And I thought there might be more data as well as other clues back at Alistair's float house. What we needed was some sort of whaddayacallit, that thing they used to decipher hieroglyphics—oh yeah, the Rosetta Stone. I would try to run over there in the morning.

I tried to sleep but couldn't. Long dormant thoughts about Billy's disappearance re-awakened old memories and they triggered a new resolve to get some answers, and that made me wonder what I would find at Alistair's float house. As the queries chased answers that refused to come out and play, my mind tired of the game and settled into more comfortable thoughts of warmth and softness, and then I suppose I slept.

Four

The next morning exploded with a roar. Huge diesels thundered to life and shattered sleep into shards of confused consciousness. My noise-bludgeoned brain placed me back on the *Maple Leaf C*. A few seconds passed before the starting roar subsided to a comfortable throbbing. I switched on the light and surveyed my stateroom. If this had been the fo'c's'le of the *Maple Leaf C*, the space would have been smaller, the occupancy larger and the odor greater. Four bodies would have been bumping into each other as they groped for pants and shirts and gumboots. I felt a little alone as I donned my clean and non-smelly DFO fleecy gear.

Upstairs on the bridge, I could have been back on the *Maple Leaf C* or any seine boat. It was still dark, and the only light was the green glow from the radar, blue and red from the sounder, and yellow from the instrument panel. Five radios crackled with static and snippets of conversation. Four of us stood quietly, grasping steaming cups of coffee as we completed our transition to full consciousness.

One of the radios hissed static and then burst into speech. "*James Sinclair, Western Marauder*. You guys awake yet?" One of our test boats. I reached up and grabbed the mike.

"*Western Marauder, James Sinclair*. Morning, skipper. What are you gentlemen up to this morning?"

"We're at the top end of Spiller. We've been sounding since four and we've identified maybe a thousand or fifteen hundred tons. As soon as it's light we'll try a set and see what we get."

"Thanks for that, skipper. We're especially interested in the size of the females, so measure as many as you can." I glanced inquiringly at Pete and he took the mike.

"Hi Jimmy, it's Pete here. One other thing. We want to make sure the samples are as representative as possible. Could you ask your power skiff crew to grab a few buckets from along the cork line?"

"Roger that, Pete. We're gonna have breakfast now and then get to work. Talk to you later."

Another radio came to life. "*James Sinclair, Northern Queen.*" That was our other test boat, farther south toward Seaforth Channel. As I reached for the mike to answer him, the sideband issued its typical metallic buzz and the northern report began from Prince Rupert. And then a second VHF began issuing the marine traffic report at the same time as the seven o'clock weather report started on weather channel 2.

I'd lost the knack of listening to five radios at once but there were enough of us there to absorb all the pertinent information. A single seine boat skipper could have listened to and processed all the information as a matter of course. I didn't like to think about what this implied about the ability of a few DFO personnel to manage hundreds of fishermen.

Streaks of red began to appear over the eastern mountains. The white peaks of the coastal range took on an orange tinge against the brilliant blue sky. It was going to be a beautiful day. I looked at George Kelly, captain of the *James Sinclair*. "Let's go for a cruise. See what we can find."

He nodded and picked up the intercom. "Can we get a couple of guys to pull the hook?" It wasn't really a question, and almost instantaneously we heard a click and a hum as an unseen deckhand engaged the hydraulics. As the anchor chain rumbled onto the winch, George casually positioned himself at the wheel. He turned on the Wesmar sonar and adjusted the range on the sounder. The anchor clunked on board, and George raised an eyebrow at me. I looked at Pete, who shrugged.

"Let's head up Spiller and look at the eastern shore," I said. "I want to see if there's anything schooling up in the shallows."

George pushed the throttle forward and the powerful engines quickly accelerated the big grey boat to her cruising speed of twelve knots. It was quiet in the wheelhouse, but I knew that the engines were producing almost as many decibels as horsepower, which was why fishermen liked the *James Sinclair*. It couldn't sneak up on anyone. As we headed for Spiller Channel, all eyes were on the sonar and the sounder. The sonar showed a pattern of radiating lines, like the sun's rays. If schools of fish were present, the lines would become brighter and indicate the direction and distance of the school. The sounder gave us a picture of what lay directly beneath the boat. Usually it just showed the ocean bottom as a solid red line, but if schools of fish were beneath us they would show up as light blue or yellow smears depending on their density. Really dense schools, such as big bunches of herring, would show up as solid red just like the bottom, so you had to know the bathymetry of the area.

When we were about one mile off the eastern shore, the sonar lines flickered and intensified, indicating a large school about forty-five degrees to starboard and about a quarter mile away. George turned us toward the fish and, as we closed on them, our eyes turned to the sounder. As we passed directly over the school, the flat red line of the bottom bulged into a red semi-sphere that started at about thirty fathoms and ended just above the bottom at sixty fathoms.

"Fifty to seventy-five tons," I said. "What do you think?"

"Maybe a little more," said Pete. "Definitely worth setting on."

"Depends on how much time in the opening. And how lucky you feel."

And that was how we spent the rest of the day. We covered a transect about a mile off, all down the eastern shore of Spiller Channel. We saw four more schools in the fifty- to one-hundred-ton range and one big school of about three hundred tons.

At intervals during the day, the two test boats came on the air with details of their sets. The fish they caught were sampled and then released, or more accurately, samples of fish were taken from the sets, tested for roe content and then dumped overboard. Unfortunately for them, they were not at that point, active swimmers. All the tests showed roe percentages from eight to ten and an even split between males and females. No spawned-out females, and no slinks or spawned-out males. The females were a little on the small side, ranging from sixteen to eighteen centimeters.

Through no design of mine, we ended the day at the southern end of the channel, near Yeo Cove. I suggested we drop anchor and spend the night there, and no one objected.

When Pete and I held our pre-conference conference, we both agreed that it was early yet, that there were no indications of mass spawn, but that it was time to send the plane up looking for early spot spawns. If the plane saw short stretches of shallow water turned white by milt, it would start to give us an indication of where the major spawn might occur. And if it reported miles and miles of white water, we would know that our estimations were wrong and we damn well better get the fleet ready to go.

That night we updated the fleet, fielded a few questions, refereed a couple of arguments and noted that the fleet stress level was just starting to build. No frothing at the mouth yet, but stomach acid was starting to rise.

Later, as I lay in my bunk, I started going over Crowley's journals in greater detail. I was still only skimming them, but getting a good idea of the type of information they contained. The daily entries were mostly about prawns. He was, after all, a prawn fisherman. But if he saw a fish jump, he reported it. He was very specific about species and abundances of marine mammals, as well as birds. And all species information was correlated with information about weather and sea state, tide, temperature, and salinity. As well, he made occasional comments on unusual events that might affect the marine environment; things such as heavy boat traffic, unusual amounts of garbage, and oil slicks.

I went over the last journal even more carefully, looking for indications of changes in his mental state or specific events that might have caused a suicidal depression. There was nothing that even hinted at depression, or any change in mood or personality. There was nothing unusual at all until the last four days of the journal.

April 8: After several references to seeing large herring balls, he ends the day's entry with the cryptic comment *Kelp is late.*

April 9: At low tide, he collects several sunfish, which he will dry and use for prawn bait. Comments on Mergansers feeding in shallows. He finishes the entry with, *Still no Kelp.*

April 10: He works on gear, comments on abnormally warm water temperature, and writes, *I wonder what's the problem with the Kelp?*

April 11: The final entry. I couldn't help but pore over every word. These were the last observations of a dedicated scientist who was recording information about a unique area with a thoroughness that would never be repeated. His final words: *I can see the Kelp.*

These references puzzled me because in April you would not expect to see very much kelp anywhere on the coast. It was not the growing season. At best, you would find straggling remnants of the previous summer's crop.

On April 12, Mark had dropped by and asked to borrow the journals. The next day, Crowley had shot himself. I tried to arrange the bits of information into a coherent pattern but nothing made sense. I couldn't accept that Crowley's mind, orderly and rational and disciplined, could have unraveled so quickly into the nihilistic scream of suicide. On the other hand, his inexplicable concerns with kelp might have been the first hint of a mind reeling into chaos. The end might have been as predictable as it was inevitable: the blood-spattered triumph of entropy over the ordered system that had been Alistair Crowley.

I stared blankly at the bottom of the bunk above me. Every time an emergent thought threatened to coalesce into meaning, it dissolved just as quickly. Eventually so did my consciousness and I drifted into sleep. I should have dreamt about Crowley, been confronted by his pale ghost festooned with fronds of bull kelp. And screamed silently as he wrapped me in his cold embrace. But I slept a dreamless sleep and woke before the engines did.

Five

It was only six when I shuffled into the galley expecting to have to fumble around with coffee makings, but the aroma of brewing coffee greeted me like an old friend. George was already up and the first batch of mud was almost ready. I shouldn't have been surprised. Skippers don't sleep much and are always the first up. I was never sure if they became skippers because they didn't sleep much or didn't sleep much because they had become skippers.

When the coffeemaker gurgled to the end of its cycle, I poured two cups and took them over to the table.

"Morning, George. Looks like it could be a nice day." I spoke in the slightly hushed tone of one who knows there are others still sleeping.

He took one of the mugs and sipped it black while I diluted mine with canned milk. "Cheers. Yeah, the forecast says the high pressure will hold for seventy-two hours anyways."

"George, I want to poke around Yeo Cove. How 'bout I take a Zodiac and meet you guys back at Shearwater? You can check out the west side on your way back."

"You're the boss, but hell, there's no problem with that. Just take a portable VHF in case you run into trouble."

I nodded and took another sip of coffee. I felt a quiet surge of excitement.

"You think you might find something important Crowley left behind?"

I'd forgotten that George had been around long enough to know all the stories and have heard all the rumors. I felt embarrassed and a little ashamed now at the prospect of poking through a dead man's effects. George had a different slant on it.

"He was a strange guy. Watch out for booby traps." He rose and headed for the wheelhouse. I could hear him turning on radios as I sat and tried to think. I thought I should go and brush my teeth, so I did.

The red streaks of dawn were just beginning to fade from the sky as we launched the Zodiac. A cold yellow orb masqueraded as the sun. Shivering, I took my bag of sandwiches and large thermos of coffee and jumped into the boat.

The Zodiac was eighteen feet long, very light, and powered by twin 150-horse outboards. I turned the key and the engines burbled into life. Blue exhaust smoke wafted in gentle eddies. *Well,* I thought, as I grasped the throttle, *let's see what this little baby will do.*

What it did was thrill me indecently. In about two seconds, I was skimming over the water at thirty knots but it felt like fifty. My job didn't afford the same access to big-boy toys that some guys enjoyed. DFO didn't have, for example, any F-16 jet fighters, so this little Zodiac would have to suffice. I always appreciated the occasional fantasy fulfillment that came my way as part of an otherwise dull job. And because Angelina Jolie was unlikely to show up asking about sockeye enhancement, going fast in a rubber toy was about as fulfilling as my fantasies were going to get.

The wind was cruelly cold and I soon had to slow down. With the windchill factor reduced to a bearable level, I cruised into Yeo Cove. Tucked into a little nook within the bay was a rickety float to which was tied the *Jessie Isle*, a beautifully maintained forty-five-foot wooden ex-troller that was, or had been, Crowley's boat. And at the far end of the float, behind stacks of prawn traps and coils of ground line, was the neat little float house that had been Crowley's home.

I tied up behind the *Jessie Isle* and sat for a moment, looking around. My skin warmed in the absence of wind and it occurred to me that a coffee would go down well. My numb fingers unscrewed the thermos cap and I slopped coffee into the cup. I held it with both hands and sipped slowly. I considered having a sandwich, but my stomach was not in an accepting mood. I was, I realized, hesitant to step onto the float.

Where had the body been found? Would there still be bloodstains? I shook off my squeamishness and carefully set foot on the slippery planks. I walked past the *Jessie Isle* and admired her unblemished hull and varnished cap rails. *I should have a look at the log,* I thought, and climbed aboard. As I reached for the galley door handle, I heard the whine of an approaching outboard and guiltily stepped back.

A Zodiac approached, bigger than mine, and as it neared, I could see that it carried two RCMP officers. As it got nearer still, I could make out that one was female. When they came alongside, I saw her face flushed with wind and cold, and when she flashed a smile and threw me a line, I was smitten.

When she stepped onto the float, she stuck out a hand and introduced herself. "Staff Sergeant Louise Karavchuk, Bella Bella Detachment. And this," indicating the boat driver, "is Aboriginal Community Constable Gordon Wilson."

I explained who I was and, hedging a bit, why I was there. "Alistair was sort of a colleague, or ex-colleague, of mine. I can't believe he killed himself." And then, hesitantly, "Who found the body?"

She gave me a direct look. Her eyes were an ordinary brown but they sparkled or glimmered or shone, or something, in a way that needed studying. I forced myself not to stare as her lips formed words. "He was found by the Heiltsuk Fisheries Guardians who stopped by regularly to share information with him."

I took longer to respond than I should have. "I thought he committed suicide. Is there some question about that? Is that why you're here?"

She smiled. "We're just trying to cover all the bases. We take any unnatural death seriously. We thought, for example, that we should have found some records or journals or data of some kind."

"I've got those." I explained the circumstances in what I hoped was a rational manner. It had been a long time since I had cared so much about not sounding like a twit.

"You'll have to give those to us, at least temporarily. I know it's probably really important scientific data and we'll make sure you get it back."

I tried to look sincere. And trustworthy. "It's all on the *James Sinclair*." And in what I thought was a flash of brilliance, "Maybe I can go over it with you, see if there's anything anomalous or anything."

She gazed at me levelly, as Raymond Chandler would have said. Although he would have erred, due to Louise's five-foot-fourish stature. "And where is the *James Sinclair* now?"

I replied perhaps a touch too eagerly. "It's sounding herring now, but it'll be back in Shearwater tonight."

"I'll see you there," she said. She shook my hand, leapt back into her Zodiac, and thirty seconds later I was left with a rapidly diminishing image of bright yellow and orange, framed by white spray.

Sergeant Louise hadn't told me not to poke around. Maybe because I was DFO and she regarded me as a fellow enforcement professional. So, in the absence of anything better to do, I wandered up the dock toward the float house. Before entering the cedar-shaked building, I circled it uneasily. The solar panels on the backside of the roof, the southern exposure, were inconspicuous but for a brief glint of sunlight.

Inside the house, I saw neatness and tidiness and cleanliness and order, all overlaid by a soft accumulation of recent dust and a baby cobweb here and there. Coleman lanterns. No electrical appliances. I looked for the computer that must have been the rationale for the solar panels. It's not that hard to follow wires. Beneath the floorboards of Alistair's bedroom I found it. The equipment was encased in a cedar box hung beneath a trapdoor covered by a scrap of cheap rug stuff. The central processing unit, an old Dell, and a slightly more modern monitor, were dry and, I hoped, functional. The RCMP had missed them.

My first thought, embarrassingly puppy-like, was to present this potential evidence to Louise. In my mind, we were on a first name basis. But paranoia overcame infatuation. I better check this stuff out, I thought. If there's anything relevant, I'll show it to her. I gave the computer monitor the float test and it failed. I found a garbage bag to protect the CPU from salt spray, put it under my arm, and walked out of the float house.

As I passed the *Jessie Isle*, I remembered that I had wanted to check the log. Beyond feelings of guilt now, I stepped over the cap rail and pulled open the galley door. Standard working boat configuration: table and benches on the starboard side, fridge and counter portside, oil stove against an insulated wall forward. I realized I'd never seen a different arrangement and wondered why.

I walked through the galley and forward to the wheelhouse. Again, everything was standard. Windows in front and on both sides, steering wheel in the middle, and lots of electronic equipment mounted wherever would be handiest. At the back of the wheelhouse, portside, was the chart table, and under it, several drawers. In the top drawer, I found the ship's log, almost full, with page after page filled with Alistair's cramped but tidy writing. I shoved it in my pocket and left.

As I untied the Zodiac, I glanced at the sun and reckoned it to be about two. It was less than an hour back to Shearwater, so I had time to kill. I rummaged around in the locker under the seat and was rewarded by finding a variety of cod jiggers. I remembered several jigging hotspots in Seaforth Channel where we used to stop when running home from Prince Rupert, the urgency of home momentarily overcome by the prospect of fresh fish.

I better check those spots out. Research. Catch-per-unit effort. New data compared to old.

I smiled inwardly and decided not to bullshit myself. I would steal a moment of enjoyment and refuse to feel guilty about it. I flashed up the Zodiac and headed south out of Spiller Channel and into Seaforth. There was a reef halfway to Bella Bella, almost a net length off the south shore, where I'd never failed to come up with some form of seafood delight—a halibut, red snapper, lingcod, or rockfish.

The crème de la crème of bottom fish, black cod, usually lived more offshore and really deep. I'd never caught one on a jigger and relied on friendly long-liners to give me the occasional feed. But I hooked one now, obviously a wandering outcast, and as I pulled him into the boat, I was already planning the garnish.

It was three-thirty and would be gathering dark by four, so I roared for home. As I passed Bella Bella, just around the corner from Shearwater, I saw the RCMP Zodiac headed for its berth. I thought I could make out Louise in the stern, so I altered course and headed to cut them off. I caught up to them just as they slowed to approach the downtown Bella Bella dock. As I came alongside I held up the ten-pound black cod and grinned at Louise. "Why don't you come out to the *Jimmy Sinc* and I'll cook dinner?"

She thought this over carefully, obviously balancing "appearances" against the opportunity to take advantage of my keen intelligence. "You can cook it at my place." She pointed at the big squat grocery store just up from the wharf head. "Four houses north of the store. Faded green. Bike in the driveway. Bring the journals." She jumped onto the float to tie up, and I turned and headed for Shearwater with a large grin on my face.

When I got back to the boat, I casually sauntered into my stateroom with the computer under my arm and stowed it in the drawer under my bunk. I went back out on deck, filleted the black cod, put the fillets in a plastic baggie, then put the guts and head in a crab trap and lowered it over the side. Waste not, want not. Not want too much meatloaf.

By the time I'd showered and put on my cool DFO fleecy, it was five-thirty. I grabbed the box of Alistair's journals and, after some hesitation, removed the one with the hieroglyphics and stowed it, along with the log of the *Jessie Isle*, under my pillow.

In the galley, I nodded to the four guys playing crib. "Going ashore," I said. "Won't be long. Pete, would you mind doing the eight o'clock update?" He nodded. When they saw me take the bag of fillets out of the fridge, they exchanged knowing looks.

I took my stuff out onto the back deck and lowered it into the Zodiac, then climbed in, started the engines, untied the bowline, and moved off. If the crew was looking out the galley window, they might or might not have been surprised to see me steer, not for the Shearwater pub, but around the corner toward downtown Bella Bella.

By the time I tied up at the wharf, dusk had turned to dark and cool air to cold. I just had time to nip into the store and buy a lemon, a bag of salad, and a bottle of BC chardonnay. Then I set out on the trek to Louise's house, and thirty seconds later was there. When she let me in, I raised the bottle of wine and said, "Hope you're not still on duty."

"By the time you put that in the fridge, take out the chilled one, and open it, I'll be off duty. What excellent timing you have."

I followed instructions, noting Louise's fridge art as I did so. There was a photo of a serious-looking Louise with her arms draped over the shoulders of an older couple. Parents. Another of a smiling Louise hugging a furry animal. Dog. And a couple of Far Side cartoons that hinted of an encouragingly skewed worldview. I poured two glasses of wine and raised mine in a wordless toast. "Are you hungry now, or should we wait a bit?"

She considered this seriously, obviously taking internal readings on The State of the Appetite. "How long to cook the fish?"

"I was planning on steaming it, maybe twenty minutes."

"Let's take a quick look at the journals, and then we can relax and enjoy dinner."

I placed the box on the kitchen table while she tucked one foot under her and semi-sat on a rickety chair. As I removed the journals, I looked around the small interior: living room/kitchen and two doors opening to the bathroom and bedroom. Clean and tidy but very sparse. "You haven't been here long?"

"Three months. Posted from Winnipeg. First time in BC, although my folks are planning to retire out here."

"Welcome to God's country." I finished stacking twenty-six journals on the table, more or less in order, pulled out a chair, and sat down. "I've gone through these and I couldn't see anything unusual except for the last one." I opened the last journal and showed her the final entries, the strange references to kelp.

She hitched her chair closer to mine and leaned in to read the entries. When she finished and raised her head, she was very close to me.

"What's strange about that?"

I tried not to sound like a university lecturer. "Kelp grows in the summer and dies off in the winter. Alistair knew that it wouldn't start to grow again until July or August. So why the references to the kelp being late and his concern about not being able to see it?"

She nodded and held out her glass for more wine, then leaned back in thought. I poured myself another glass and watched her think. I hesitated to break the comfortable silence, but finally said, "You're suspicious about something. What's up?"

She chewed on her lower lip, tapped fingers on the table. "I'm going to light a fire. Why don't you put the fish on?"

Not bothering to reply, I sprang into action. "I have sprung into action," I noted with satisfaction. Louise looked at me oddly.

I found a large pot. There was no steamer so I improvised by placing a round cookie rack in the bottom. I added an inch of water, placed the fish on the rack, put the pot on the burner, and gave it full throttle. By the time I'd made the salad, by opening the bag, she had the kindling blazing and was adding a couple of large logs.

"I don't mean to be unforthcoming, Danny, but this is a police investigation. I have to be a little bit careful about what I say. But I can tell you there's no smoking gun anywhere. Sorry, bad metaphor. There're just a couple of things that don't quite fit."

I nodded. The water was boiling so I put a lid on it and turned down the heat. "Twenty minutes." I remembered to slice the lemon and then topped up our wine. We both sat down again and she asked me for my life story, not in those words, of course. More like, *So where are you from?* Accompanied by slightly widened eyes looking at me over the rim of her glass. I gave her the Coles Notes version and she reciprocated.

By this time the fish was done, and I could tell at a glance it was perfect. While she fetched two plates, I opened the second bottle of wine. I put a fillet on each plate and we sat down to eat. The fillets had just slightly separated into tender oily flakes. She followed my example and squeezed some lemon juice over the fish, then placed a forkful in her mouth. "Ohmigod! This is so so good."

Aha, I thought. You're mine now. Out loud, "It's black cod," I said. "The best whitefish you'll ever taste."

We ate mostly in silence, sipping wine and eating just enough salad to feel virtuous. She ate steadily and seriously but even so, I finished ahead of her. I had almost but not completely overcome the seine boat habit of two-minute dining. We sat back, satiated. When I offered to do the dishes, she looked at the two plates and the pot and indicated that she could probably handle it. But I knew I'd scored even more points, and was beginning to plan my "Don't fall in love with me too quickly" speech.

"Danny, is there anything else of Crowley's I should have?"

Like an overconfident boxer, blind to the lethal left hook. "No, I don't think so."

"What about his boat's logbook?"

Guilty silence.

"It occurred to me to check his last fuel-up, so I went back. Who else would have taken it but you?"

Trying to perform a combination of anger and hurt, unlikely to be nominated for any award. "I didn't realize I was being tested."

"It wasn't a test, Danny. More of a trust-building exercise."

"How 'bout I fall over backwards and you catch me?"

"And then the group hug?"

I'm sure my eyes betrayed my sudden yearning. "Considering the group, a hug would be nice."

"The possibilities are endless. But we have some work to do."

I looked at her and she looked implacably back. I sensed a shift in mood and tried for a recovery. "To err is human, etcetera, etcetera. But I usually get things right the second time around."

"I'm sure you do." She opened the door and stood by it.

I decided to demonstrate understanding and cooperation. I donned my jacket, walked through the door, and turned to face Louise. "Good-bye?"

"For now." And the door shut.

As I walked back to the boat my breath froze in the air. I was glad my cool DFO fleecy was warm. I considered the report card of my "date." *Danny tries hard but there is much room for improvement.* Still?

Six

The *James Sinclair* pulled the hook at seven the next morning, right after I'd pulled up the crab trap, removed six large males, and thrown the females back. I'd lost track of the number of times we'd pulled anchor and steamed off trailing a crab trap behind. When a crab trap gets wound into the propeller, it's generally considered to be a bad thing.

We cruised through the narrow gap that leads into Seaforth Channel, and turned the sounders and sonar on. The brilliant stars faded as the sky lightened. The ocean was still a blanket of black, flecked with the white of small waves. A freshening breeze was kicking up a bit of chop but the three hundred tons of *James Sinclair* pushed imperviously through the water. Our heading was west, and by the time it was fully light we were turning north up Spiller Channel.

We zigzagged up the middle, all eyes on the sounder. Every blob of red indicated a school of herring, and we estimated the size and noted it. The two test boats were performing the same exercise along both shorelines. By noon, we'd formed a rough estimate of the amount of herring in the area. The central coast seine quota that year was thirty-five hundred tons. Between us and the test boats, we'd identified six to eight thousand tons.

We'd sent the plane up and the spotter had seen thin streaks of white in the green water along the Spiller Channel shore. Light spawning had started.

The other key factor in the equation, the roe content, had risen to twelve percent in the northern part of the channel, although it remained at about ten percent in the south. This probably meant there were still fish moving into the spawning area from the open ocean. But

D-day was getting closer. There would probably be a run on Rolaids and Tums at the Bella Bella store.

About four o'clock, we headed back to Shearwater for the evening conference. George was somehow handling the boat without my assistance, so with nothing better to do, I plugged my computer into the sat-phone network and went to the DFO website. I'd meant to check some of the stats from the Gulf opening but was waylaid by an icon for the Strategic Policy Working Group. Guided by some masochistic impulse, I clicked on the icon and it opened the report of the Special Policy for Licensing Abalone Group (SPLAG). After reading for a couple of minutes, I burst out laughing. "Listen to this. The policy guys have come up with a solution to the abalone problem. They're going to introduce area licensing."

Area licensing was a method by which DFO attempted to correct their screwups. It could be they'd issued too many licenses for a fishery, or mismanaged a fishery to the point where there weren't enough fish to support the same number of boats that had once made a good living. What they did was divide the coast up into little boxes and tell everyone that, whereas before they could fish the whole coast, now they could fish only in one little box. And if someone wanted to break out of the box, he could do so only by buying another license from a fellow fisherman. Result: one less fisherman and more expense for those remaining.

But this was ludicrous. Abalone was a dead fishery and the licenses were worthless. Pete and George rolled their eyes. They'd spotted the obvious flaw. Why would an abalone fisherman with a worthless license want to buy another one? "Stay tuned," I said. "It's a work in progress. I just know they'll come up with a brilliant solution. These are, after all, Policy Guys."

Silence. Sort of like when your dim-witted uncle acts up at the town picnic and embarrasses the whole family. Maybe this should be number two on my list of "Reasons Our Bureaucracy Keeps Screwing Things Up." The people who are affected by a policy should have some input into it.

We cruised along in silence for a while. I wrestled with my thoughts but we were booed out of the ring. I stared out at the shoreline fading in the dusk. Eagles festooned the trees like large fierce flowers. Seine boats weren't the only predators gathering to feast on the herring.

And so my thoughts returned, laudably but late, to work. "Pete, when do you think it'll happen?"

He rubbed his jaw. "Well, I don't know if George will agree, but things look pretty much on schedule to me." George nodded without taking his eyes off the water. "Tomorrow's Sunday," Pete continued, "I think we can afford to take the day off. But we'll send the plane up and I think we'll see more spot spawn, maybe fifteen, twenty miles of it. There's bigger tides starting on Monday and they'll push those southern fish farther up into the channel. I'm thinking maybe Wednesday we should let 'er go."

"Okay," I said, "maybe tonight we should put the fleet on forty-eight-hour notice." George and Pete both nodded. "Congratulations gentlemen, we have formulated a plan."

Dinner that night was an impromptu experience that only fishermen and us parasitic bureaucrats could ever experience. We started with the crabs I'd caught, then got into a bucket of clams that someone had dropped off. George brought out some sockeye that he'd smoked last summer, and we finished with grilled halibut donated by one of the company scout boats, obviously trying to curry favor.

After genuflecting before Alex, the cook, I headed to my stateroom with the intention of perusing Alistair's computer. I realized I'd need a monitor and turned toward the wheelhouse. George was there, picking his teeth. "How much you figure that meal would have cost downtown?"

"You couldn't have got it downtown," I said. "Not that good. I need to borrow a computer monitor. Do you mind?"

"Take the one off the GPS. It's the best one."

"Thanks. I'll have it back in a couple of hours." I performed a quick lobotomy and lugged the monitor into my stateroom. In no time, I had it hooked up to its new brain, and powered up Alistair's computer. As I'd feared, though, the computer asked for a password. I tried to bypass it but Alistair had been much too canny for that. Prawns? No. Hmmm. Shrimp? Crustacean? Wait a minute. Latin. What the hell was the Latin for prawn? That didn't work either. Shit! A flash of memory: Chimera. Bingo! I was in.

The password allowed me access to the desktop. I looked at the array of program icons and clicked on Excel, and then "open." The drop-down menu showed a list of files and I opened the first one. I was now looking at a database like the ones pasted in the journal. I opened more files. More of the same and I still couldn't make heads nor tails out of it. I closed Excel and considered the other program icons. There was Word, Access, Adobe, Eudora, Internet Explorer, Photoshop, and all the assorted junk stuff that no one ever uses. I opened Eudora, knowing there wouldn't be much because he didn't have a phone line. His inbox, surprisingly, ran to seven hundred and thirty-eight messages, courtesy presumably of landlines in Bella Bella. Most were of the "Cheaper prescription drugs from your best friendly guys in Nigeria" or "Drive your women crazy in bed" variety. There were a few messages from colleagues, invitations to conferences, and family updates from a daughter in Ontario, but nothing to interest me.

I opened Word. There were three files and every one of them was gobbledegook. Alistair had encrypted them. Ergo, they were really important. Ergo, I had to read them. Ergo, I'd have to enlist someone more computer literate than me. Maybe this was a problem for Super Bette, girl computer whiz.

There was a rap on the door. "The conference starts in five minutes."

"Okay, be right there."

I shut everything down, disconnected the monitor, and took it back to the bridge. Alex handed me up a coffee and I took a sip as I looked around. The usual suspects were gathered and all five radios were crackling away. I turned all of them off except for the VHF tuned to channel 78A, and picked up the mike.

"Attention, the roe herring fleet. This is the *James Sinclair*. Stand by for an announcement." I released the mike key and looked at Pete and George.

Pete shrugged. "Go ahead and put them on forty-eight hours' standby. Then we'll get down to the details."

George raised a finger. "Forty-eight hours takes us to Monday night, which is a bad time to open a fishery. Make it thirty-six hours and they'll be ready to go Monday morning if necessary."

I nodded and keyed the mike button again. "Attention, the roe herring fleet. We are giving notice that the fleet is now on thirty-six hours' notice with the earliest possible fishery on Monday morning at eight, but with an anticipated fishery on Wednesday at 0800 hours. Here are the results of today's test fishery."

I then read off two pages of numbers: tonnages, percentages, male/ female ratios, number of slinks, amount of spot spawn, and all the other arcane data that, taken together with a healthy amount of pure intuition, would allow us to pinpoint the optimum time for the fishery. I finished with, "Please come back to the *James Sinclair* with any questions."

"*James Sinclair, Dawn Dancer.*"

One of my favorite boat names. "Go ahead, *Dawn Dancer.*"

"Yeah, well, so how come if you're thinking about opening on Wednesday, you're putting us on standby for Monday?"

George rolled his eyes. "Jesus, who's running that boat this year? Must be a goddamn rookie."

I made sure George was finished expostulating before I transmitted a reply. In a carefully neutral voice, "Skipper, all our information points to a probable Wednesday fishery, but the fish have fooled us before. We don't want to see a panic on Monday morning if a major spawn does start then."

There were more questions but everyone seemed fairly comfortable with the idea. Fortunately, weather was not a major part of the equation for this particular fishery. Spiller Channel was a fairly sheltered area and these were the seine boats, the big boys. Thank God I wasn't running a gillnet fishery somewhere off the west coast. That could be a real high-wire act. One slipup and you'd lose more than the Flying Wallendas.

When the last query had been queried, and the last reply replied, I bade goodnight to my fellow inmates and returned to my stateroom. I hadn't learned much from Alistair's computer but thought I might be able to glean a clue from his logbook. Many fishermen keep a ship's log and a separate fishing log. Alistair combined the two. A typical entry would look like this:

April 3
0500: left base
0630: set one string, Blarney Rock
0715: set one string, Mulcher's reef
0820: set two strings, 80 fm hole.
1230: picked 1st string—63 lbs large
1345: picked 2nd string—52 lbs large, 15 jumbo
1430: picked strings 3 & 4—115 lbs large, 42 jumbo, bycatch—two China rockfish
1435: left for Shearwater
1730: arrived Shearwater, delivered
1900: fueled up—84 gal.
1930: tied up

The log covered the last four years. A quick skim-through showed that almost all entries followed the same format. Sometimes entries referred to a simple cruise without all the set data, but other than that, there was nothing even remotely unusual. For lack of anything intelligent to do, I took the logbook to the copier and spent fifteen minutes copying every page. Then I placed the book in the inside pocket of my floater jacket so I could give it to Louise and get back to first base, or at least line up to get tickets to the ballpark.

Seven

The next morning, the main engines remained silent. There was only the comforting hum of the auxiliary engine as it powered the generator. But I was up early anyway and greeted George at the galley table. Sitting across from him, I sipped my coffee. Rain pattered on the roof. We could hear the weather station on one of the wheelhouse radios. Southeast winds, strong to storm force, two-meter swells at Idol Point, barometer falling; outlook—winds rising to gale force and continuing overnight.

I looked at George and grimaced slightly. He nodded. Definitely a harbor day.

"I think I'll go visiting, George. Okay if I take the Zodiac?" He shrugged and got up to pour us both another coffee. We sat for awhile. Finally, tired of the constant chatter, I got up, donned rain gear and life jacket, and jumped into the Zodiac.

I revved up to full speed but the rain stung my eyes. Not wanting to proceed at full throttle with my eyes shut, I slowed down and idled over to the *Coastal Provider*. As I tied up, my salivary glands leapt into action at the smell of frying bacon. Feeling like Pavlov's dog, I opened the galley door and stepped inside.

Mark and his crew were sitting at the table, just about to tuck into copious amounts of bacon, eggs, and real hash browns. "Hey Danny, grab a plate and help yourself." Graciously acquiescent, I filled my plate and joined them at the table. "Gentlemen, this is an old friend of mine, Danny Swanson. Danny, that's Randy, Johnny Jr., Sid, and Jarrod." As he went around the table, I nodded hello and hoped I'd remember their names.

We concentrated on the food for awhile, and then, because I had the only seat not blocked by the table, I got up and poured a round of coffee. As the piles of food dwindled, conversation swelled. Many comments on the weather and how it boded for the fishery, much speculation about the timing of the fishery and speculating about the myriad ways that DFO could screw it up. Mark hurriedly interjected that I was in fact a DFO employee, but because of my past was not a "real DFO guy." I tried to look reassuring and the talk continued. At the first lull, I told the story of SPLAG, the Special Policy for Licensing Abalone Group, and their stellar work on matters of complete irrelevance. There were a few chuckles at that, and then the devil took control of my mind. "You know," I said, "their website is interactive and anyone can post policy ideas. We should post something completely off the wall and see how they react to it."

"Couldn't they trace it and you'll get into trouble?"

"We could sign a false name, or"—I felt a surge of evil glee—"we could sign a real person's name, like, say, Fleming Griffith." Appreciative chuckles all around the table. "Okay, they're talking about area licensing for worthless licenses. What can we add to that to make it even stupider?"

Mark chimed in, "DFO says to the license holders, buy out two other licenses and we'll give you an experimental license, sort of like send in two box tops and we'll give you a free coupon."

Johnny Jr. enthusiastically joined in. "But the experimental license has to use different gear." Abalone were harvested by divers and I couldn't imagine any other way to do it, but Johnny Jr. could. "We'll say they have to experiment with traps."

I was sipping my coffee and almost choked when he said that. Abalone were, sort of, mobile. They could cover up to ten or eleven inches a day. It would take weeks for more than one to find its way into a trap. It was just ridiculous enough to appeal to the policy gurus.

The other guys were jumping in now. "But we must have strict trap regulations—minimum mesh size and four-inch escape holes.

No more than thirty traps per boat. And traps must be constructed of North American bamboo." Six adult males were sitting around in a very no-nonsense seine boat, giggling like children. "And the traps have to have legs so they don't sit on the bottom and squash things." We dressed it up in linguistic clothes of appropriate bureaucratic hue, making references to peer-reviewed monitoring methodologies and adjusted catch-per-unit effort, and presto: we had A Policy.

This may seem ridiculous to anyone who lives in the real world, but in DFO land, truth is much, much stranger than fiction. I couldn't help but remember the great Sointula abalone experiment. DFO had just finished one of their occasional pogroms directed against fishermen and were as usual surprised at the public outcry. Collapsing coastal communities, unemployed fishermen, bankrupt businesses, and broken families are difficult to justify as "good results." So DFO consulted their flaks and came up with a "transition policy." This, of course, involved throwing large lumps of money at the problem. Sointula was awarded a modest pile of money and decided to invest it in BC's first abalone farm. DFO approved the plan but, apparently not realizing that abalone are incapable of spontaneous generation, refused to grant a license to collect some brood stock.

Finally, the co-op armed themselves in common sense, collected twelve adult abalone, and dared DFO to charge them. Refusing to surrender to this attack of rationality, DFO did so. Charges were later dropped at trial but the co-op had to pay the legal fees. And DFO extracted a further pound of flesh by demanding that up to fifty percent of the total production be returned to the ocean to build up wild stocks.

Abalone are slow growing and it would be at least four years before the animals were of marketable size. After two years of operational costs, the abalone co-op was broke. Volunteers kept it going for two more years. In year four, DFO approached the co-op and asked for five thousand animals to return to the wild. In return, the co-op asked for permission to sell some abalone to raise money to cover expenses. Unfortunately, by this time DFO had listed abalone as a species at risk and therefore they couldn't be sold. Never mind that these abalone weren't at risk because they had been raised in tanks, and never mind that if the co-op couldn't raise money, it would fold and the primary source of abalone for transplant to the wild would be lost.

By the time DFO sorted out its internal inconsistencies, and allowed farmed abalone to be sold, the co-op was broke. Defeat had been snatched from the jaws of victory.

Fishermen were used to this level of thinking, if that is the right word, from DFO. That is why we were totally convinced that the nonsense that we had concocted would be accepted as rational. Mark went to the wheelhouse and typed our gibberish into his computer, signed it as Fleming Griffith, and posted it. He came back to the galley grinning. "I wonder how long before Griffith sees that and deletes it."

"It might be awhile," I said. "I believe he's in Brussels telling the Europeans not to worry about the east coast cod because they can fish our west coast cod. We'll log on tomorrow and check the response."

The crew began to bicker about their own policy issue, whether or not rain gear was allowed in the galley, so Mark and I grabbed a coffee and retired to the wheelhouse. Mark settled into the swivel chair by the wheel and I lounged on the padded bench by the chart table. We stared out the window at the wind-driven rain.

"Hey," I nudged Mark's chair with my foot, "how's the vow of celibacy holding up?"

"Nothing to it, as long as there's no actual female within visual range. It gets a little tough if I have to tell them about it, because then they're all over me, like it's a challenge or something. Actually, it's the ultimate pickup line. I wish I'd thought of it in junior high."

I laughed. "As I remember it, there wasn't an overwhelming need for a vow of celibacy because you were already under a sentence of celibacy."

"Well, you were in the same jail I was."

"Yeah, but I was pardoned sooner. Good behavior and all."

He snorted. "Good behavior? You used to leave trails of drool up and down the halls. My mongrel dog showed more dignity than you did." We lapsed into silence as we remembered the "difficult years"; sexual arousal as a state of being.

The voices from the galley were getting louder. "Fifteen two, fifteen four, a pair is six, and a run is nine."

"Stinkhole!"

"We're not playing stinkhole!"

"We always play stinkhole north of Cape Caution."

"You lie like a hairy egg. Shut up and deal."

The rain was easing. Mark stood up. "Let's go for a ride. There's a couple of herring punts in Bella Bella I want to look at."

We grabbed our rain gear and went out on deck.

The Zodiac was a lot faster than Mark's power skiff so we used it. Mark wanted to go to the fishermen's wharf where most of the boats were tied up, rather than the government dock downtown. As we got close to the dock, we could see Native guys in rain gear hanging herring gill nets. "Native guys" was my internal terminology. Publicly, I attempted to use the terminology of the day: Aboriginals or First Nations or whatever. Normal Native guy terminology for Native guys was "Indian."

Bella Bella, a village of about fourteen hundred people, was home to the mighty Heiltsuk Nation. At one time, they had a pretty fair-sized fleet. That was before Fleming Griffith conned the Fisheries Minister of the hour, an ego in a suit named Fred Mifflin, into decimating the salmon fleet. Actually, decimate isn't a strong enough word. How about "triagimate," since a third rather than a tenth of the fleet was killed off.

As we tied up, we could see close to a hundred boats of all shapes and sizes. Mark wanted to look at herring skiffs, which were used for gillnetting herring rather than seining them. You couldn't catch as many gillnetting as seining, but the fish were of better quality, there were a higher percentage of females, and therefore more roe, so you got a better price.

As we wandered down the dock, we ran into an old buddy. Cecil Brown was a Native guy from Metlakatla, up north. We knew him because he used to run a packer for JS MacMillan Fisheries and we would offload our salmon onto his boat.

He smiled under his Sou'wester. "Mark, Danny, good to see you. Hey Danny, if Mark sets early, are you going to bust him?" He laughed and wiped rain from his face.

"Actually, I'm here to bust you because you're way out of your territory."

He winked. "It's okay. I've got cousins here so I'm legit. And you know what? I've got cousins everywhere so you can't give me a hard time. C'mon, I'll buy you a coffee." He led the way to his boat, a fifty-two-foot packer that at one time had been the largest fiberglass boat built in BC. The *Waterfowl* was well maintained and gave no hint of its long and arduous history. The boat had probably transported more fish over the years than any other packer still working. And because Cecil considered any wind under forty knots a summer breeze, the boat had probably had as much green water over the bow as under it.

We doffed our rain gear and entered the cozy galley. The oil stove radiated a pleasant warmth. The coffeepot was full and there were bannock and smoked salmon set on the table. "Make yourself at home, guys." He placed three mugs on the table, poured extremely black coffee into each of them, and pointed at the sugar and can of condensed milk.

We settled around the table and customized our coffees. "So Danny, how's Ottawa? You look like you're still halfway sane anyway."

"Ottawa is Ottawa, unfortunately. It sure feels good to be back out here."

"Yeah, well you sure earn your money. I wouldn't work back there for anything. So how come you guys got brave enough to leave Shearwater and sneak into Heiltsuk territory?"

Mark answered, "I heard there were a couple of herring skiffs for sale."

"Yeah, the Glenning boys are selling two ten-ton skiffs. They're three fingers over, right behind the *Cape Morrisey*. So you want to quit the big boat stuff? Become a stiff in a skiff?"

"Jimmy only lets us have the one seine license. I like to fish it here, but gillnetting is good up north. If I can get a good deal on some gear, I might give it a try."

"Finish your coffee and we'll wander over and have a look. The sun's almost out."

The sun might have been out in Tahiti but it sure as hell wasn't out here. However, the rain was now merely a drizzle and the sky was light enough that you could almost read a newspaper. We walked down the float to the header float and then along it to the third finger. Just as we turned to walk down the outside float, something caught my eye, and I stopped in amazement. A battered aluminum crew boat, maybe twenty-four feet with a forward cabin, and the name in just slightly faded red letters. *Kelp*.

Mark and Cecil turned to look at me. "What's up?"

I pointed at the *Kelp*. "Mark, did you read to the end of Alistair's journals?"

He shook his head. "I didn't get a chance to finish them."

"I'll explain later, but we need to find out who owns that boat."

"Okay, let's take a quick look at the skiffs, and then we'll find the wharfmaster. He'll have a record of the owner."

As we walked farther down the float, Cecil looked at me questioningly. I shrugged. "It's a long, strange story, Cecil. I'll tell you about it some time." By this time, we were passing the high bow of the *Cape Morrisey* and could see two flat-bottomed herring skiffs tied side by side. The inside skiff had a FOR SALE sign on it with a phone number. Mark made a note and then began to clamber over the skiffs, inspecting hull condition and welds, as well as the gear. Finally he finished and climbed back onto the float.

"Let's find the wharfmaster." We walked toward the wharf head and up the gangway to the parking area. Cecil stopped by a phone booth and began fumbling for change.

"No lineup. Better phone the wife. See you guys later." We waved and walked toward a vinyl-sided shack displaying a sign. WHARFMASTER. When we entered, I could see that the sign should have read WHARFMISTRESS. She was Heiltsuk, maybe some white blood, and extremely attractive. As she rose from her desk and approached the counter, I noted, hopefully without staring, her burnished brown skin, high cheekbones, and long glossy black hair.

"Can I help you?" Her voice was as attractive as the rest of her.

I leaned on the counter and gave her the full benefit of my coolly intelligent but warmly open and honest gaze.

"I wonder if you could tell us who owns that aluminum crew boat, the *Kelp*."

"Mac McPherson used to have it. Used it to run back and forth to his A-frame show. He sold it about a year ago, but I've never seen the guy that bought it."

"Do you have a name and address?"

"Hang on." As she walked away toward a bank of filing cabinets I prayed my gratitude to the inventor of blue jeans. I glanced at Mark. He must have been struggling with his vow but he was concealing it well. When she reached the filing cabinets, she bent over to pull open the second from the bottom drawer, and I had to avert my eyes. She extracted a file and walked back toward us.

She smiled and I felt all warm inside. "Trevor Holbrooke. Apartment 237, 892 West 41st Street, Vancouver, BC. He mails us a money order for the moorage fees every month."

"Thanks for the info. My name's Danny, by the way."

"Melissa. Melissa O'Rourke. Pleased to meet you."

"Well, thanks. You've been really helpful." Out of habit, I tried the standard line. "Maybe I could buy you a drink, just to say thank you?" Without looking, I knew that Mark was gazing heavenward.

"That's not necessary. I'm always happy to assist DFO in the ongoing performance of their duties."

I looked at her for a hint of a smirk, but she had an absolutely straight face. "Well, see ya."

She nodded and went back to her desk. When we were outside, I said to Mark, "Pretty cute, eh?"

"Yeah, I know her boyfriend."

"Really?"

"Oh yeah, he's this big Native guy. Used to play lacrosse for the Victoria Shamrocks. Killed a guy in a fight during the '97 play-offs. No charges, but he's still got a really bad temper."

I bit. "I don't remember anyone getting killed . . ." I broke off when Mark burst out laughing. "Bastard."

"Gullible twit."

We ambled back toward the wharf. "Let's take the boat downtown. Maybe you can arrange to meet the Glennings and talk prices. I've got a couple of errands to run."

Five minutes later, we were tied up at the downtown dock. We walked up the floats, past kids fishing, using more sophisticated gear than I'd ever had, but with the same expressions of unquenchable optimism. The odd one even had a fish lying on the wooden planks, vivid colors fading to dull lifelessness. I waited while Mark used the pay phone, and when he hung up, he said he'd meet me back here in an hour. When he was around the corner and out of sight, I headed for the RCMP building. I pondered briefly why I was being so damn surreptitious, but I arrived at the door before I arrived at an answer.

Inside, I asked for Staff Sergeant Louise Karavchuk, and was told to wait. I perused the WANTED posters on the wall and was pleased to see none of my relatives. Should I point that out to Louise? Maybe not. No need to be completely on the defensive.

She appeared at the counter and nodded hello. "What can I do for you?"

"Can we talk in private?"

She glanced behind her and considered a minute. "Let's take a walk." She donned a rain jacket, unlatched the gate, and joined me on the public side of the counter. "I've been stuck in the office all day. You're a good excuse to get out."

I was thrilled. I'd been upgraded to a good excuse. "I want to apologize again about last night," I said once we were outside. "I've got a lot of suspicions but no evidence. I don't want to make wild accusations and I guess I wanted to have first crack at the logbook just to see if I could see something that would have been meaningless to an outsider. But I don't think there's anything there at all." I took the book out of my inside pocket and handed it to her. She slipped it into her pocket.

We walked up the hill, then turned left toward the bighouse. We studied the façade, painted brightly in a Heiltsuk motif. There were forms within forms within forms, and each larger form merged seamlessly with all the others. "Tell me about your suspicions."

I took a deep breath. "Alistair might have been involved in something at DFO that was highly illegal. The people he was involved with might have killed him to keep him quiet."

"Alistair hadn't worked for DFO for seventeen years. Why kill him now?"

"Don't know."

"Who killed him?"

"Don't know."

"If Crowley was on the run, why come here?"

"Don't know."

"What do you know?"

"Eight years ago, we caught a mutant fish tagged by DFO. After we caught it, my buddy took it to DFO lab. They say he never arrived there, but a picture of the fish, taken after we caught it, showed up in a DFO database recently. And my buddy disappeared into thin air."

Somehow we'd ended up walking quite close together. Narrow sidewalks or something. She nudged me with her elbow. "I can understand why you were holding back a bit. No one likes to come across as a conspiracy nut. Do you have anything concrete at all?"

"Maybe. Remember those references to kelp? Like he was waiting for it? There's a boat at the fishermen's wharf called the *Kelp*. No one's seen the owner but I've got an address in Vancouver for him. We should check it out but we've got to be careful not to alarm him."

"Really? Not alarm him? Good thing you pointed that out."

I decided to be quiet for awhile. But just a short while. "Why are you guys suspicious?"

"Highly confidential, okay? There are a number of ways to commit suicide with a long gun, but you need to pull the trigger with something, usually a finger or toe. There was no powder residue on any of Crowley's extremities, although his fingerprints were on the trigger."

"You were right, suspicious but not definitive."

"Give me that address. I'll have it checked out. We'll try and match it with a phone number and any utility bills, like hydro. We can do that just by checking the cross-registry files, you know."

"Yeah, I knew that. I just wanted to see if you knew that. What time do you get off work? You owe me a dinner."

"God, you're smooth." She smiled at me and the world seemed a better place. "I trust my credit card more than I trust my cooking. I'll meet you at the restaurant around seven. I've got to talk to someone up the street here. See you later."

I waved and turned back toward the wharf. It was a small town, I reflected, if someone could offer to meet you at "the restaurant." As further evidence of the small-townness of the place, I deduced that the attractive young woman approaching me was the same attractive young woman who had come on to me so blatantly at the wharfmaster's office.

"Hello again," I said cleverly.

"Why, it's Danny DFO." She gave me a taunting stare. "Wanna check me over? You know, for violations or anything?"

I was beginning to detect a certain level of antipathy. I gave her my best hurt smile: not "wounded puppy" but "carrying-on-in-spite-of-the-wounds."

"Sometimes I'd like to burn my DFO jacket," I said. "But then I wouldn't have a job and the whole world would be worse off."

"That would be awful, Danny. Then what would we do? We certainly couldn't manage our fisheries all by ourselves."

Irritation dictated my reply. "I was a fisherman for ten years. I know how everyone feels about DFO. I signed up because I thought I could change things. I was young and stupid. What the hell."

It was if a mask disappeared from her face. "I'm glad to know you're not a typical DFO dickhead. Now, if I knew you weren't just an everyday dickhead, I'd feel comfortable talking to you."

An assortment of responses flashed through my mind. "Yeah, well, I'm not just an ordinary dickhead," seemed not entirely satisfactory. I was saved from the necessity of an intelligent response by the arrival, stage left, of another actor on the scene.

Middle-aged Native female, comfortably round like my favorite aunt, carrying an umbrella, which hadn't prevented her glasses from streaking with rainwater. She stopped and removed her glasses, gazing owl-like at us. "Hello, Melissa."

"Hello, Auntie." Then addressing me, "This is my Auntie Rose." And then, with just a hint of non-disapproval, "Auntie, this is Danny Swanson."

I knew that in Native society, the terms "Auntie" and "Uncle" had a wider meaning than in our European kinship system. The terms extended to various relationships by marriage as well as to older cousins and second cousins. So I thought I was on firm ground when I asked, "How exactly are you guys related?"

Rose wiped her glasses and looked at me. "I am Melissa's mother's sister. Her aunt." And then she let me off the hook. She smiled gently, "I am her Auntie in all senses of the word." She stared at DFO crest on my jacket. "Perhaps you knew Alistair Crowley?"

I was surprised. Crowley was, according to popular opinion, a loner at best, if not an outright hermit. "I knew of him, mostly as a working scientist. I was shocked to hear about his death."

"I work at the Heiltsuk Health Centre. Alistair used to drop in and give us a hand. He was putting together a comprehensive database for us." She bowed her head. "I liked Alistair. If he was one us, we would know what to do. Are his remains being looked after?"

Damned if I knew. The body was probably lying rent asunder in a drawer in the Bella Bella morgue. The sister in Ontario, had she been notified? Hopefully. And what sort of acknowledgment would be made of Alistair's life? Death, or rather the end of a life, was heeded with significant attention in Native communities. Band offices would be closed for at least a day. Meetings would be canceled, no matter how important. Why? Because every human being was recognized as being a member of not only a family, but a community. And therefore the community would mourn.

I resolved at the very least to gather members of Alistair's sub-community and drink some scotch. Scientists, as ego-driven and contentious as they could be, were always ready to recognize their own: in death, if not in peer-reviewed journals.

"I guess procedures are being followed, Rose. His family will organize the funeral; I'll organize the wake."

She smiled. "Ah yes, the Celtic approach. Our legends speak of a lost tribe that disappeared on a journey. I've always thought that they ended up in Scotland. The Scots are so tribal, they could only have originated from us. The bagpipes must be their way of channeling the ancestors."

I couldn't help but laugh. "Or talking to the wolves." The amusement on her face encouraged me. "Did Alistair just show up out of the blue and start working for you?"

"He was an old university friend of my father's," Melissa said. "Dad was the doctor here for years. Alistair dropped in to talk to him, not knowing my parents had split up and my dad was back in Vancouver."

Rose continued "And when he saw me struggling with my filing system, he offered to computerize everything for me. He used to drop in and spend a day every couple of weeks or so. I found it very helpful."

"Is your Dad still in Vancouver?"

"Yeah, he runs a drop-in clinic on East Hastings. Dr. James O'Rourke. Dr. Jimmy to everyone who knows him."

I looked at my watch. "Jeez, I gotta run. Nice meeting you, Rose. Thanks for introducing us, Melissa." I waved and strode briskly down the hill. Mark was waiting, not too impatiently, by the wharf head.

"Did you buy a skiff?"

He shook his head. "We're still dickering. They want to sell the skiffs only, no licenses. I'd prefer a package deal, so we'll see what happens. If the price of herring goes down again this year, there'll be lots of gear and licenses for sale. Mind you, if that happens, I'd be a fool to buy one."

"The old catch-22," I laughed. "If you can afford the license, you shouldn't buy it. If it's worth buying, you can't afford it."

Somehow I'd missed lunch and dinner wasn't until seven. Fortunately, man is a foraging animal. I pulled Mark into the Zodiac and we set a course for the fridge on the *James Sinclair*. On the way there, I asked Mark if he knew Pete and George and the rest of the crew. "Pete almost busted me once. It was two years ago on herring. I made a set close to the line but I had to turn a bit to miss that asshole on the *Pacific Aggressor*. About a quarter of my net, at the most, was over the line. Pete roars up in the Zodiac and tells me to backhaul. We were already closed up, so I said I had the right to check and record my Loran readings, to see if he was right. While I was pretending to do that, I radioed my power skiff and told him to tow us full bore. Pete knew what was going on. Three minutes later we were on the right side of the line so he just waved and took off. He could have made a big deal about it but he didn't."

"You're lucky it wasn't me. I would have had to follow through just because some people know I fished with you."

"Maybe you're better off in Ottawa. You can't cause trouble there."

"Yeah, but I can sure get in trouble.'

We tied up to the *James Sinclair* and climbed aboard. In the galley, Pete and George turned as we entered. They were hunched like surprised vultures over a plate of fresh blueberry muffins. I pointed. "Stay away from those. They're for the good people. And here we are."

I introduced Mark and named his boat, and Pete grinned. "I'd like to take a look at your Loran some day. It must be really old-fashioned to take so long to read."

Mark parried. "It has really small print and sometimes it takes awhile to find my reading glasses." He sat down and innocently helped himself to a muffin.

George grabbed a muffin in self-defense as Pete and I lunged politely for the plate. "Have you looked at your computer today, Danny? That Abalone License Policy whatever website is getting to be beyond a joke. Fleming posted a discussion paper suggesting people apply for experimental licenses to fish abalone with traps."

I stared hard but not at Mark. "And then," George continued, "Some ass-kissing dimwit replied what a great idea that was and proposed a twenty-five-cents-per-pound royalty."

I'd always been curious as to what exactly constituted a genuine guffaw. I had my answer, as all four of us threw back our heads and roared.

Pete wiped tears from his eyes. "Don't these guys realize that it would take thirty-seven years of fishing abalone with traps to raise enough money to pay for the stamps to mail out the licenses?"

"You're exaggerating. With the new DFO-designed traps, it might only take sixteen years. Mind you, it will take DFO nineteen years to do the paperwork to get the new traps approved." And we were off again, gasping and choking with laughter like adolescent boys.

Alex the cook emerged from his stateroom. "You guys discussing the organization again?" He shook his head. "You know, when I was working on seine boats, I thought that DFO was fucked. But now that

I've been working for them for six years, I can see the error of my thought. They're not the fuckees, they're the fuckers. By the way, didn't I make some muffins half an hour ago?"

"You should have made the kind that lasted."

"Oh, I can do that. My next batch will last a long time."

George backtracked hurriedly. "No need for that, Alex. These were just fine." None of us considered it even passingly curious that the skipper would kowtow to the cook. The first rule on any working boat was, don't mess with the cook. The second rule was, if you break rule one, slip your plate to the guy next to you. And the third rule, obviously, was don't sit next to the guy who messes with the cook.

Mark stood up. "Thanks for the BS, guys. It was fun. See you on the grounds."

When I got back from returning Mark to the *Coastal Provider*, the galley was deserted. Nap time, I guessed. It was only four, so I went to my stateroom, intending to follow my shipmates' example. But my brain insisted on worrying at the puzzle. I lay on my bunk and thought back to the questions Louise had asked.

Why had Crowley been killed now? If the killing was connected to some dark secret in the West Vancouver lab, why not kill him seventeen years ago when he retired?

Who killed him? Figure out why and who would probably fall into place.

And why had he come here, fifty miles southeast of the middle of nowhere? To hook up with Dr. James O'Rourke? Unlikely, I judged, but worth looking into.

By the time I had pondered these questions to the point that they knew damn well that they'd been pondered by a not inconsiderable ponderer, it was time to shower and get ready for my big date.

As I took advantage of the *Jimmy Sinc*'s ample water tanks for my shower, I considered whether or not I should rethink my principle of not sleeping with anyone until the third date: at least, anyone who had been a principal on the date. Play it by ear, I decided.

The sky had cleared before a ridge of high pressure and the temperature had dropped at least five degrees. The water was black and so was the sky. Suspended just below the roof of the sky were countless sparkling ice crystals, and below them the pale glow of a three-quarter moon. I was wearing my DFO fleecy and my DFO floater jacket, and glad of them. I wished I had worn my DFO woollen watch cap. Fortunately, it was a short ride and I still had some feeling in my ears when I arrived at the dock.

I tied up the boat and set off for The Restaurant, more properly referred to as Alexa's. I arrived before Louise, helped myself to a mug of steaming coffee, and sat with my hands cupped around the mug. My cousin Ollie came in, saw me, and sat down. "Danny Boy, what's up?"

"Just waiting for the fish, same as you. Have you got your boat here?"

"No, I'm shaking with Lenny Gravino on the *Seeker*." Shaking was what herring gillnetters did, literally shaking the net so that the fish fell out and into the bottom of the skiff. It was bloody hard work.

"How's the shrimp business?"

"It's okay. Price isn't great but the stocks seem pretty stable. It's a pretty basic fishery. I cruise out into the Gulf of Georgia, find my favorite spot on the McCall Bank, do a few drags, and head home to Steveston." Louise approached the table and I introduced her to Ollie. He got up and shook her hand. "Nice meeting you, but I've got to get back to the boat. See you later, Danny." He limped toward the counter, just another casualty of the in-seine boat wars.

Louise sat down and smiled at me as she waved good-bye to Ollie. "You want the good news or the bad news? Actually, you don't have a choice. The bad news is that the owner of the *Kelp* gave a phony address and probably a phony name. The good news is that this info, plus the lack of powder residue on the body, has persuaded the higher-ups to designate this as a suspicious death. We've talked to the Credit Union and they're finding out where the money orders were bought. The next time Melissa receives a payment for the moorage fees, she'll hand the envelope to us, and we'll try to get some prints off it and trace the mailing origin."

"You've been busy."

"We always get our man."

Before I could think of a clever reply, the waitress arrived to take our order. We both settled on halibut cheeks and a green salad. The salad arrived first, which was about all you could say for it.

I pointed out to the waitress that it wasn't really green.

"Oh," she replied, "we just call it a green salad. You wouldn't expect us to hire someone Greek just to make our Greek salads, would you?" I couldn't argue with that, and the halibut cheeks more than compensated for the lack of support from the salad department.

"There's something else we could check out. You know Melissa O'Rourke? Crowley was a university buddy of her father's. That may be why he showed up here. The father is practicing in Vancouver now. I'd like to talk to him when the fishery is over."

"Bit of a problem there, Danny. You're not supposed to be part of the investigation. Hell, technically you're a suspect, even though you've got a really good alibi: namely, you were still in Ottawa when Crowley was shot."

"If this murder is tied to the science branch of DFO, you're going to need me to navigate through that maze, both the bureaucratic and the scientific side of it." I could hear the ire inflecting my voice. "Crowley's friends and colleagues will open up more to me than you guys. If I'm going to help out, assist you in your inquiries or whatever, you can't just treat me like a trained seal."

"Danny, I would never treat you like a trained seal. And dammit, I won't let my fellow officers treat you like one either. The first time they throw you a fish, I want you to let me know." She paused a beat, gauging my reaction. I was too righteously indignant to smile.

"But Danny, we can't have a civilian running around questioning witnesses in a possible murder investigation."

"Louise, you need my help. I know stuff you don't, I know people you don't, and I can open doors for you."

Louise gave me a bit of a smile. "You want to be a doorman, you'll have to change your uniform. Okay, Danny, you're right. I need your help on this case. But you're enough of a bureaucrat to know there's protocols involved. We can stickhandle through them but it'll take teamwork."

"As long as I'm on the team and not in the penalty box. C'mon. Walk me back to the dock."

Two minutes later, we stood on the float, sheltered in the shadows of some pilings. I desperately wanted to hug her but settled for standing there awkwardly. Finally Louise told me I had to go and I reluctantly obeyed. On the way back to the *Jimmy Sinc*, I reflected that this date was an improvement on my last one. There was a lot to be said for bureaucratic liaison.

Eight

In the morning, I nursed a coffee and gazed inattentively out the starboard porthole of the galley. A sleek red hull was momentarily framed in the opening as the *Racer* slipped into the harbor. The diagonal white stripe amidships on the hull identified it as a Coast Guard vessel. It was Christine's boat, or the one she served on, at least. My spirits rose as I contemplated a reunion.

The anchor chain rattled as the *Racer* dropped its hook about halfway between us and the *Coastal Provider*. I'd give them a little time to get squared away, do their chores and such, then I'd pick up Mark and go over for a visit.

George and Pete wandered down from the wheelhouse where they'd been listening to the radios. Radio chatter, on a harbor day with a large fleet anchored up, can be very entertaining. Even fishermen get bored after awhile with talking about fish. So they start telling jokes, some of which would be repeatable in polite company, or they tell stories or sing "Happy Birthday" to their buddies, or broadcast short spurts of their favorite tunes.

George sat down while Pete rummaged through the fridge. "Did you hear those two Native guys talking a while ago?" I shook my head. "They were talking about the weather and all the signs that they relied on to predict a blow. They talked about the red sky in the morning and the feel of the air and the seabirds heading for shelter and so forth. And then the one guy says, but don't forget to look at the white men's anchor lines. If they've got long anchor lines, you know it's going to blow. You've gotta check all the signs." He chuckled. "You've gotta check all the signs. I like that."

A meatloaf sandwich joined us at the table, with Pete hanging off the north side of it. "Too bad all of our cross-cultural relationships can't be that positive."

I raised an eyebrow. "Cross-cultural relationships?"

"Hey, I always get philosophical on Sunday mornings, but you know what I mean."

Yeah, I knew. Relations between white and Native fishermen were generally pretty good. They had to be. When you might have to call on a guy to tow you off a rock sometime, you wanted to be sure you hadn't called him a stupid Indian at some point. But aside from self-interest, there was a genuine bond among almost all fishermen that stemmed from the fact that they were all trying to scratch a living in the most dangerous profession in the world. There were some rednecks in the fleet, though, and sometimes tensions rose when a particularly misguided bit of DFO policy seemed to favor one race over another. However, most guys realized the Natives had some catching up to do. They just didn't want the entire cost of Native reconciliation to come out of their pocket.

George nodded his head. "My favorite time when I was fishing was hanging around the net floats on the weekend. You'd have Japanese and Natives and white guys and Swedes"—I kicked him under the table—"and they'd all be helping each other with their nets and BS-ing and having a great time. I never knew how to make a proper mesh knot until Harvey Scow's wife showed me. And I showed a few Native guys how to throw in a window patch."

We all ruminated about this for a few minutes. Pete commented, "There should be Natives working with us, on all the patrol boats."

"Too bad there's not a few Natives in that big DFO building in Ottawa," George said.

"Christ," Pete replied, "they've got too much self-respect for that."

We ruminated on that as well. Finally, I said, "I'm going over to the *Racer* for a visit. You guys want to come?" I knew George would never leave the boat, but Pete demurred as well, mumbling something about reports.

Just as I stood up, there was a faint thud and a familiar voice yelled, "Ahoy, anyone awake in there?"

When Mark poked his head in the door, Pete said, "Oh, hi. We were just going to stand down after a fourteen-hour shift. But if there's anything at all you need, we are here to serve."

"What I need, Pete, you ain't got. But thanks for the offer. Danny, you want to go for a visit?"

I grabbed my coat, waved good-bye, and followed Mark out onto the deck.

His tugboat-like power skiff was moored alongside. We jumped in, and with a roar and a cloud of black exhaust smoke, we set off for the *Racer*. When we came alongside, I made sure we had lots of bumpers hanging over the side. Didn't want to chip the paint; not ours, we didn't have any. Mark took care to make an extra gentle landing and we tied up, bow and stern.

Christine must have seen us coming because she appeared on the back deck and waved us aboard. She looked good in her uniform, trim and competent. I couldn't help but see her in a fresh light. She was no longer our shipmate, swaddled in a sort of brother/sister protectiveness. She was an attractive mature woman, and I wondered if she had a boyfriend.

She beamed at us as she pushed her still uncontrollable hair out of her face. "Hey guys, it's great to see you." She held out her arms and we hugged and pounded each other on the back. "Rumor has it Fergie's in the area. Have you run into him?"

"Not yet. Some of the gillnet fleet's still in transit. They don't fish until after the seines."

"Yeah," she laughed, "same as always. The poor old gillnetters get the leftovers after the seines have creamed most of the quota."

Mark poked her shoulder. "You rag pickers always got double our price with less expenses, so you gotta let us have a few fish."

"Well, you can have 'em all now. I've got a real job."

I pointed at the stripes on her shoulder. "You look real important. Are you an admiral?"

"Just about. Come on in and we'll grab a coffee." She led the way into the *Racer's* spacious and well-equipped galley. Some of Christine's crewmates were seated at the table and she did introductions all around. By the time we'd all heard and forgotten everyone else's name, mugs of hot coffee had appeared in our hands and we joined the uniforms at the table.

"What have you guys been up to?" I threw the question out expecting Christine to answer, but a guy with one more stripe on his shoulder picked up the ball.

"We've spent the last five days doing a search and rescue operation. SAR. Unfortunately, we didn't quite manage the 'R.'"

I looked at him and belatedly picked up on the prevailing aura of fatigue, and something else—defeat, I guess. These guys had obviously taken the search for Les Jameson a lot more seriously than I had. They'd found his boat but not him. Presumably, he'd been the victim of a FOTAL event: Fallen Overboard Taking A Leak. Not a very glamorous way to die, and decidedly unpleasant, but the lot of many a fisherman.

Mark was curious. "Was the boat floating or on the beach?"

Christine answered this time. "It was drifting but it had some hull damage and a badly dinged prop. We think it must have hit the beach, probably after Les had fallen overboard, and then drifted off when the tide rose. We did all the tide and wind calculations, trying to figure out where the boat might have beached relative to where we found it, and where a body might have drifted compared to where the boat did. And of course we cruised every inch of beach in case he'd got ashore."

I entered the discussion. "If he fell in south of Cape Calvert, there's that strong outflow that comes out of Rivers Inlet, tide and wind. He would have ended up way the hell offshore. No hope of finding him. But I know you guys gave it everything."

I looked at Christine. "Are you too tired to come for lunch?"

"Not if you're buying."

"Not me. Mark is. He hasn't spent all his grub money yet."

"Yeah, and that's from the '91 season."

We excused ourselves and stood up. I tried to think of some bon mot that would dispel the gloom, but I couldn't. Mark offered, "You guys should catch some zeds." We left.

Once in Mark's skiff, heading for the renowned dining room of the fabulous Shearwater Hotel, I yelled over the diesel's roar. "They take it seriously, don't they?"

"Yeah, and they beat themselves up over it. We did our best, worked thirty-six hours after we'd been ordered to quit, and we couldn't find him. So that's that and we move on to the next job."

Christine had fished her own gillnetter for three years and it showed. The point is not that she is tough, although she was, but that she was realistic to the point of fatalism. And I admired her for it.

"Here we are, folks." Mark landed the skiff in front of *Sexy Sue*, a dilapidated old yacht whose stays were slumping and makeup was peeling. But someone still cared. Pots of flowers graced her stern deck and the tie-up lines were almost new. A live-aboard, unless I missed my guess.

The three of us walked briskly up the dock, thinking lunch-like thoughts. Seated in the restaurant, doing the waitress wait, I took note of the other customers. At two adjacent tables, a group of fishermen engaged in one loud conversation. And in the corner were two guys I took to be locals. I wondered why I assumed that, and decided it was because they were about as laid-back as you could get without being laid out. One of them, a sixty-five-year-old belt and suspenders type, was slowly stirring his coffee. The other, sporting the full Stanfields set, in classic grey, was examining a well-used toothpick.

Belt and Suspenders: "That bloody McTaggart! Hey?"

Mr. Full Set: "Damn right."

B & S, shaking his head: "What are you gonna do, eh, eh?"

Mr. FS: "You're damn rights."

B & S: "Had the nerve! Had the golderned nerve.

Mr. FS: "There you go, eh, there you damn well go."

I missed the denouement because the waitress arrived, left to get her pad, and arrived again.

"Soup's good today."

"Special?"

"No, but it's not bad."

"No, is there a special?"

"There was yesterday. Probably some leftover. It wasn't very good."

"That's okay." I felt the urge for a large chunk of dead animal. "I'll have the steak, medium rare. Green salad." Comparison shopping. How would Shearwater's green salad stack up against Bella Bella's? The implications of that decision overwhelmed me. "Make that fries."

Christine decided on a clubhouse while Mark dithered. "Tell me about the soup again."

"It's pretty good."

"No, what kind is it?"

"Hang on, I'll check."

We stared at each other until she returned. "Clam chowder."

"Local?"

"No, I'm from Cache Creek."

I put my forehead on the table. "Wonderful," I heard Mark say. "I'll have the clam chowder then."

When her footsteps had gone away, hopefully taking her with them, I raised my head and looked at Mark. "I'm glad you didn't discover page two of the menu. We'd still be waiting for you to make up your mind."

Christine slapped the table with glee. "He knows all about page two. Remember that year we were in here and he lost a bet, and he had to eat page two? What was the bet?"

I laughed as the memory flooded back. "Billy bet him he couldn't chug a beer no hands in ten seconds He got beer up his nose and sneezed all over my sweet and sour mystery balls. Waitress wouldn't bring me new ones."

"I'm just glad I had to eat page two and not page three."

Christine nodded eagerly. "Yeah, desserts versus appetizers. You could have died from piella."

"You mean paella. That's a Spanish food, not something you get from eating pie, you idiot."

"Who're you calling an idiot? If you ever need to call on my professional capacities, I will be the searcher and you'll be the searchee. That's why I have a pension plan. I'm much more likely to need it."

Mark was still sputtering when the food arrived. After we'd taken the edge off our appetites, I nudged Mark. "Tell Christine about the abalone license policy."

Mark's eyes lit up. "You'll love this." He orchestrated the story properly, as fisherman do, using his knife and fork as twin batons while building toward the climax. He concluded with a timpani roll and a clash of cymbals. "And then we signed that nonsense with Fleming Griffith's name."

Christine had to cover her mouth so as not to expel food as she laughed. "Jesus, I should have known you delinquents were behind it. We've been sort of following it and it's the only comic relief we've had."

"But don't forget, Christine, we only contributed one small piece to the grand strategy. The rest is all straight from the policy group."

"When Griffith finds out he'll freak!"

"Oh, I don't know. He might be happy to take credit for our brilliant ideas."

"I bet they shut the site down. Or at least password-protect it so the barbarian hordes can't deface it."

She was right. When we got back to the *Racer*, Christine's shipmates had all turned in, so we kept our voices low. Even so, we eagerly linked to the SPLAG website, where we found that Griffith's supposed contribution had been deleted and there was a sign-in process that demanded a password to access the site.

"I'm sure there's a way around that," I said. "I'll have to consult my geek friends."

Mark asked Christine if she'd heard about Crowley.

"That was sure a shock," she said. "I never figured Crowley as a suicide type."

"Maybe he wasn't."

Two pairs of eyes locked onto me. I was unsure of whether or not to unburden myself, but in the end, what it came down to was just the need to share something with friends. I thought about limiting the story to Crowley, but everything came out. It had to. I couldn't talk sensibly about a murder without some motive, and that led to the West Vancouver lab and Igor and Billy.

After my twenty-minute monologue ended, there were several moments of silence. Finally Mark stood up. "Let's take a ride. I don't feel comfortable talking in here."

We climbed into his skiff and he idled slowly away from the *Racer*. "I've always felt that Billy was dead," he said. "But I figured he was probably rolled while trying to score some coke. This means he was murdered by someone at the lab, or at least connected with the lab. Were they worried about that fuckin' fish, trying to cover it up?"

Christine shook her head. "No, lots of people saw that fish: us, guys that walked past the boat while we were doing network. Billy showed it off like a sideshow geek. He must have seen or heard something at the lab that was supposed to be a secret."

She looked at me. I shrugged. "There were some dodgy things going on there, but Christ, nothing worth killing someone over. Let's concentrate on this end of the thread. If we can link the *Kelp* to its owner, we might have the last person to see Crowley alive."

"In other words, his murderer. And maybe Billy's murderer." Mark looked almost angry as he guided the skiff through the maze of anchored boats. We were getting the odd wave from people on the boats, and I waved back unconsciously as I concentrated on the significance of Crowley's visitor. Crowley had obviously expected him, having made what I now realized were several references to the *Kelp* in his journal. And the visit was late. Why?

"Here's something we can do," Christine said. "Whoever owns the

Kelp obviously used it to visit Crowley, probably on a semi-regular basis. Someone at the dock may have seen him on the boat. Let's go ask around."

Christine and I staggered back a step as the skiff surged ahead. Mark had rammed the throttle wide open and we were heading for Bella Bella.

Nine

We surged toward the fishermen's dock, our broad bow casting aside three-foot furrows of water. Mark was obviously deeply preoccupied because he broke the most basic rule of boating courtesy; he didn't slow down to minimize our wake, and boats were crashing and banging all around us as we tied up. We looked around sheepishly but there was no one present to chastise us.

When we were a hundred feet down the float, a window flew open and Cecil Brown stuck his head out. "I didn't know it was going to blow today. It feels like it's blowing fifty but there's no wind. Hey, maybe it's one of those tsunamis. It couldn't possibly be some ignorant twit's wake, could it?"

"Tsunami. It was on CBC. Predicted to hit right about now."

"Oh, that's all right then. Long as it wasn't some ignorant twit. Hey, Christine, long time no see. Who's that with you?"

"Two ignorant twits."

Mark made as if to push Christine in the water. "Sorry, Cecil, I was trying to think and drive at the same time."

"Think? You're forgetting you're a fisherman. Chase things around and sometimes catch them. But think? Be serious."

"Sorry. Lost my head. Where is everybody?"

"Canucks are playing. Who are you looking for?"

I looked up and down the dock before I spoke. "Cecil, you need to keep this under your hat. That boat I was curious about earlier, the *Kelp*, it might be connected to Alistair Crowley's death."

As the operator of a packer, collecting fish from a variety of highly competitive fishermen, Cecil kept more secrets than a priest or a beautician. And he didn't ask questions, which would only have increased his burden of secrets. So he didn't ask any questions now, merely pondered the implications of what I'd said. "We're trying to find someone who might have seen the owner, or anyone on the boat or connected with it in any way."

"I'm down here twenty-four hours a day, at least until fishing starts, and I know everybody. If anyone knows anything, I'll find out and let you know."

"We're just going down to look at the boat. See you later. And thanks." He nodded and shut his window, and we continued down the dock. When we got to where the *Kelp* was moored, I was pleased to see Louise standing on her stern.

"Glad you're here, Danny. We're going over this boat for clues. You can help us spot anything unusual."

Christine patted my shoulder. "And you're asking a DFO employee? They're known for being clueless."

I introduced Louise to Mark and Christine, and explained how they were involved with the case. The boat's back door was open and there were two guys inside, one taking pictures and one doing something that may have been lifting fingerprints. Not wanting to appear too eager, I tried to keep my voice casual. "Find anything yet?"

"No. You guys take a look and tell me what you think."

Mark was busy looking through the windows into the cabin. Christine had strolled slowly up to the bow, and was strolling slowly back, scrutinizing every exterior detail of the boat. I asked, "Is there a logbook on there?"

"No."

I looked at my watch. "Holy shit! I've gotta get back for the test boat updates and then the eight o'clock conference. I'll talk to you later."

As we walked away, Christine observed, "Gee, Danny, I think she likes you."

I ignored her. "Did you notice anything unusual about the boat?"

"You saw the towing bridle, right?" Christine replied, "Brand new half-inch double-braided poly. That stuff is very popular with the gillnet fleet. Either the boat's just been towed or someone expected to have to tow it."

"There's a fairly new plotter on there," Mark added. "I'd love to have a look at it. It might show everywhere that boat's been in the last while."

"Unless someone's erased the waypoints," I said.

"On that model, even if it's just turned on for a reference, it'll record tracks automatically and store them," Mark said. "A lot of guys don't realize that."

"Wow, that could be very interesting." I thought for a moment. "After the cops are through with the boat, maybe we can have a look at it."

"If we fish tomorrow . . ." Mark's voice trailed off.

I considered the options. "You know, guys, if fish stuff starts happening, we're not going to have any more time to play detective with that boat. Maybe I should ask the RCMP to impound it so we don't lose whatever information might be on the plotter."

Mark nodded. "Louise seems pretty bright. Explain to her about the plotter and make sure they get an expert to retrieve the info. You don't get a second chance if you screw it up."

"I'll go see her tonight," I said in what I hoped was a resigned voice.

Back on the *Jimmy Sinc*, I walked into the wheelhouse in time to hear the start of the test boat reports. In North Spiller Channel, most of the tests were around twelve to thirteen percent, with one at sixteen percent. Farther south, the percentages were down around ten, but things were definitely percolating. There were at least fifteen thousand tons of fish in Spiller and ten to fifteen miles of light spawn along both shorelines. It was getting uncomfortably close to decision time. If it was a gillnet fishery, we'd probably wait a day or two until more fish moved into the beach, but that wasn't necessary for the seine fishery. Theoretically, things were good enough to fish tomorrow, although some might want to wait for the roe percentage to go up a bit. I looked at Pete in an interrogative manner.

He looked equivocal. "Let's hear what the company guys have to say."

I didn't really like letting the company guys have too much input, but they were the ones buying the product and naturally they wanted the best possible quality, which meant the biggest roe.

"Well, guys, biologically speaking, there's no reason not to fish tomorrow. But we're not the ones paying the license fees. As much as possible, I'd like to let the fleet make the call. If we get any sort of consensus on the eight o'clock conference, we'll just go with it."

George looked up from the radar. "Consensus? I thought we were talking about fishermen. Gillnetters don't like seiners who don't like trollers, but northern gillnetters hate southern gillnetters more than they do seiners, who aren't too fond of west coast seiners, and everybody agrees that draggers are Satan's spawn except the draggers, who consider themselves beneficent providers for a hungry world, and sports fishermen look down on everyone unless you tie your own flies out of Tibetan monk whiskers, and everyone absolutely detests anyone who ever caught one more fish than they did."

"Yeah, but I took a mediation course," I said, trying to look confident. "Gentlemen, this is the dawning of the Age of Aquarius, and the lion shall lie down with the lamb and verily the mouths of men shall speak no ill."

And I was right. Either the company guys had whipped the fishermen into line, or maybe because they hadn't spent all their grub money yet, a solid majority agreed to wait at least one more day. Mind you, the dissenting minority was extremely vocal and there was language used that would have resulted in mass arrests in a more normal setting. But for fishermen, it was undoubtedly a consensus. And the best part was that I didn't have to make a decision.

That and the fact that I had dodged a potential slangfest brightened my mood considerably. Perhaps more than was justified, because I still had to visit Louise and negotiate some reasonably acceptable version of the truth while concealing the fact that I was guilty of withholding evidence in a criminal investigation. Again.

As I jumped into the Zodiac to run ashore, I thought about how much I should reveal. Why not tell all and give her the computer files? One, she'd be really mad. Two, she might arrest me. Three, it might have a negative effect on what I insisted on thinking of as "our relationship." What the hell, I might as well come clean, start afresh, get everything off my chest and begin a new era of trust and reconciliation. For five seconds, I was buoyed by a sense of relief, which quickly sank into the sea of despondency. Feeling like a guilty schoolboy, I tied the boat up at the Bella Bella dock and directed my steps toward Louise's little bungalow.

She answered the door, which hadn't even spoken, and looked at me for a second with the warm light of the fireplace behind her. "Hi, Danny. Nice to see you. Come in."

"Hi, Louise. There's a few things we need to discuss about the case."

She led the way toward the kitchen table, which was cluttered with files.

"I'm just going over the reports about what the techs found on the boat. Sit down. Glass of wine?"

"Sure." I hung my jacket over the back of a chair and pulled it up to the table. "Anything interesting?"

She handed me a glass of white wine and I looked at her attentively as she sat down facing me. She wore jeans and a white blouse and slippers with no socks. Her ankles were extremely attractive.

"Nothing interesting. Lots of fingerprints but no matches with known criminals, no suspicious residues such as gunpowder. Nothing helpful at all. But I thought you and your friends might have spotted something. You know boats and I don't."

"Yeah, a couple of things. There was a brand new towing bridle rigged up on the bow. The guy was either towed recently or expected to be towed. Also there's a new plotter in the wheelhouse. It may contain a digital record of the boat's last few trips."

"Wow, I'm glad you came by. This sounds important. What's a plotter?"

I took a few minutes to explain as she gazed at me appreciatively and I basked in her gaze. "A plotter establishes the position of a boat and displays it on a screen. It can also remember different positions and show them as a course line. So I think we should impound the boat and get an expert to look at that plotter." She nodded.

"And I've been thinking about the guy who ran the boat. He seems to be pretty smart. We might never trace him from this end. But if there's a connection to the DFO lab, it has to be someone who worked there at the same time as Crowley. We need to look at DFO personnel files. And we need someone to talk to Dr. James O'Rourke. If he and Crowley were really close, Crowley might have told him something."

"Yeah, he was on my list of people to talk to, as well as the sister in Ontario. You've been very helpful, Danny. Thanks a lot."

"Before you demonstrate your gratitude in a more meaningful way, which I'm sure you're dying to, we have a slight problem. Crowley had a computer hidden in his float house. You guys missed it. I found it and I've looked at some of his files. But we need a translator."

"Well, aren't you the clever one? I'm going to assume you just found the computer yesterday and this was your first chance to tell me about it. That way I won't have to handcuff you. Unless of course you want me to."

I leaned over and kissed her gently on the mouth. She put her hand on the back of my neck and pulled me toward her. I resisted, but only because I didn't want to fall off my chair. I stood awkwardly and pulled her up and into my embrace. She hugged me tightly as I touched her closed eyes with my lips and slid my hand under her blouse and caressed the bare skin of her back. After a moment, we pulled apart slightly and she looked up at me and smiled. "You should go. But come back tomorrow and bring that computer."

I considered saying something clever but I didn't want to spoil the mood. This was obviously one of those times when natural charm would get you further than natural cleverness. So I brushed her forehead with my lips, waved good-bye, and left. And all the way back to the boat, I registered naught but the ineffable lightness of being.

Ten

Tuesday morning, we had the plane in the air at first light. It reported more and heavier spawn. Obviously some herring had never heard of foreplay. The *Western Marauder* reported in that they too were seeing lots of spawn, as well as herring flipping in the shallows along the beach. The boat was lining up a set on a big school of maybe a thousand tons. The *Northern Queen* said they'd run farther north before setting.

I looked at George and Pete. "Looks like tomorrow for sure."

"Yeah, everything looks really good," Pete said. "Let's see what the percentages are."

George nodded agreement. "Even the weather looks not too bad. Bit of a low, probably rainy and breezy, but nothing to worry about."

We sipped our coffee and drummed our fingers while waiting for the test set reports. Finally the *Western Marauder* came back on the VHF. "*James Sinclair, Western Marauder*. Five tests—thirteen percent, thirteen percent, seventeen percent, fifteen percent, eighteen percent. Twenty-one slinks, nine spawned-out females. Average length—twenty-one centimeters. We're seeing more fish than yesterday and they're closer to the beach."

I keyed the mike. "Thanks, skipper. We'd like one more test later this afternoon, maybe farther south, but you could be finished after that."

"Roger, Danny. We'll be happy to take our charter fish and head home." He was talking about the one hundred and fifty tons of herring he would be allowed to catch to pay for his test fishing work. None of the test boats got paid in cash because DFO didn't have the money. At least they didn't have the money to spend on fisheries management, which was supposed to be their primary mandate. I wondered how much they were paying the boy wonders of SPLAG. I made a mental note to check on their latest flashes of genius.

I was forced to flip back a few pages on my mental notepad when the *Northern Queen* reported in with a burst of static. "*James Sinclair, Northern Queen*. Well, guys, we got a little ambitious here. We were on a really big school so I tried to just take a piece of it. I took a little bit too big of a piece. We had a hell of a time drying up. But they were beautiful fish, twenty-two to twenty-three centimeters; all the tests were thirteen to fourteen percent. It broke my heart to let them go."

I replied. "Thanks, skipper. I know how hard it is for you guys to release fish. But with any luck you'll find the same bunch when it's time to take your charter fish."

"No chance of that," he replied dolefully. "Even if I was that lucky, which I definitely ain't, these fish are too smart to be caught twice. Oh well."

"That was a fine whine," I noted. "Full-bodied and mature, with a hint of an edge. But not his best work. I've heard him in the past where he's brought tears to my eyes."

"The guy's caught more herring over the years than all these young guys put together," George added. "The only reason he's still fishing is because he's genetically programmed to do it. That and the fact that he needs something to moan about."

"My, aren't we unsympathetic today," I said. "I happen to know that if it wasn't for his old-age pension, he'd have to rely totally on his investments. But let's get serious. We have a fishery to plan. We'll wait until this evening, but I'm thinking we should announce that we anticipate a fishery tomorrow. We'll ask the fleet to hold at anchor so they don't go roaring around and scatter the fish. We'll release them tomorrow morning and open the fishery at say, two in the afternoon. What do you think?"

Pete nodded. "By God, a fishing plan. Did you think of that all by yourself?"

"No, I read your notes."

"I thought it sounded familiar. In that case, I agree."

I looked at George and he nodded with absolutely no hint of a lack of enthusiasm. So it was unanimous. Just as I was thinking about how easy fisheries management was, Alex yelled up from the galley. "Danny, there's someone here to see you."

When I poked my head into the galley, it took a bit of effort to recognize the clean-cut, dignified-looking gentleman helping himself to coffee from the pot on the stove. "Fergie, for Christ's sake. When did you get here? When did you get so respectable?"

Gone was the long hair and the Fu Manchu and the ripped jeans. But the grin was the same and so was the booming "hey, you" as he grabbed me and pounded my back into submission. "Goddammit, Danny. You don't look like a bureaucrat."

"Well, you don't look like a responsible adult. Actually, you do. Hey! It's great to see you. Sit down. If a strange guy offers you food, eat it. It's good."

"He already did. I don't really care for wild blackberries in a chocolate sauce spread over potato pancakes, but the genuine maple syrup topping kind of won me over."

"Yeah, you're easy as ever. Have you seen Mark and Christine yet?"

"We anchored right beside Mark, and he yelled that you were here. I haven't seen Christine yet, but I need to talk to her about the Les Jameson thing."

Several of my synapses flared inquiringly at that, but I decided to leave it until later. "Hey, Fergie, we need to talk to you about a bunch of stuff. Let's get together for lunch at the hotel. One o'clock?"

"Right on. I've been looking forward to this. It was a good crew, Danny. We were a really good crew. The truth is, I jumped on a boat to come up here just because I hoped we'd all get together again." He stood up from the table, grasped my hand with one of his paws, and pulled me in so he could pound me again with his free hand. He gave me a thumbs-up as he stepped over the transom to the back deck. I leaned out the galley door and watched him jump into a standard piece of fishing aluminum and surf off in a non-shoreward direction.

I had things to do. There were the reports to fill out. I approached this with all the verve and panache of the Leafs defending a three-goal deficit. I was looking at several standard forms that were supposed to encapsulate the fisheries management situation for roe herring in Area Seven. But I couldn't fill in the blanks, not on this form nor any other, in such a way as to describe what was actually happening with real fish and real humans in this blessedly real area of the world. But paper was winning, over rock, scissors, and the conduct of life in general.

The imposition of the paper world onto the real world had always struck me as the first tragedy of bureaucracy. This was the third entry on my list of "Reasons Our Bureaucracy Keeps Screwing Things Up." We'd forgotten. Paper could be shredded but reality could shred us.

I struggled with it for far too long. Finally Form 42P1A2 got the best of me. There comes a point where "none of the above" doesn't seem quite pertinent enough. Impertinence won out. In answer to line 27, reasons for variance from projection, I scribbled "reality rules" and went for lunch.

I was the last one there and the gang had obviously enjoyed a few barley-based appetizers. As I approached the table, Fergie finished a story with a rude hand gesture and they all roared with laughter. I sat down to shouts of, "Danny Boy, your round, pal."

We BS-ed for awhile, studied the menus, and got the ordering out of the way. As the waitress left, Fergie remembered what he wanted to ask Christine. "You guys found Les Jameson's boat but no sign of him, right?" Christine nodded. "Was there any sign that there was another person on the boat?"

"We didn't have any reason to think so," Christine sat up a little straighter. "What makes you ask?"

"We were at the fuel dock in Port Hardy the afternoon that Les pulled out. He was there fueling up and I just had the impression that there was another person on his boat. He was standing on the back deck and it sorta looked like he was talking to someone in the cabin. But I couldn't be sure. And if no one else is reported missing, I guess I was imagining things."

We all mulled that over for awhile. "I guess what we could do is go back and look at the boat for a sign that there was a second person on it," Christine said finally. "We never really considered that before. I'll do that this afternoon. And now, Fergie, Danny's got a story to tell you."

By the time I finished, our food had arrived and been unconsciously inhaled. There was silence for quite some time before Fergie swore viciously. "Those cocksuckers! Those pencil-necked, scum-sucking shitbags! I don't care who they are, we're going to find them and make them suffer. Billy was too good a guy to have his life taken away by some dipshit fucking with fish."

"We're not sure of anything yet," I said, trying to calm him down. "We don't know what any of the connections are, but we've got things we can follow up on, and we can all make damn sure that we won't let it go until we know what the hell happened. Mark, we're going to fish tomorrow, and then you and I will be heading for Vancouver. Fergie will still be here waiting for the gillnet opening. Christine, do you know what the *Racer* will be doing?"

"We'll stay until the gill nets are finished. Fergie and I will have a few days to poke around here. You and your RCMP friends can follow things up in Vancouver."

Mark was fidgeting impatiently. "I need half an hour on that crew boat. If there's any info on the plotter, I can get it."

"Are you certified?"

"At what?"

"Anything."

"Fuckin' right."

"Okay, I'll call Louise and tell her you're certified and she'll let you look at the plotter. At the same time we can check in with Cecil and see if he's found out anything about who was using the *Kelp*."

As we queued at the cash register, I noted that Fergie was so shocked by what he'd heard that he was paying for his share of the lunch. I stopped in the lounge to phone Louise, and, thankful that I wasn't lying to her face to face, told her that Mark was certified to play around with the Didsat Model MFD6 plotter, and suggested she meet us with the keys to the boat.

"That's great, Danny. I couldn't find any of our guys who knew anything about them. See you in half an hour."

Fergie was driving a thirty-foot herring punt. Mark went with him, Christine came with me and we roared back to the *Jimmy Sinc* to pick up Crowley's computer, and then around the corner to Bella Bella.

We found Cecil on the *Waterfowl* and invited ourselves in for coffee. Cecil and Fergie shook hands and grinned at each other.

"Jeez, we've gone from the Dynamic Duo to the Three Musketeers to the Four Horsemen of the Apocalypse," Cecil observed wryly. "Any bad guys better look out."

"Speaking of which, has anyone been seen hanging around the *Kelp*, that aluminum crew boat we were asking about?"

"No. Nobody's seen anyone, heard anything, smelled anything, or seen, heard, or smelled anyone who has seen, heard, or smelled anything. Which tells me one thing for sure: if anybody's been using it, they aren't local. Now, there's two ways into this charming little hideaway: boat or plane. Nobody would come by boat to pick up a boat that was stashed here. Which means they flew in. But nobody saw anything during daylight hours. Plane gets in at four in the afternoon. So if anybody flew in to use that boat, they would have had to hang around until after dark. Foreigners don't blend in easily here. So, if you had an idea when the boat was used, you could ask around about strangers in town, as well as check the airline passenger lists."

"I know one date it was used for sure, according to Alistair's journal. April 11, that's when he saw it. And probably April 13, the day he was shot. I'll get Louise to check those dates."

No sooner had I said her name, than I saw her walking down the dock. I gestured to the porthole. "Here comes Louise. Thanks for the help, Cecil."

We climbed over the rail of the *Waterfowl* and stood on the dock as Louise approached. She looked at the computer tucked under my arm, smiled at me and my heart skipped in waltz time. "Which one of you people is the certified, Danny-approved, Didsat plotter technician?"

Mark stepped forward. "That's me. Glad to help. If there's any trip information on that plotter, I'll get it for you." He led the way down the float, stepped onto the *Kelp*, and waited as Louise opened the cabin door.

She raised a cautionary hand before letting Mark enter. "You're dealing with evidence that may be involved with a murder case and you may be required to testify regarding anything you discover. In other words, we need to certify the chain of evidence. I need to document everything you do. So you need to tell me exactly what you do, key-stroke by keystroke."

Mark nodded. "I understand. It would be handy if you could tape this."

"I can do that." Louise laid a compact tape recorder on the cabin dashboard and pressed the record button. "April 19, 2004, Staff Sergeant Louise Karavchuck, Bella Bella government dock, extracting evidence from an electronic navigation device on the motor vessel *Kelp*. Please proceed, Mr . . . ?"

"Angastouri; Mark Angastouri." He walked to the front of the wheelhouse, reached up to the plotter, and pressed the power button. "I pressed the on button and the plotter is now opening up the initial display. Press menu button and then 'display waypoints.'"

The screen displayed a long list of geographical points referenced by their latitudes and longitudes, obviously going back to when the *Kelp* was owned by Mac McPherson. Mark scrolled down to the bottom of the list, selected the last fifty waypoints, went back to the menu and selected "trip plotter." The screen morphed into a chart of the area, with squiggly lines all over it. These lines represented voyages that had been made by the *Kelp*. Many of the lines were almost identical, overlaying each other so that they formed a thicker track line running from the dock at Bella Bella to Yeo Cove with a stopover at Morehouse Bay in Return Passage. It was obvious that the *Kelp* had made many return trips to Crowley's float house. Other tracks started at the dock, ran together for awhile, then fanned out to cover many small bays on the north and west coasts of Campbell Island. A half dozen or so tracks wormed down Lama Passage into Fisher Channel, entered Lagoon Bay, and came back.

Mark looked at the display and chewed his lip. "The trick now is to display these trips by date. The only thing I remember is that if I do it wrong, we'll lose everything." He looked at Louise who looked at me. I laughed and Louise visibly relaxed.

"Try April 11 and April 13."

Mark punched a few buttons and the course the *Kelp* had followed on April 11 came up on the screen. It was strange in that it didn't start at the dock, or at the end point of a previous trip, but in the middle of nowhere: the lower end of Fitz Hugh Sound. It traced a line through Lama Passage, past Bella Bella, and then the familiar track to Yeo Cove via Morehouse Bay and back to Morehouse Bay. The plotter showed nothing for April 12, but at 5:00 AM on April 13, the day of Crowley's death, the *Kelp* had gone to Yeo Cove and then back to Bella Bella.

"Bingo!" Mark slammed his fist on the bulkhead. "I think Crowley's murderer drove this boat and all we have to do is find out what happened to him when he got back to Bella Bella. He must have flown out." He looked at Louise.

"Sorry to disappoint everybody. We already checked the passenger list for the thirteenth and there were no foreigners on it: just some fairly non-suspicious local types, mostly elders going out for medical stuff. Same the next day. And for three days previous to that, there was fog in Port Hardy so everything was grounded."

"He's still here," I said. "And that means he's probably a fisherman, or posing as one." I looked at their faces as they thought it through. If the killer hadn't left, he would stick out like a sore thumb, unless he had an excuse for being in the area. There wasn't much to camouflage an outsider, no circuses in town, just the herring fishery.

Louise pulled out her notebook. "There're sixteen rooms at the Shearwater Hotel and another eight at B&Bs in the village. They're all full and I've got all the names. We'll go over them later. Are you finished here, Mark?"

"One more thing. Okay if I start her up?" He turned the key and the engine roared into life. He pushed the shift lever into forward for just a second. The boat surged gently against the tie-up lines and then relaxed. Mark shut off the motor. "Don't see any need for a towing bridle. Runs fine."

"Can you disconnect the plotter so we can store it? It's important evidence now," Louise said.

Mark nodded and began the shutdown process.

I stepped off the boat onto the dock and handed Crowley's computer to Louise. "I'll see everyone later. Got a herring fishery to run." But as I walked toward the Zodiac, I was thinking not of the opening tomorrow, but of what the hell the attraction was in Morehouse Bay. The *Kelp* had been there at least eight times in the last year.

Back on the *Jimmy Sinc*, I gobbled a bowl of Alex the cook's clam chowder and went up to the bridge for the evening conference. The test boats started their reports. Things were pretty much the same, except that there were now more fish in the southern end of Spiller Channel. Everyone assumed new fish were moving into the area. I looked at George and Pete. They achieved consensus that we should stick with Plan A.

I keyed the mike. "Attention, the roe herring fleet in Area Seven. This is the *James Sinclair*. Stand by for an announcement." I waited ten seconds to give everybody a chance to move from their respective galleys to their respective wheelhouses. I gave an update on the test results and sounding information, then got to what everyone was waiting for. "We anticipate a fishery at 1400 hours tomorrow afternoon in Spiller Channel. We ask the fleet to remain at anchor tonight. We will convene an advisors' meeting on the *James Sinclair* at 0800 hours tomorrow. If the advisors agree, we will release the fleet and commence the fishery at approximately 1400 hours. Come back to the *James Sinclair* with any questions or comments."

"*James Sinclair, Point Kelsey*."

"*Point Kelsey, James Sinclair*. Go ahead, skipper."

"Yeah, *James Sinclair*, just wondering here, why can't we head up there now and do a little scouting?"

"*Point Kelsey, James Sinclair*. At last year's post-season review, it was agreed that too many boats running around scatters the fish. So this year, we'll keep it to a minimum. Everyone should have two or three hours prior to the fishery so it's a level playing field."

We went back and forth for awhile. No one was too exercised about anything. The complaints committee had evidently taken the night off, and I eventually crept into my bunk with a pleasantly goose-bumpy feeling of anticipation.

Eleven

When I woke and put on a clean pair of socks the next day, I had no way of knowing that that would be the high point of my morning. Coffee in hand, I sidled into the wheelhouse and nodded at George. Pete joined us almost immediately and we slurped contentedly while waiting for the test boat reports.

At 0630, the *Western Marauder* came on the air. They were at the north end of Spiller Channel and they couldn't see any fish. The *Northern Queen*, at the south end of the channel, reported some scattered schools but no more than one hundred tons total.

Oh shit. It was a fishery manager's worst nightmare: a fleet vibrating with the anticipation of a fishery and the goddamn fish had disappeared. Worse, I was the messenger. I'd be lucky if they only shot me.

I tried to sound, if not unconcerned, at least not on the verge of panic. "We'll wait until 0730. If the guys haven't located anything by then, we'll cancel the advisors' meeting and go looking."

I wondered which herring had been the leader, the trendsetter. One of the millions had obviously become dissatisfied with the attractions of Spiller Channel and communicated that feeling to his immediate neighbors. "Hey guys, this place is, like, so yesterday. But I know this cool little ecosystem that hasn't been discovered yet." Before anyone realized what was happening there was a mass movement. Bloody fish were worse than humans.

At 0730, I went on the air, canceled the advisors' meeting, and stood the fleet down. I heard myself using the words "non-critical decision sequence" and "temporary dispersion event." I hadn't spent all those years in Ottawa for nothing. The airwaves were immediately alive with electromagnetic indignation. I tried to listen to all five radios as they cataloged in detail my stupidity, inadequacy, moral degeneracy, my most astounding physical defects, and the lack of formal recognition of my parents' relationship.

A half-hour later, the quality of the vituperation began to wane. There are only so many metaphors that can be constructed around a person's resemblance to male or female genitalia. I told the fleet to stand by for the 8:00 PM update and nodded at George. The *James Sinclair* pulled anchor, and we slunk out of the harbor.

Pete was the first to speak. "That was a pretty good fleet rant, but not the best. I remember when Sam Mattingly had to close the Skeena sockeye fishery so the sporties could catch more steelhead. He couldn't get a word in for at least three hours. Mind you, there were more boats there."

George reassured us. "Don't worry, guys. The fish are still around somewhere because we know they haven't spawned yet. We'll find them."

"And if we don't, I've always wanted to emigrate to Patagonia." My eyes didn't waver from the sounder as we cruised all down Seaforth Channel, going out as far as Susan Rock. Nothing. As we cruised back on the opposite shore of Seaforth, I acted on a hunch. "Let's head up Return Passage," I said.

About halfway up the channel, we started seeing substantial numbers of fish, and then more all along the top of Chatfield Island. There were more big schools, two hundred to five hundred tons, all around Cunningham Island as well. My knees spaghettied with relief. Maybe my name wouldn't be immortalized as "The DFO Dimwit Who Blew the 2004 Central Coast Herring Fishery." My main concern now was that if the fish stayed here and didn't return to Spiller Channel, could we fish in this area? Was there enough room and were the shallow spots sandy or rocky? I called the two test boats and told them to sound the north and west sides of the island, not just for fish but for fishable bottom.

Still mentally genuflecting before the Gods of Fish, I almost forgot to check out Morehouse Bay as we passed it on our way back. It was nearing four and the sun's rays came at us low over the water, outlining in shadow anything on the surface of the water. The bay opened off Return Passage, encompassing maybe twenty hectares with the inner portion guarded by a shield of islands. We were about a quarter mile off an imaginary line that joined the two opposite points of the bay. Close in to the islands, I saw a familiar though unexpected sight. I started to point it out to the others but for some reason stopped myself. Rolling through the water, noticeable only because of the angle of the sun, were the backs of thousands of sockeye, a bunch as big as any I'd seen. Of course, they weren't supposed to be there, but somewhere out in the middle of the Pacific. I almost doubted myself, but I'd always had good fish eyes and I knew damn well what I was seeing.

A minute later, I lost them as the angle of the sun changed, or they dived. Was that what had attracted the *Kelp* here? But I had to save that thought for later. For now, I allowed myself only herring thoughts.

"Let's anchor in Wigham Cove. We'll start sounding real early in the morning and try to figure out if these fish are going to hang around here or move back to Spiller. And if they're going to resume the spawn, or hold off for a bit."

"I guess last night, those fish that we thought were moving into Spiller were really leaving," Pete ruminated. "Leaving the same old bedroom to have more exciting sex in a strange motel room." He shut up when George and I both stared at him.

We dropped the hook and had time to enjoy Alex's clam fritters with crab salad and freshly baked sourdough bread. I went to bed too early and couldn't convince my body to relax or my mind to mellow. I lay almost rigid and stared at the bottom of the upper bunk as a stampede of woolly thoughts raised dust clouds in my brain. Just as I was getting most of them into a corral, the alarm went off.

It was two in the morning and, for the first time, I was the first one up. I dressed warmly and went out on deck for a pee. As my knees braced against the cap rail and I looked out over the water, I could appreciate what a snug little refuge Wigham Cove offered. Black hills formed a full circle around us except for the narrow opening. The small saucer of sky wasn't big enough to show the moon, but the stars were bright and the air still. I shivered, but lingered despite the cold. The only sound was the gentle lapping of water. I wished the moment would last forever.

A light came on in the galley, and I knew George was up. Minutes later, I could smell coffee and I went inside. We exchanged quiet good mornings and waited for the coffee. Just as George began to pour two cups, Pete joined us and George poured a third. We sat at the table and didn't say anything for a while. Finally, I began to ask questions. Had there ever been a fishery where the fish appeared to be holding now? Were there any boundary issues? Had there ever been a spawn here, or was it just a holding area?

George deferred to Pete. "There's room for a few boats to work the top end of Chatfield and the east side of Cunningham. They used to fish around here during the reduction fishery, but I don't ever remember there being much of a spawn."

"I'd definitely feel more comfortable back in Spiller," George agreed. "I bet the fish would too. I think we need to give them time to move back there."

Great. Another two or three days of rising tension and rising tempers. I guess this is what I got paid the big bucks for. "Well, let's go look around and try to figure out what the hell they're doing."

As it turned out, they weren't doing much of anything, but at least I was able to report to the fleet that the fish hadn't disappeared. Some of the cooler heads led the discussion and it was agreed that as long as a large spawn didn't start, we would wait and hope the fish returned to Spiller Channel where there was room for the whole fleet to work in familiar waters.

By Friday, the bulk of the fish were back in Spiller Channel and they were starting to spawn. I flew back to Shearwater that evening for an advisors' meeting. We decided to release the fleet Saturday morning with a fishery anticipated for noon. As I flew back to join the *James Sinclair* in Spiller Channel, I could see that the water was white with spawn. Biology had become destiny. There would be no turning back.

Twelve

Saturday morning, pre-dawn, there was a mist low over the water, but I knew it would burn off by nine or ten o'clock. Because of the mist, the planes were still on the water when the fastest of the seine boats began arriving.

Power skiffs were being launched and rigged to tow, bow up behind the seine boats. Plastic tarps that had covered the nets were removed and rigged to protect windows and shiny areas from slime and scales. Pumps and pipes were rigged to pump, hopefully, thousands of tons of herring into hatches. Herring, in the modern fishery, were sucked out of the net via a vacuum pump lowered down into the bag once the net had been dried up.

Soon, the whole fleet was sounding the channel like hounds scenting for a fox. Twelve or so boats had opted to work on the fish that remained in Return Passage, that lessened the congestion in Spiller Channel slightly. By 0930, at least six planes were in the air. The airwaves crackled with cryptic messages, everyone's voices sounding strained. There were occasional angry exchanges and it was still two hours before the fishery.

The *Racer* was up at the top boundary and we were at the southern end of Spiller Channel. We'd dispatched two Zodiacs to patrol the fishery in Return Passage, even though the boundary was completely arbitrary and we weren't particularly worried about strict enforcement.

By 1100 hours, we were running the southern boundary. Pete was gobbling Tums and George's grip on the wheel was just a little tighter than normal. I scanned the fleet with the binoculars and noted Mark's boat, the *Coastal Provider*, motionless close in to the beach. He'd obviously found some fish and was sitting on them, hoping they wouldn't move.

Between us and the shore, the water came alive. A school of herring boiled to the surface and the green water turned to silver, like the body of some prehistoric monster writhing in the shallows. Squadrons of gulls shrieked as they dive-bombed the almost solid mass of tiny fish.

A half hour to go. The fleet of about fifty packers was hovering anxiously just outside the boundary. When the fishery opened, they would come charging in to assist their partner boats by sounding for fish, supplying new nets for ripped ones and functioning power skiffs for broken ones, by holding corklines threatening to sink with the weight of fish, and by pumping fish out of nets once they were dried up.

About two minutes before noon, all radio chatter stopped. Everyone was anticipating the announcement. Even if there had been a reason to, I wouldn't have had the nerve to disappoint them. I squeezed the mike button and tried to sound calm. "Attention, the roe herring fleet in areas seven-dash-thirteen and seven-dash-fourteen, this is the *James Sinclair*, please stand by for an announcement." I looked around, checking for any false starts. Boats were circling at ever-increasing speeds but no one had released their skiff yet. "Attention, the roe herring fleet in areas seven-dash-thirteen and seven-dash-fourteen, fishing for herring by means of seine net is now declared open until further notice." Before I could finish the announcement, every seine boat lucky enough to be on fish was revving full speed ahead and their power skiffs were revving full speed astern. I finished my little speech even though I knew no one was listening. "Any boat fishing must be licensed for the area and all crew must have personal fishing licenses. Any boat wishing to change nets must notify the *James Sinclair* and do so in a designated area."

There were five boats within a half mile of us and each was peeling off a set. Since each net was about a third of a mile long, the exercise would obviously take some cooperation and planning. Unfortunately, cooperation and planning were not in the lexicon of most herring skippers. Three of the boats managed to complete adjacent circles. One boat was forced into a lopsided oval of a set and the fifth boat was forced outside. Unable to complete a circle without enclosing another boat, he was forced to backhaul.

The boat that was forced to haul back his net was essentially crippled since he couldn't use his propeller without sucking his net into it. Powerless, he was drifting close to the corkline of another boat. His power skiff attempted to pull him away but in doing so entangled his prop in another boat's net. Much consternation ensued.

A big steel boat came roaring over and started a set right in front of us. George was forced to veer to starboard to miss the guy's power skiff. I grabbed the mike. "*Susan Marie, James Sinclair.* You're right on the line now, skipper. You don't want to go any farther south."

A curt "Roger that" acknowledged my warning. And when he finished the set, a long tangent of his net lay right on the boundary line, but not over. God, these guys were good.

Many boats had started to drum in now and seal bombs were exploding like mini depth charges. Meant to scare the fish into the net, they boomed and lit up the water. Smoke drifted over the water like a battle scene. I scanned the binoculars in Mark's direction and could see them drumming in, everything seemingly under control.

It was now 1245. I talked to the *Racer* and the two test boats. We deployed all of our Zodiacs to start gathering hails, each skipper's estimate of how many fish he had, so we could figure out how long to leave the fishery open. One of our Zodiacs in Return Passage came on the air, his voice muffled by the whine of his outboards. "Everybody's heading your way, Danny. The fish here were too skittish. They're hoping to get into Spiller before it closes."

"Thanks for that. They should get here in time but there're no guarantees."

And then things got interesting. Because the Hailing Game had begun. If a guy had any amount of fish at all, it would take hours to dry up and pump out and get ready for another set. Therefore it would be in his interest if the fishery closed and reopened again later. To that end, he would tell us that he'd caught a hell of a lot of fish, hoping to panic us into thinking that the quota had been caught. We'd close the fishery, later these guys would "reassess" their catch downwards, and we'd re-open the fishery when they were ready to go again.

In contrast, guys who had a fast few hundred tons on board and were operational again would want the fishery to stay open, so they'd hail low. And boats with no fish yet, like the guys racing down from Return Pass, could only pray that no one else would catch very much so we wouldn't close it.

We started to get preliminary hails. Some forty and fifty tons, a few in the two-hundred- to three-hundred-ton range. I noticed Mark was hailing four hundred and fifty tons. Good for him. There were a few outrageous hails, over a thousand tons. Pete and George and I collectively raised our eyebrows at these, but you never knew for sure. Sometimes fishermen told the truth.

We were two hours into the fishery now and—in spite of some obvi-ously inflated hails—had only caught about twenty-five hundred tons of the thirty-five-hundred-ton quota. Every one of the boats that had been here at the opening gun had got its net wet. About thirty boats were pumping big sets and the rest were running around, ever more frantically, looking for a school of fish worth setting on. Looking south, I could see the rump fleet from Return Passage racing toward the boundary line.

Those twelve boats plus the fifteen or so already here and still opera-tional represented considerable catching power. I didn't want to go over the quota. The fishery would have to close soon. "We'll have to update the hails. I'd like to be no more than five hundred tons behind the real-time catch. Then we'll close at three thousand tons hailed and hope the final number is not too far over."

The first of the latecomers roaring across the line flew a blue JS Macmillan flag. We weren't supposed to have the company's secret chan-nels, but some previous techie had scanned them into our multi-band radio. We heard the JS Macmillan pilot screaming at the skipper that there was a big school just inside the boundary on the western shore. The big steel boat, which I could see now was the *Jeanna B*, heeled hard over and headed for the beach. She made two circles and then dropped her skiff and began a set. I knew her skipper, Sam Milosevic, and I knew he wouldn't set on nothing.

One of our Zodiacs reported a new set halfway up the channel that looked very promising. The fishing boat had called for one of his packers to go alongside the corkline and hoist it up, the sign of a big set. The newcomers were now peeling off sets—probably "hope sets"—but some of them would get fish.

I took a deep breath, looked questioningly at Pete and George, and seeing no response to the obvious question, picked up the mike and closed the fishery.

"Attention the roe herring fleet in areas seven-dash-thirteen and seven-dash-fourteen, the fishery is now closed until further notice. An update relating to possible further openings will be provided on a radio conference call on channel 78A at 1800 hours this evening."

The fishery had been open for two and a half hours, pretty much standard for a modern herring seine fishery. I hadn't done anything except look out the window of the *James Sinclair* and use the radio-phone, yet I was totally drained. Things had gone well after the initial panic over the misbehavior of what were obviously some herring juvenile delinquents. All the boats were still floating and none of the humans had needed to be medivacked out. In the next few hours, we'd find out if we were under or over the quota, but I was confident that we would be pretty close to thirty-five hundred tons.

"Gentlemen," I said, "allow me to buy you a coffee and offer you the delights of Chez Alex."

As we started to shuffle out of the wheelhouse, a fax began to whirr from the printer. I lagged behind, idle curiosity directing me to wait for the two pages that slowly scrolled into the receiving tray. My bullshit antennae perked up when I saw the SPLAG letterhead. When the whole document had been printed, I read it and laughed. Pulling it from the printer, I took it back to the galley for the amusement of my colleagues.

Alex had boiled some prawns as a pre-dinner snack. There was a variety in the species belonging to the shrimp family: side-striped, hump-back, pinks, and the spotted prawn, which was publicly known and sold as the "prawn," while the other species were called "shrimp." The deck crew had already done serious damage to what had been a ten-pound bag. Now Pete and George were seriously engaged in the prawn ballet: rip head off, tear breastplate, squeeze meat out, dip in garlic butter, and succulentify. I partook of a few squeeze-and-dips, succulentified to at least a temporary sufficement, and then waved the fax with greasy fingers.

"You guys will love this. The latest from the Special Policy on Licensing Abalone Group. It says right here, hard to believe but true, that all abalone caught under the new licensing regime must be indi-vidually identified." I selected a large humpback prawn in time to save it from one of Pete's grapplements. "So, if you manage the paperwork to obtain a license, design an abalone trap that fits the new rules, and if you were to actually catch an abalone, you would have to name it: Alice, Herman, Brunhilda?"

"Don't be silly," George waved a large side-stripe prawn at me. "You're assuming the DFO policy gurus would do something stupid. Has that ever happened? Aside from the odd mistake on the east coat, the west coast, the Arctic Ocean, the Great Lakes, plus some very large lakes in western Canada?"

"Yeah, I hate to be critical. To err is human, to fuck up beyond all possible belief in the face of overwhelming advice on the right course of action is not divine, it's DFO."

The radios started to chatter with the latest hails. The *Pacific Gambler*, which had originally given an estimate of six hundred tons, had ripped its net while drying up and most of the fish had escaped. I felt bad for the crew. They'd thought they had something, had busted their ass in adrenaline-fueled toil and sweat, and then lost everything. I wondered if they had a license for up north. That could make the differ-ence between severe depression or a we're-still-in-this-ball-game attitude.

Or maybe their pool partners had done well. In the modern era of short openings and high license fees, boat owners often resorted to pooling as a way of evening the odds in the ever-more-risky and high-stakes crap game that the coast herring fishery had become. Hopefully the *Pacific Gambler* had partnered with a couple of other boats and those boats had caught something. The catch would be shared and the crew of the *Pacific Gambler* wouldn't go home completely broke.

The *Coastal Provider* was still hailing four hundred and fifty tons, and I knew Mark wouldn't bullshit. Other hails were being adjusted as hope gave way to reality, and the time for bullshitting was over anyway. The boats that had the big sets, like Mark's, would be pumping their fish for hours. The numbers were becoming more concrete as time passed. We wouldn't get the final tally until the fish were delivered to the processing plants in Vancouver and Prince Rupert and weighed on actual scales. But I knew that the hails were usually accurate to within twenty or thirty percent. So we had caught a little under or a little over the quota of thirty-five hundred tons. This had been a successful fishery and I felt like congratulating myself even though I knew it had been mostly luck. And other matters were crowding into my consciousness.

I needed to talk to Mark and I couldn't do it on the air as Danny DFO. I grabbed the radio mike. Altering my voice just a bit, from BC midcoast drawl to Steveston third-generation Japanese twang, I called the *Coastal Provider* from a garbled boat name. One of Mark's deckhands answered and asked me to repeat my boat name. I held the mike close to my mouth and gargled and hissed to imitate static, and then said "Mr. Billy says pump everything." Normally Mark would pump the fish he couldn't carry himself onto packers and head south with the rest. But I needed him and the boat here.

Pete was still back in the galley scoffing prawns, but George had reclaimed his territory in the wheelhouse and could not have missed my somewhat odd radio exchange. I looked at him as he recalibrated the radar but he radiated incuriosity. "Fun's over here. Let's head back to Shearwater," I said.

He nodded and pushed the throttle forward.

Thirteen

On Sunday morning, I woke before dawn and took my coffee out onto the deck. Sleeping seagulls bobbed in the water like white corks. I paced and sipped, and after awhile glimmers of light began to struggle over the horizon. By the time full daylight revealed another scenic masterpiece, I had made a few decisions. By cup number three, I was in the wheelhouse waiting for Mark to call. By cup number four, he was on the air.

"*James Sinclair, Coastal Provider.*"

"*Coastal Provider, James Sinclair.*"

"Good morning. I'd like to give our final hail, four hundred and eighty tons."

"Thanks for that, skipper. What's your current position?"

"About a half hour from Bella Bella."

"Roger that. Thanks for your input and good traveling."

I turned to Pete. "I'm going to stick around here for awhile. Would you mind running me around the corner so I can jump on the *Coastal Provider*?"

"Grab your stuff and let's go."

I shook hands with George, thanked him for his help and wished him luck on his trip north for the last opening. In my cabin, I threw dirty clothes into my bag, took a look around for stray belongings, checked the drawer under my bunk. Jesus Christ! Alistair's journal, the odd one that I hadn't given to Louise. How the hell was I going to explain this? More groveling. I grabbed the journal and left. On my way through the galley, I shook hands with Alex and promised I'd send him my recipe for smoked oolichan pie. He almost succeeded in looking interested.

Pete was already warming up the Zodiac when I jumped in. By the time we got to Bella Bella, Mark was idling by the government dock. We went alongside, and with my bag in one hand, I clapped Pete on the shoulder with the other. "That was one of the better fisheries and I think we should take full credit for it."

"Absolutely. We were in full control at all times and never a worry wrinkled this baby-smooth brow. I'll see you in The Big Smoke."

I clambered onto the deck of the *Coastal Provider*. Pete waved and proceeded to generate a large rooster tail behind which he soon disappeared. I went forward to the wheelhouse and took a seat in one of the two captain's chairs.

"Congratulations, buddy. Four hundred and eighty tons is not a bad score."

Mark was slumped comfortably in the other chair, one eye looking forward, the other toward the radar screen off to the side. Fortunately, this temporary wall-eyeism never became permanent. He scratched absently at his week-old stubble.

"Yeah, it went well. I'm glad it's over. Now I feel like I can concentrate on more important stuff."

"Can you fly your crew home? We need the boat here."

"Sure. Why?"

"Remember how the plotter showed the *Kelp* stopping in Morehouse Bay every time it went to Crowley's place? Guess what I saw in Morehouse Bay?" I waited for Mark to crinkle his forehead into a questioning mode. "Sockeye. A huge school. Biggest bunch I've ever seen."

"You're crazy. Not at this time of the year." He paused. "And so? You want to catch a few of them?"

"Exactly. We'll take Christine and Fergie, Louise if she wants to come. We need some samples of those sockeye. They're not normal or else they wouldn't be here. So dollars to dandelions, they're related to Igor. Then we'll head for Vancouver and start following up on some of the leads there. We need to look at the personnel lists for the DFO lab back in 1996. I honestly don't think Crowley killed Billy, at least not single-handedly. So I want to know who else was working there."

"I think you're right. Crowley seemed genuinely surprised when I told him Billy had gone missing."

It took just a moment for this to sink in. "Jesus Christ! You told Crowley that Billy went missing?"

"Yeah, about three weeks ago, when we first got here. I went to see him just to pick his brains about what was going on, fish-wise. We started BS-ing and I told him the story of our last great salmon season. I had to include Igor and how Billy took it to the lab and we never saw him again. Crowley seemed genuinely shocked, which seemed a little odd because it's not like he knew Billy or anything."

"Did you ask him if he knew anything about Igor?"

Mark took a second before he replied. "Yes, but looking back, he kind of dodged the question. Or more that he ignored it and just focused on Billy."

"This could be important. One of the big questions has been if Crowley's death was connected to Billy and Igor and the lab back in 1996, why was he killed now? What was the catalyst? What precipitated the killing? It could have been your telling Crowley about Billy's disappearance. Say Crowley was involved in nefarious activities at the lab with at least one accomplice. Billy shows up and is killed by the accomplice. Crowley doesn't know anything about it until you tell him. Immediately after you tell him, he contacts the accomplice and raises shit. The accomplice gets nervous, comes up here, and kills Crowley. What was the date when you told him?"

Mark stood up and consulted the calendar on the back wall of the wheelhouse. "April 8."

He sat down and put the boat in gear, idling toward an anchoring spot. I followed these maneuvers with about ten percent of my brain, while the other ten percent churned and cogitated and eventually spewed forth a theory.

"How's this sound? Crowley finds out from you on April 8 about

Billy's probable murder. After you leave, he contacts his accomplice. How does Crowley contact him? Gotta think about that. Anyway, he says, 'hey buddy, we gotta talk this over, you better get up here.' So this bad guy makes a date to come see Crowley using the *Kelp*. We know that's true because Crowley's journal says he was expecting the *Kelp*, plus the *Kelp*'s plotter says the boat was there on the morning of the murder."

I sat and thought as Mark went to the bow to drop the hook. When he came back inside he went to the chart drawer. "What was that other place that showed up on the plotter tracks of the *Kelp*? Lagoon Bay?" After some rustling and snapping of large pieces of paper, he laid a chart on the chart table. It showed lower Fisher Channel and in particular Lagoon Bay. If we continued straight after exiting Lama Passage, we'd enter the bay. It was an interesting-looking place. The center of the bay's shoreline was broken by a narrow, shallow pass that led into a large, deep lagoon: Codville Lagoon. The lagoon, in turn, sheltered a large island. "Man, if someone wanted privacy for something, that would be an ideal place. You ever been in there?"

I shook my head. "Never had the need to. And I bet that's true for most people."

We sat and thought some more. I remembered something that had been bothering me. I grabbed the mike and called the *Racer* on channel 16. Christine didn't answer, but they went to get her. When she came on the air, I asked to switch to channel 22. Mindful that anyone could be listening in, I phrased my question carefully. "Miss Farnsworth, it's Danny Swanson here. Last time we talked, you said you'd look for the second parcel that came in from Port Hardy. Did you find it?"

"Yes, I did. Shall I mail it to you?"

"I'll be in Shearwater in an hour. Can you meet me at the office?"

"Roger on that."

I switched the radio back to channel 16. "There was a second person on Les Jameson's boat. I wonder what she found that makes her think so." I played around with this new piece of the puzzle and was repulsed by the picture that began to emerge. "Jesus, I think our boy's pulled off the hat trick."

"How do you figure?"

"Our bad guy gets a call from Crowley that makes him desperate to get to Yeo Cove before Crowley spills something. But it's foggy in Port Hardy, and the planes are grounded for three days. But being DFO, or DFO connected, he knows half the fishing fleet is on their way north. So he hangs around the dock until he sees someone he knows, Les Jameson, and bums a ride. But because he's already made up his mind to kill Crowley, he has to kill Jameson, and it's easy to make that death look like an accident."

Mark nodded. "I'm thinking of the plotter tracks. Let's say our bad guy kills Jameson and throws him overboard somewhere, say Cape Calvert. Then he continues on in Les's boat and sneaks into Bella Bella late at night. He rigs up a towing bridle on the *Kelp* and heads back south with both boats. In Fitz Hugh sound, he starts up the *Kelp* and casts Les's boat adrift. That explains why that last trip of the *Kelp* starts in the middle of the sound. Then he heads north, kills Crowley in the wee hours of the morning, takes the *Kelp* back to Bella Bella, and disappears somehow."

"Almost right, but not quite. Crowley saw the *Kelp* on the eleventh. So probably the killer stopped by for at least one visit before killing Crowley on the thirteenth. He wanted to check things out before he acted. Hey, did you see a computer when you were there?"

"Yeah, right on the kitchen table."

"It wasn't there later. Our bad guy obviously took it, but that one was bait. Crowley was suspicious of his accomplice. The computer with all the info was hidden. Then the killer spent the night of the twelfth in Morehouse Bay, so no one in Bella Bella would have seen him."

"And he's probably still in the area, maybe Lagoon Bay."

"Yeah, but I'm almost scared to come face to face with him. In fact, I am scared to come face to face with him. He kills people."

I lurched to my feet in what I hoped was a decisive manner. "And the truly scary thing about all this is that Fleming Griffith was running the lab when all this started. What if he's involved in the murders?" Wordless pause. "I'm going to talk to Louise. Can you get hold of Fergie and meet us at the bar in an hour?"

"See you there."

When I barged into Louise's office, she was on the phone, or rather, talking into it. When she hung up, I leaned over her desk and kissed her with awkward passion. "Want to go fishing?"

"Explain." I did. She groaned. "A minute ago, I was working on an unsolved homicide. Now you tell me we've got a mass murder on our hands."

"Yeah, but just one murderer. And together, we can nail him."

"And you want me to go where? Morehouse Bay?"

"It's where the trail leads. Besides, you'll get to see the old crew in action. It'll be like reuniting the '94 Oilers."

"Give me a little time to arrange some stuff. Pick me up at the dock."

By the time I got to the bar, the rest of the crew was seated at a table, untouched beers going flat in front of them. Mark raised an index finger in greeting. "I've brought these guys up to speed but they're having a hard time digesting it."

Christine spoke through hands covering her face. "I'm having a hard time, not so much digesting it, but believing it. It seems completely unreal. Three people killed over a science experiment gone wrong?"

"Just one, really: Billy. Then Crowley was killed because he found out that Billy had been killed and Les Jameson was killed because he could have fingered Crowley's killer. The big mystery, the thing that's driving me crazy, is why was Billy killed. It just doesn't make sense."

Fergie straightened up and slapped the table. "I don't care if it doesn't make sense. Maybe we're dealing with a deranged lab rat. I just want to get the bastard and kick his balls up to his tonsils." We all sat silent again.

A question occurred to me. "Christine, how do you know there was a second person on Les Jameson's boat?"

"I started going through his gear. There were two carryalls full of clothes and personal stuff. One definitely belonged to Les because it had his wallet. The other bag was full of clothes that were too big to fit Les, and it had a toilet kit that included a hairbrush."

Les Jameson hadn't had hair for even longer than he hadn't had morals. "Have you got the bag now?"

"Yeah."

"Give it to Louise. We'll pick her up in Bella Bella. You guys ready?" We left the beer on the table and walked out.

Twenty minutes later, I helped Louise over the cap rail of the *Coastal Provider* and led her up to the wheelhouse. She smiled at everyone. "Hi, everyone. Thanks for volunteering your time on this."

"We were a pretty tight group," Christine said with a smile, "the crew of the *Maple Leaf C*. I guess this seems to us just a case of helping out an old shipmate."

I didn't know if she was referring to Billy or me. Didn't really matter. Mark put the boat in gear and we headed north into the gathering dark.

With five people in the wheelhouse, it was a little crowded, but not uncomfortably so. We bantered companionably for ten or fifteen minutes, and then I suggested that Christine and I do a wheel shift. Mark yawned and headed for his cabin and Fergie went to claim a bunk in the fo'c's'le. Louise stayed with Christine and me. Soon we were heading westward in Seaforth Channel.

The wheelhouse was dark, lit only by the dim, comfortable light of the instruments. I was at the wheel with Louise standing beside me, staring with interest at the radar and sounder and GPS display, and Christine lounged on the bench along the port bulkhead. I spoke quietly. "Mark must have been a little tired. They were pumping fish all last night."

"Seine boat guys are such sissies," Christine snorted, "which I realized when I started gillnetting. Gillnetters stay up for days at a time."

Louise turned to her. "You're joking. That's not safe."

"You're right, but working on a boat alone is not safe. Setting a net is not safe. Drumming in is not safe. Being on a slippery deck at night is not safe. But that's gillnetting. So staying up for a few hours past what most people would consider a normal shift is just part of the game."

"What's the longest you ever stayed up?"

"I used to do forty-eight hours regularly, but after that, I'd start seeing the phantom deckhands. About fifty-six hours was my absolute limit. But I knew guys who swore they could do three days."

Louise shook her head. "Good God. I had no idea that fishermen did stuff like that. After doing fifty-six hours, did you take a couple of days off?"

"No, I'd set the alarm and have a fifteen-minute catnap, do another few hours, another catnap, and so on. The only problem was that during those catnaps The Bad Things would appear."

"What do you mean?"

"Oh, the thousand and one things that can screw things up: a slight shift in the wind blows your boat onto the net, a riptide sinks your net, a huge log drifts into the middle of your net, a boat comes around the corner and runs over your net. Shit like that."

"I can't imagine why anyone would want to fish for a living."

"Masochists, I guess. But when things are going well, fish hitting your net, you're making the right moves, and you out-drum some guy to get the next set, there's absolutely nothing that compares to it."

I silently agreed. After about half an hour, I altered course to head into Return Channel. At the wheel of a boat, in the company of friends, I felt better than I had in a while. I told Louise about our SPLAG scam. She chuckled softly. We ran northeast for an hour before I turned into Morehouse Bay. Christine was dozing on the bench, but when she heard the engine slow, she woke up and helped me drop the hook. Then we all found a bunk in the fo'c's'le, I kissed Louise goodnight, and we snuggled into our respective bunks and waited for what the morning would bring.

Fourteen

I was the second one up in the morning. It was almost daylight. We had slept in but that was okay because this wasn't real fishing. We only needed to make one or two sets, catch a few of the refugee sockeye for specimens, and call it a day.

Mark and I sipped coffee and watched the eastern sky lighten and the scattered cirrus clouds start to turn pink. The boat sat quietly at anchor. There wasn't a sound, but you could almost hear something whisper the meaning of life.

The pink dawn gave way to soft golden daylight and the sounds of human animals awakening drifted up to the wheelhouse. Soon everyone was there. Louise broke the silence. "I won't be much help today so the least I can do is cook breakfast. Do you have eggs and stuff, Mark?"

"On this boat, we've always considered food as safety equipment. We never leave the dock without it."

"Is a Western omelet okay with everyone?"

There was not a single objection so Louise went down the ladder, and soon we could hear pots banging in the galley. Fergie was staring intently out the window. "I don't see any sockeye, Danny."

"They're around here somewhere. We'll find 'em after breakfast." I went down to the galley to get another coffee and stayed to watch Louise bustling competently around the stove.

"I thought you said you weren't much of a cook."

"If I was rich, I would have lied about that too. I want you to be interested in me, not my incidental attributes."

"I happen to be very attracted to your incidental attributes." I got up and kissed her. She kissed me back.

"Some attributes are more incidental than others. Does the uniform attract you?"

"Take it off and I'll see how I feel."

"You feel aroused." She turned back to the stove. "I don't want to burn the omelet. Why don't you make the toast?"

By the time I had made ten pieces of toast, the omelet was ready, so I called the others to the table. We ate quickly, even though there was no need, and when we were finished, I told Fergie it was his turn to do the dishes.

"What do you mean, it's my turn?"

"I did them last. It's your turn after me."

"We haven't been together on a boat for eight years. Are you telling me you remember who did the dishes last?"

"I wrote it in my diary."

"Even so, this is a different boat. Different rotation. Law of the sea."

"Rotation is invoked by the last doer of the dishes. Chapter twenty-three."

"All right, but I get the last piece of toast."

Christine grinned. "Some things never change. It's nice to know you can count on a certain amount of consistency, even if it's only childishness."

Mark went back to the wheelhouse and the engine roared into life. Christine and I went to pull the hook, and then we had a quick conference in the wheelhouse. "Let's take a look in behind those islands. That's where I'd be if I was a sockeye."

"If you spend too much time in the West Van lab, you might be."

The boat moved slowly forward as Mark kept his eye on the sounder. There was a string of three or four islands in the outer bay, and two more on the inner southeast shore. In between the two sets of islands, we found the fish. Mark stared at the sounder. "It looks deep enough for a set. Let me sound it out for a couple of minutes."

We went out on deck to get everything ready. I told Louise to stand on the upper deck behind the wheelhouse so she'd get a good view. Professionals in action, I told her.

We checked the myriad of things that needed to be checked so that the complex activity of launching and recovering a quarter mile of net could be achieved without disaster, and then assumed our positions. I would run the drum in Billy's absence, Fergie would run the skiff, and Christine was at her old post on the deck winch. Mark poked his head out the back door and yelled some last-minute instructions. "There's a lot of fish and we only need a few. I'm going to do a quick circle set so Fergie won't have to tow much."

He gunned the engine and the boat sped up. I felt the familiar butterflies signaling my rising excitement. I gave a thumbs-up to Fergie standing in the skiff and Christine by the winch and then Louise behind the wheelhouse. The horn sounded and Christine let the skiff line go. The net started to peel off the stern and I watched the line of corks as Mark started to draw a big white circle in the water. When the net was almost completely off, Mark poked his head out again. "Don't even use the tow hook. Just start drumming slowly when the last cork hits the water."

As the last cork dribbled over the stern, I placed the second roller in the spooling gear and draped the towline between the two rollers. Fergie had towed his end of the net back to the boat. He passed the end of the tow-off line to Christine who wrapped it onto the deck winch. Fergie had jumped back onboard, and he released the blondie before dragging the purse line sternward where he fed it into the pursing block. Christine started pursing and I started drumming. I certainly wasn't an artiste of the caliber that Billy had been, but I knew the basic moves. While Christine and I were performing our parts in the dance, Fergie swung the boom to port and hooked up the hairpin.

Mark joined us on deck and stood beside Fergie and me next to the drum. "This is completely ass backwards. I'm trying to catch as few fish as possible." Then he looked at me. "Hey, do we need a permit for this?"

"I can issue a scientific permit," I said, wondering if I could.

"Rings coming up!"

I ran the spoolers over to my side and stopped the drum. The purse line pulled tight. "Whoa!" Fergie rammed the hairpin into the neatly bunched brass rings. "Goin' up!" Christine raised the hairpin to a convenient height, pulled the deck winch out of gear, and I started drumming again. Soon there were only six rings left and I slowed the drum. When there were only two rings left, Mark grabbed them and Christine lowered the hairpin while Fergie ran to untie the end line. Mark stooped and carefully passed his two rings around the horn, even though we weren't really concerned with losing fish, and Fergie did the same with the end line. I stopped the drum and Mark pulled out one of the spoolers so the fish wouldn't be squished passing between them.

Mark peered over the stern. "There's a couple hundred," he said.

I lowered the stern ramp until the roller was almost in the water and then went ahead on the drum. A neat little bag of flopping fish came over the stern, and I raised the ramp and stopped the drum. Fergie and Mark pulled slack through the end rings. I went ahead on the drum again, and the neat little bag of fish spilled onto the stern.

"Come and look at this," I shouted to Louise. Almost immediately, we spotted two Frankenfish, then three more, and then too many. Some of the fish were normal, at least in outward appearance. But the deformed specimens, writhing on deck, made my stomach heave. I looked at my shipmates and they all displayed expressions of distaste, like they were watching unusually offensive porn.

I was in a quandary. I wanted to save the Igors and maybe a dozen of the normal-looking fish. But what to do with the rest? Throw them overboard? Alive or dead? When I voiced these questions, Mark was unequivocal. "We can freeze a few of these but I don't want the rest on my boat. And if they're mutants, they shouldn't go back into the ocean alive."

"Okay, let's save the obvious mutants and a dozen normal-looking ones to autopsy." The "autopsy" consisted of slitting open the bellies to check the gonads. Christine and Fergie and I grimaced as we handled the misshapen mutants. Their flesh was soft and repellent, but we willed ourselves into a clinical detachment.

We quickly discovered two things. All the "normal" fish were males and they all carried radio tags, little cylinders the size of a vitamin pill. It now seemed prudent to open up the deformed fish. They weren't Igors, they were Igoresses, and they were radio-tagged as well.

Fergie shook his head. "Wow, all females are mutants. Who knew?"

Christine kicked bloody water at him. "You may want to re-phrase that slightly."

"We need to take a good look at the islands," Louise said to Mark. "Can you cruise around them real close to the shore."

"It's too shallow. But we can use the skiff."

Christine offered to tag and bag our specimens, so Louise and I climbed into the skiff. As we cruised toward the innermost of the islands, I asked what we were looking for.

"Clues."

"Oh."

We slowly circumnavigated all of the islands in Morehouse Bay. Every one was heavily vegitized, so we looked for openings in the underbrush, anything that resembled a trail. We saw nothing that would indicate the hand of man had ever set foot on any of the islands.

I did take the opportunity, when we were out of sight of the *Coastal Provider*, to snuggle with the local law enforcement. Much more than the quick grope of my previous amours, it was a searching embrace that left us flushed and yearning. It was with some reluctance that we headed back.

When we got alongside the big boat, I spread my hands wide and shrugged. I threw Fergie the skiff line, and he threw it over the drum to Christine, who put it on the winch and pulled the skiff up tight to the stern of the *Coastal Provider*. Louise and I climbed aboard and looked enquiringly at Mark. He checked his watch. "It's ten-thirty. We can be in Lagoon Bay by four. It'll still be light enough to look around."

Mark went up to the wheelhouse and the *Coastal Provider* began moving out of the bay. He headed northeast up Return Channel, so he could turn south down Johnson Channel on the way to Lagoon Bay. Sometimes you had to head in one direction so you could make progress in the opposite direction.

Our mood lightened when we were joined by a small group of harbor porpoises. They shot toward us like torpedoes, then turned and ran with the boat, surfing in the bow wave. I took Louise out to the bow so she could lean over and look at them. We could almost touch them. They were such amazing creatures, zooming through the water with no discernible movement of their bodies. They could have been jet-propelled, and they were having such fun! If ignorance is bliss then oblivion must be golden rapture. And the porpi were completely oblivious, to our concerns at least. I felt jealous but Louise was entranced. Soon they grew bored with us and shot off on some other adventure. Louise took my hand and we went back into the warmth of the wheelhouse.

Mark and Fergie and Christine all looked at me as we entered. "A few questions have arisen," Christine said. "Perhaps you'd like to try to answer them?" I shrugged.

"Those little pill things we found in the fish? They were radio transmitters?"

"Yeah, they obviously wanted to track the fish, because they were worried they wouldn't follow a normal pattern. Or, they were programmed not to follow the normal pattern."

"Okay. Second question: why are all the mutants female?"

"We can only guess, right? It could be an unforeseen consequence of the genetic manipulation. Or maybe it was deliberate because they didn't want these fish to breed with normal fish."

"But even ugly humans reproduce." Fergie was on thin ice here and I ignored him.

Mark put his two cents in: "I'm betting the deformities were unintended. They wanted this whole experiment to go unnoticed, not have their fish picked out and scrutinized and brought back to the lab for identification."

There seemed to be general agreement on that. I advanced the question that was really bothering me: "Crowley came up here to monitor the experiment. That means he knew the fish would be here, which meant they'd been genetically programmed to stay inshore, on the central coast. Don't ask me why."

The *Coastal Provider* continued to part the waters, down Johnson Channel and then into Fisher Channel. The beauty of the day reproached us for our imperfections. Louise disappeared down to the galley, and twenty minutes later came back with a tray of sandwiches. We didn't actually snarl and snap over them, but there were a few hand slaps and exhortations to take just one at a time. They disappeared very quickly.

Soon we could see Burke Channel opening to the east, and we knew Lagoon Bay was just ahead. Anticipation crackled between us like an electric charge. Mark cut close by Nob Point and did a transect from north to south across the bay. We saw nothing unusual, so he headed for the narrow gap that led into Codville Lagoon. Throttling back to half speed, he watched the sounder closely as the bottom came up to two fathoms and then dropped back down to forty-five. We were in the lagoon.

If you turned the chart sideways, the lagoon was shaped like a toadstool. It was deeper than most lagoons, with a large island at the eastern side. Mark turned to port, intending to cruise the shoreline. As we neared the island, I could see wisps of smoke drifting up from somewhere near the center and my heart skipped a little. Mark saw the smoke too. "Don't tell me someone lives here."

I touched Louise's shoulder and pointed at the smoke. I could feel her tense, and I read her thoughts: *What if the bad guy was here?* Mark continued to cruise the beach, and in doing so circumnavigated the island. We saw no sign of a boat, which lessened the chances that there was someone on the island. When we had followed the shore all the way around to our starting point, Mark put the boat in neutral and waited for instructions.

I was adamant: "We need to land on the island and find the source of that smoke."

Louise was more hesitant: "The book says in situations like this, you call for backup. Mind you, backup a long way away."

"If we'd seen a boat, I'd say call for reinforcements," I said, pressing my case. "But I don't think there's anyone there. Besides, there's five of us."

"Okay, here's the deal," she said. I could see her thinking carefully. "I'll get my pistol and two people will come with me to the island, and two will stay here. When we get to the island, one person stays with the skiff, and the other comes with me. Any sound or sign of trouble and the skiff person comes back here. If there's no radio contact between the land party and the boat after thirty minutes, you guys take off and establish radio contact with Bella Bella ASAP. Ask for help."

"I'll run the skiff, and after I drop you on the island, I'll stand off a net length or so," Christine said. "I won't move back in until I see you, and you give me the okay."

"That's pretty close to a foolproof plan," I nodded agreement. "I'll go with Louise."

"Foolproof?" Fergie laughed. "Considering the personnel, it better be."

"I'll be right back," Louise said, heading for the fo'c's'le. When she returned, she was in uniform, wearing a protective vest with her sidearm on her belt. "Let's go, guys."

We went out to launch the skiff, and five minutes later Christine was steering us toward the island. Louise raised her voice over the sound of the engine.

"Let's cruise all the way around it, before we decide where to land." Christine nodded and stood on her toes to get a better view as she steered.

When we got to the other side of the island, we spotted a break in the wall of salal. It might have been a trail. Christine kept going around the island, but we saw nothing else that resembled a trail. When we got back to the break in the salal, Christine headed straight in toward the beach. Twenty feet offshore, she cut the engine. We glided in silently, until there was a crunch as we grounded on gravel. Louise was the first out of the boat. I followed, and then turned and pushed the skiff back out. Christine started the engine and reversed out until she was well off the beach. Louise waved her even farther back. "I want her out of easy gunshot range." Gunshots? In this Pacific Eden? But I knew the serpent was looming around us and the old rules no longer applied.

The break in the salal was indeed the start of a trail. We could see that, after about fifty feet, the salal gave way to scrub pine. After that was the unknown.

"I'll go first," Louise said. "You keep about twenty yards back."

"I've got a better idea." I realized we were whispering. "I'll go first. That way, if someone jumps me, you'll be able to rescue me with guns blazing."

"Okay. Go slow. I'll stay behind enough to be out of sight."

I nodded, and crouching, started to bushwhack my way along the ill-defined trail. It was by no means a Parks Canada-approved hiking trail, and I was soon scratched and sweating and swatting away bugs. I clambered over a couple of deadfalls and once took a wrong turn into a salmonberry thicket. But after about two hundred yards of painstaking progress, I could see a lighter area ahead. I emerged into a clearing and whistled in amazement. There had been a building here, more than a building, an installation of some kind, but whatever it was had been reduced to smouldering ashes. Louise was soon beside me and she repeated my whistle.

"We missed him by twenty-four hours. I'm guessing that's how long ago this fire was set." She stepped out into the clearing. "The surrounding trees were just too green to burn; not that it makes much difference. The killer is covering his tracks. I wonder what was here."

I examined some familiar metallic shapes. They were blackened but recognizable. "We've got two generators here, and that metal latticework; if it was standing up, could have been a radio tower. I think this was the monitoring station." We began to walk the perimeter of the clearing. On the eastward side, we almost stepped on an electrical cable that snaked into the trees in one direction and back into the center of the burned area in the opposite direction. I tried to follow it into the bush, but soon gave up. "We should be able to pick this up where it reaches the beach."

We tried to examine what would have been the interior of the building, but it was still too hot. So we stood there and looked around. "Any chance we'll find useful evidence here?"

"No fingerprints or DNA evidence," Louise said, shaking her head. "Nothing biological. I guess that was the intent. But when we sift through the ashes we might come up with something. Not everything is flammable. Where do you think that cable goes?"

"Let's go look."

When we had retraced our steps back along the trail, and arrived at the beach, we looked to see if we could find the electrical cable. We did. About a hundred yards north of where we'd landed, the cable came out of the bush, ran across the intertidal area, and disappeared into the water. We waved to Christine and she idled in to pick us up. "Well?"

"There was some kind of monitoring station in there but it looks like the bad guy torched it. He's cutting his losses and covering his tracks. There's an electrical cable running into the water. I want to see if it comes out on the mainland beach, over there."

Christine aimed the skiff at the spot I'd pointed out: a bay within the lagoon within the main bay. It was about half tide, and a lot of the gravelly beach was exposed. It was there that we discovered the last and the most unexpected of the implausibilities we'd come across that day. The beach was littered with familiar red carcasses: spawned-out sockeye salmon.

Louise didn't realize the implications of what we were seeing, but Christine did. Sockeye, like all salmon, are supposed to spawn in freshwater streams and rivers. In the fall, not the spring.

"Christ Almighty!" Christine gestured at the carcasses. "Goddamn scientists are breaking the laws of nature."

"I'll let you guys worry about that." Louise was grim. "I'm more concerned with them breaking the laws of the Criminal Code of Canada."

We headed back to the *Coastal Provider* in silence. Parts of the puzzle were becoming clear to me, but certain areas were still obscured. It was like running a boat in the fog. Sometimes you could sense things, shapes in the fog that you couldn't quite see. Sometimes you saw things that weren't there. And the more you concentrated, the more the lines blurred.

It was five-thirty and almost dusk by the time we got back to the boat. Mark had dropped the hook. We described what we'd seen while Mark and Fergie listened calmly. The troops were getting impervious to shock.

"No sense rushing off anywhere," Mark said finally. "We might as well have a relaxing supper."

Fergie had something in the oven. It smelled roastlike. There was a bottle of red wine on the table, so I sat down and poured myself a glass. Louise retired to the fo'c's'le to slip into something a little more comfortable, which meant divesting herself of her .38 Special, but she soon returned, and we all sat around the table and sipped wine reflectively.

"The lagoon must have really low salt content," Mark said, "more fresh water than salt. That must be what enabled the fish to spawn there. It's obviously all part of the plan, but what the hell is the plan?"

Fergie delved into the wine cellar under the forward bench and produced another bottle of red and one of white. It was completely dark outside, and the galley windows showed only our reflections. The oil stove produced a comfortable warmth and the smell of the roast intensified. The five of us sat close together around the table, insulated from the vastness outside. Self-sufficient. It was boat life.

We batted around theories about the case, but soon ran into the wall of the unknown. Conversation shifted to more mundane matters; movies we'd seen, the last good book we'd read. Before hunger had progressed to the point of drooling on the table, Fergie took the roast out of the oven, along with sourdough biscuits and roast potatoes. He'd boiled some peas, so as not to discriminate completely against chlorophyll-based life forms, and while he made the gravy, I carved the roast.

The two of us sitting on the outside of the table served the three trapped on the inside along the wall, and then served ourselves. There ensued a scene of serious nutritioning. The roast never stood a chance. When the only clues to the roast's erstwhile existence were some bits of fat and stained string, we celebrated our victory over meat by finishing the wine. We then launched the desert campaign, plotting the destruction of a gallon of chocolate ice cream topped with frozen strawberries. Having achieved total food domination, we celebrated our success with coffee and Baileys and brandy.

When it was bedtime, Mark offered Louise his cabin so she wouldn't have to sleep with the rabble in the fo'c's'le. She demurred, saying she was third-generation rabble herself. She again took the bunk above mine, and gave me a quick kiss before nimbly climbing in. As I lay below her, separated only by some plywood and a mattress, I tried to keep my thoughts pure. I failed.

Fifteen

In the morning, we were forced to invoke the anti-hangover clause. (If you ignore it, it doesn't exist.) Nevertheless, many crew members were unusually contemplative.

The consensus was to skip breakfast, so Mark brought the engines to life, we rattled the anchor chain onto the winch drum, and set forth for Bella Bella, where we tied up at the government dock and gathered in the wheelhouse for a conference.

It was agreed that there was, at present, no more need for the boat here. We'd discovered what there was to discover. Mark could head back south, taking Fergie and Christine. Louise and I would fly south.

Louise and I grabbed our bags and jumped off the boat. I untied the lines and waved as the *Coastal Provider* backed away. It was noon. "What next, Commandante?"

"I want to check in at the office," Louise said. "And I'll send my dive crew back to the lagoon to check out those cables."

"Okay, I'll wander around in a purposeful manner." We were walking up the hill. Louise peeled off into the RCMP building and I carried on alone with my thoughts. I began sifting through the latest amalgamation of knowns and unknowns.

Known: Someone, probably our bad guy, had burnt a building where no building should have been, in isolated Lagoon Bay.

Unknown: How had he gotten there? I was sure we had his boat, the *Kelp*. Had he stolen another one?

Known: There was a thick electrical cable running from the burnt building into the ocean.

Unknown: What was it for?

Known: Sockeye salmon were spawning in a saltwater lagoon, at the wrong time of year.

Unknown: How was this even possible?

I wandered thoughtful as a cloud and eventually found myself down at the public dock. The afternoon sun warmed my shoulders and glinted off the water. The water taxi had just landed and some people got off the boat and some got on and some just stood and talked. A clap on my shoulders distracted me and I turned to see Cecil Brown grinning at me.

"Herring season's over, Danny. It's too late to bust anyone now."

"There's no statute of limitations on serving bad coffee."

"Or impersonating a Fisheries Officer." The grin disappeared. "You find anything out about that boat?"

"Not yet, but we're on the guy's trail."

"I used to pack Crowley's prawns. I sort of know his routine. Did you find his logbook?"

"Yeah, I've got a copy of it" I said.

"If I could take a look at it, I might be able to spot something. I know he'd had a few run-ins with other prawn guys."

"Like who?"

"Not mentioning any names, but someone with the initials Joe Vukovitch, in particular."

"A Yugoslav prawn fisherman. Bound to be trouble" I said.

"That sounds racist to me."

"No, just gear-typist. I'll make another copy of the log and drop it off at your boat. I'm flying out tonight so call me if you pick up on anything. You've got my cell number?"

"It's written on the ceiling above my bunk," he said, deadpan.

"I'm touched."

"I know that. Your number is right there with all my other emergency numbers, search and rescue, oil spill response, late-night pizza delivery."

"What sort of emergency am I supposed to respond to?"

"Bad fisheries policy."

"I'm surprised you haven't called before now."

"I have. Your secretary wouldn't put me through."

"I don't have a secretary, just voicemail."

"Silly me. If I'd known that, maybe we could have avoided the whole sorry mess that we're in."

"Yeah, well, I guess that makes it all your fault. I'm gonna go and copy Alistair's log. Catch you later."

I headed back to the RCMP building. Louise was out. While I waited for her, I made a copy of Crowley's log to give to Cecil. I then charmed the office staff for an hour or so, until Louise returned. I joined her in her office. "Has anyone reported the theft of a boat?"

She shook her head. "Why?"

"I was hoping that our bad guy stole a boat from here to get down to Codville Lagoon. The alternative is another Les Jameson scenario. I don't want to find any more bodies."

"He could have stolen it and returned it the same night so it wouldn't be missed. That means he flew out of here yesterday, maybe the day before, or he's still here. I'll check the Pacific Coastal passenger lists, but he wouldn't have used his real name." She gestured to the window and I turned in time to see a government green pickup truck pull into the parking lot. Two guys in drysuits jumped out of the back and I deduced they must be the divers. We went out to meet them. I recognized one as the constable who'd been with Louise when I first met her at Crowley's float house. I went up to him and said "Hi," and he introduced me to the other guy, Calvin Reid.

Louise greeted them. "That was quick, guys. Find anything interesting?"

Calvin held up a large baggie with a black box inside. As I peered at it, I could see two wires sticking out of the box.

"The cable ran for about one hundred meters under the water. There were four of these boxes attached to it by wires. We cut this one off and bagged it. We were wearing our diving gloves so evidential integrity is intact." He grinned and I could tell he got a kick out of sounding so officially correct. A potential bureaucrat.

"Good job. I'll take it to Vancouver and let the all-stars check it out. Do you know what it is, Danny?"

"Radio receiver. That cable was set up to receive signals from those little transmitters in the fish. I think the cable ran to an amplifier, maybe an on-site recorder, and then to an aerial for long-distance transmission."

"So Crowley could have received the information at his float house? And someone in Vancouver could have received it?"

"Crowley definitely could have received it. Maybe he relayed it to Vancouver." I thrust my hands firmly into my pockets and thought hard. Louise looked at me expectantly.

"We're supposed to be on that seven o'clock flight tonight."

"Okay. You carry on here. I'll meet you at the airport."

I walked down to the dock and found Cecil's boat. He wasn't there so I left the copy of Crowley's log on the galley table. By that time, I was feeling hunger pangs. The restaurant was crowded when I got there; no available tables, but a familiar-looking guy waved me over.

"There's a spare seat here. Sit down."

"Thanks a lot." I sat down and nodded at the other people at the table. They made eye contact over their burgers and grunted greetings. I remembered who the guy was: Sam Wilson, a gillnetter of some repute.

"Hi, Sam, were you out on the herring?"

"Yeah, we were at Stryker Bay. Did good. I heard you ran a good fishery here."

I shrugged. "We can't screw everything up."

The guy at the end of the table, another familiar fishing face, piped up.

"Don't bet on it. You keep letting the seines catch all that fish in Spiller Channel and you'll kill the small-boat fishery in the outer bays. It's the same fish."

It was a familiar argument with some truth to it. Fortunately, the waitress showed up and saved me from answering. "Hey, you're Louise's boyfriend."

"Apprentice boyfriend. Haven't done the practical yet. Can I get a medium-rare steak?"

"I've never heard it called 'Doing The Practical' before. White people are strange." I must have looked sufficiently embarrassed because she asked what I wanted to drink, noted it on her pad, and walked toward the kitchen.

"So what's the deal with Alistair Crowley?" Sam asked while he played with the straw in his glass. "I'm hearing weird stuff."

I could almost see ears perking up around the table. Hell, it was their community and they had a right to know. Besides, I was getting tired of keeping secrets. "It's almost certain he didn't commit suicide. Which means someone killed him. And whoever did it might have used a boat that's tied up at the fishermen's dock, the *Kelp*. Ever see anyone using that boat?"

"Cecil Brown asked me that the other day. Couldn't help him. It kind of puts everything under a cloud, Crowley and Les Jameson, not that I care much about Jameson. He was a prick. But a death is a death and that's two of them in the same month."

Everyone's head turned as a scuffle broke out at the back table. A stocky young guy, eyes not fully focused, swore at his companions and made gangsta-like aggressive motions. A shrill young woman suggested that he fornicate away to another place and he did, rushing unsteadily toward the door. "Who's that?"

Sam answered scornfully, "One of our weekend warriors. My nephew, Mathew Wilson. Never quite grew up."

"Melissa's brother?"

"Yeah. Nice family. Every family has bad apples, I guess."

While everyone was shaking their heads, the waitress brought my steak and beer. I wasn't synchronized with my tablemates and they soon drifted off, leaving me alone to ruminate. I had two more beers, declined desert, and grabbed a cab out to the airport.

An hour later, we were shielding our eyes as the Pacific Coastal Airlines scheduled flight took off into a low western sun. We crossed a dappled Queen Charlotte Sound and followed the sun-sheened metallic ribbon of Johnstone Strait south toward Vancouver. The west was bright and the east was darkening. The planes and angles of various peaks and alpine lakes reflected fire or sucked light into blackness. For some time, I was mindless and only slowly became aware again and conscious of Louise beside me. She had the window seat and was still staring raptly at the celestial theatrics to the west. When the curtain of night had fallen, she turned to me and smiled.

Vancouver was only three degrees south of Bella Bella but at least six degrees warmer. I doffed my fleecy as I walked across the tarmac at the south terminal. We had only hand luggage so we went straight through the terminal and into a cab. Settled into the back seat, I looked at Louise and asked the question as neutrally as possible. "Where shall we stay tonight?"

Louise put her hand on top of mine. "Danny, I can't think about this case and have a love affair at the same time."

"Interesting. I've never had a problem separating mental activity from sexual activity."

"Really? You think about sex all the time."

I noticed I was coming in second in a lot of our verbal exchanges. But maybe that was good enough to make the play-offs. I shifted to what was proving to be one of my stronger events: crime, the analysis of. "Okay, action plan. In the morning, I'm going to check in at HQ and suss out the best way of penetrating the West Vancouver lab. That's where everything started and that's where the answers are."

"And I will go to my HQ and grovel to the local brass in order to get the resources we need to solve this. And we'll need to work with the Vancouver Police Department. It's their turf." She handed me a card. "That's where I'll be. Phone me tomorrow."

Rush hour was as over as it ever gets in Vancouver, so it was less than half an hour before we were deposited at the Hotel Georgia. We fumbled our way into an embrace and kissed as seriously as you can kiss in a hotel lobby. I left her there, resolving to eliminate the need for such partings as soon as possible.

I walked a few blocks south and checked in to the Chateau Granville. It was not as grand as the name suggested, though it was cheap and close to my favorite blues club. In the morning, it was still overcast but in a state of definite non-precipitation as I walked briskly along Granville Street, left on Georgia and then right on Burrard. I was therefore dry, albeit feeling somewhat wet behind the ears, as I stood outside and contemplated for a moment the grandeur of DFO headquarters. The edifice was perhaps more grand than its contents, a shuffle of bureaucrats whose numbers almost equaled the fishermen they were supposed to govern, yet was failing so miserably that it necessitated the employment of a PR department of Disneyesque proportions.

I rode the elevator up to an executive height and found my way to the regional director general's office. On my way down the hall, people shouted greetings and congratulations. "Way to go, Danny. Good job up there. That was a well-run fishery." I shrugged modestly, feeling like a football player who's just scored the winning touchdown. When I entered Paul Desroche's office, he was on the phone but quickly said good-bye and hung up, something I took to be another sign of my increased stature.

"Danny, welcome back to civilization." He stood up to shake my hand. "If we ever gave out bonuses, you'd be getting one."

"Thanks, Paul. Between Pete and George and me, we managed to fumble our way through. Bit of a scare when we lost the fish."

"Yes, well, all's well, etcetera. Listen, I hate to put a damper on things, but it sounds like Griffith is still mad at you. He's lobbying to get you assigned to the drag fleet."

The draggers were the trawlers, big boats that worked offshore in unsheltered waters for weeks at a time. It wasn't a popular assignment. "Fleming will have to find another victim. I'm going to take a couple weeks' holiday. Besides, he's just in a bad mood because someone impersonated him on the SPLAG website. By the way, who's the operations manager at the West Vancouver lab? I want to get some background for a paper I'm working on."

"It's a brand new person. We were just notified of her appointment two days ago. Bette Connelly. You know her?"

"Yeah, I do. Hey, I gotta go. If you hear from Griffith, tell him I think that abalone trap policy was his finest work."

As I rode down in the elevator, I was thinking about what a break it was that Bette was running the lab. I'd have to tell her Paul considered her a brand new person: at her age. She'd be a huge asset in digging up whatever secrets were there.

I phoned Louise from the back of a cab to tell her I was on my way over. She sounded quietly triumphant. "I've spent the whole morning working out protocol issues. I'm in foreign territory here, so I have to have a Vancouver Police liaison. It turns out he's a really good guy who's been on the major crime squad for twelve years. Inspector Tommy Yamada. Smart guy. And because he's a street cop and not a bureaucrat type, he's more or less accepted your presence as an unofficial team member."

Vancouver Police HQ was way over on Cambie and Sixth Avenue. I strode into the reception area and asked to see Staff Sergeant Louise Karavchuk. She came out to great me, didn't kiss me, and led me back to a meeting room where Tommy Yamada stood up and shook my hand. He was average height for a Japanese guy and sported a broken nose that, I learned later, was the legacy of his years playing rugby at the rep level. We all sat down around an oblong table that was scattered with papers, photos, and a box with a single doughnut left in it.

"Danny, this is a hell of a case you've dragged us into. Bodies all over the place, crime scenes up and down the coast, possible political involvement, and key players in the investigation lacking, shall we say, official credentials. It could be kind of fun. Before we talk about what our next steps are, I'd like to tie up some loose ends from the scene at Crowley's float house. Louise, have we confirmed the time of death?"

"The coroner's report says that both postmortem rigour and stomach contents put TOD at about 5:00 AM, April 13. That ties in with the time of the presumed killer's visit to Crowley, which we know from the plotter."

"You followed up on the ownership of the *Kelp*, and met a dead-end. What about the previous owner?"

"We tracked Mac McPherson to his daughter's place in Gibsons Landing. He remembers the buyer's first name as Trevor, which we know is phony, and he described him as tall, wore glasses, pallid complexion, sort of a city slicker."

Alarm bells went off in my brain, figuratively speaking of course. I'd had my alarm bells removed my second year in Ottawa. Louise and Tommy saw the same problem I did. Louise spoke hesitantly. "Mac McPherson is the only person who can ID the guy who bought the *Kelp*, who we presume is a multiple killer. Do we need to protect Mac?"

"He should be safe because he was difficult to trace after he left Bella Bella," Tommy said. "We had to use 'official channels.' Still, I wouldn't feel right if we didn't give him some level of protection. I suggest we get your guys in Gibsons to talk to Mac, warn him to contact us if he runs into the so-called Trevor, and also keep an eye on him." Louise and I nodded. He went on. "These electronic plotters, was there one on Crowley's boat?"

This guy was good. I hadn't thought of that. But Louise had. "I had it removed and brought it down with me. We need to give it to someone with the same level of expertise as Mr. Angastouri."

"Great. Now Crowley presumably contacted the killer after his conversation with Mr. Angastouri relating to the earlier disappearance of Billy Bradley. Living in that isolated place, how did he do that?"

"I've been thinking about that. He could have gone into Bella Bella or Shearwater and used a landline, but the log of the *Jessie Isle* makes no mention of it. He probably used the VHF on the *Jessie Isle* to access the Telus radio network. In which case they might have a record of the call with the phone number he called."

Tommy scribbled in his notebook. "I'll get onto Telus about their radio phone records. What else needs to be done?"

"Before I forget, here's another of Crowley's journals. It was under some stuff in my bottom drawer." I forged ahead before anyone queried this bit of lameness. "Also, we need to talk to Crowley's buddy, Dr. James O'Rourke. Then we need a top-notch computer geek to decipher the stuff on Crowley's computer. The same person should have a look at the stuff in that last journal I gave you. It looks like computer print-outs. I have someone in mind if you don't have anyone. And we need to micro-examine the logbook of the *Jessie Isle*."

"I think you and I should talk to the doctor," Louise said, nodding. "I'll set it up. Tommy, you must have some knowledgeable computer people. Can you get that computer into the right hands?"

"Sure, and if they don't come up with anything, Danny can give it to his people. Anything else? No? All right, let's get going." Louise stood up and Tommy and I followed suit. I shook hands with Tommy and followed Louise down the hall. "They've given me the use of an office. This way."

As soon as she shut the door to her office, I reached for her. She was already turning and we pulled each other into an embrace. She looked up at me and I kissed her. She put both hands on the back of my head and tried to pull me closer to her. That would have violated an important law of physics so she contented herself with running her fingertips over the back of my skull and down my neck to my shoulder blades. We were leaning together, forehead to forehead, when the phone rang and we jumped apart.

"Karavchuk. Yes . . . yes. Okay, maybe I should get an outside expert. All right, will do." She hung up, looked at me, drew a deep breath, and was silent for a minute. "I'm not used to kissing people at work. It might take me a moment to recover. How about you?"

"I don't think I've recovered yet."

She waited another second. "That was our electronics lab. I gave them the plotter off the *Jessie Isle* and asked them to look at it. They don't really feel comfortable with it. They deal mostly with cameras and audio stuff. I think we should get Mark to look at it."

"He'd be happy to."

She nodded and picked up a phone book. "Next step." After flipping through a couple of pages she noted a number in her book and dialed it. "Good morning. This is Staff Sergeant Louise Karavchuk, RCMP. We believe that Dr. O'Rourke may have some information that could be pertinent to an investigation we're conducting. Is there a time today when it would be convenient to see him? Yes, I understand he's busy. Lunchtime or after office hours would be fine. Noon? Fine, we'll be there." She hung up and pushed her chair back. "Let's roll, partner."

"One sec, I'll phone Mark." I dialed the Canadian Fishing Company office number and asked for Mark Angastouri. When he came on I asked him how long he would be there. He said he was in no hurry to get home to his place in White Rock, about forty-five minutes out of the city. I remembered the feeling of having no one to go home to.

"We might stop by and see you later," I told him. "Louise has got the plotter off the *Jessie Isle*. We'd like you to take a look at it."

I hung up and started out of the office. Louise was right behind me and she pinched my left buttock. I squealed and leapt slightly. She slapped my shoulder and by the time we were in public view we had wiped the stupid grins off our faces. On the drive over in an unmarked police sedan, Louise looked at me seriously. "Hey you, are you still holding out on me?"

"In more ways than one, sweetie." I gave her my most charming leer. "Actually, you have pillaged me of all material evidence. All I have left are my tawdry thoughts, which I'm glad to share with you." She gave me a coolly tough look. "Another thing. The person I had in mind to check out Crowley's computer is an old friend of mine who's probably DFO's top computer whiz, and coincidentally she's just been appointed operations director of the West Vancouver lab."

"Name?"

"Bette Connelly."

"Old friend?"

"Friend, as in colleague, working buddy, shipmate sort of thing."

"I'm not the jealous type, Danny. I just like to know things."

"I don't blame you. I'll fill you in on my sordid past love life when you've got twenty or thirty seconds."

The drive to Dr. O'Rourke's clinic on East Hastings was like going from the first world to the third. Chic matrons walking their dogs near the police station on Cambie gave way to disheveled street people pushing shopping carts laden with what the chic matrons had probably thrown away. Junkies nodded out on the garbage-strewn sidewalks. Drunks argued and some people screamed curses at the air. The few residents who answered to none of the above scurried down the streets looking vaguely surprised at finding themselves there.

The clinic was a single-story building next to the Native Friendship Centre. On the other side was a parking lot. Most of the cars had been turned into residences. The sidewalk in front of the building had been swept and the windows were clean. I admired the spirit of whoever was responsible, even if they accomplished nothing more than fifty feet of condom-free sidewalk and windows you could see through.

We entered and the woman at the reception desk stiffened when she saw Louise. This would have been a good time for plain clothes. But Louise put her at ease, explaining that she was the one who had phoned earlier. The woman nodded and asked us to take a seat. There were two patients waiting and they used a lot of energy ignoring us. I had gone through three *Reader's Digest*s, laughed at the "Humour in Uniform," sighed at the "Kids Say the Darndest Things," and been fascinated by "I Am Joe's Penis" by the time it was twelve-thirty and the last of the patients had tottered out the door. A man in a doctor outfit appeared, said "Hello," and beckoned us through the door to the inner sanctum.

The doctor's red hair was thinning and his face was lined and tired. But for all that, he was a good-looking guy and I could see where Melissa had got at least some of her remarkably attractive features.

"I'm Jimmy O'Rourke and I think I know why you're here. Melissa phoned last week and said Alistair had shot himself."

"Yes, sir, we're here about Alistair Crowley," Louise explained. "However, we're almost certain he didn't commit suicide. We believe it was murder."

While he considered that, I butted in. "I knew of Crowley when he worked for DFO. We always wondered where he'd got to, so I was surprised to find out he was hanging around in the vicinity of Bella Bella. Before I got a chance to ask him what he was doing there he was killed. By chance I ran into Melissa, and she told me you and Crowley were friends, that he had actually come to Bella Bella to see you. I thought you might have some idea as to why he ended up there."

"We were friends. Were. We were pre-med together at UBC and we sacrificed many a bottle of scotch on the altar of youthful dreams. But Alistair never really liked people. Fortunately, he had the wit to recognize that and wisely decided not to become a doctor of medicine."

"That's how he ended up at DFO?" I asked.

"Eventually, I guess he decided to turn his intelligence to animal biology."

"I understand it was a considerable intelligence," I prompted.

"He was extremely intelligent," Dr. Jimmy said. "Sometimes alarmingly so. When he went to work for DFO, I thought he was wasting himself and told him so. That caused a bit of a rift, but after I got posted to Bella Bella, we still kept in touch."

Louise had taken out a notebook and was scribbling things, trying not to impede the flow of Dr. Jimmy's reminiscences. Still, there was a bit of a silence before he carried on. "Then, in the early eighties, he visited me in Bella Bella." A note of regret had crept into his voice.

"Something was different on that visit?" I asked.

"Alistair had always been an intense individual, but it seemed that his intensity had increased by an order of magnitude. He was supposed to be on holiday but he couldn't relax. One night we broke out a bottle of scotch and sat up late, drinking and talking, just like the old days.

He started to tell me about the transgenic experiments they were doing, often without the proper clearances. I know enough biology that I could see the dangers and I told him he was being reckless."

"How did he feel about that?" I asked.

"He didn't like it. He got angry and said I had become middle-class cautious and conservative. There could be no progress without risk, he said. And anyway, he knew exactly what he was doing. He was really wound up by then and he finished by yelling that he didn't care if his experiments did get out of control. Any data was good data."

Louise had stopped writing but her head remained bowed. I knew she was concentrating intently on the doctor's words, letting an image form of the man Alistair Crowley had been, trying to infer his role and influence in the murders of three other men.

"And he stayed in Bella Bella after that? In the area?"

"No. He left the next day and we never spoke again. Although to give the man credit, the Alistair Crowley who showed up in Bella Bella in 1996 sounds like a mellower man than the one who was frothing at the mouth the last time I saw him. I understand he was helping Rose Wilson with her record keeping at the health center. I'm sorry he's dead. I think he's a man who wandered down the wrong path and was trying to find his way back when he was killed."

"That's very helpful, sir," Louise said. "It's the sort of background information that helps us to understand a case."

We all stood up and shook hands. O'Rourke looked at me. "And your interest in the case is . . . ? Protecting DFO interests?"

"Far from it. I believe Alistair was inadvertently involved in the death of a friend of mine, and that led to his death. It's a long story."

"And a sad story, no doubt. There are so many sad stories." The nurse knocked on the door. Dr. O'Rourke's lunch break was over. Louise and I walked back to the car in silence.

As Louise drove down Hastings Street, I looked north across Burrard Inlet to the mountains beyond. It was cleaner out there and simpler, the forces more elemental than the half-hidden influences that disrupted the affairs of men. I gazed at Louise until my gloomy thoughts dissipated. "The doctor's story doesn't really advance things at all, but it reinforces my theory that bad things were going on at the West Van lab and that's the crux of this whole case."

She nodded. "I'm starting to worry about the political fallout on this. I just know there's a whole bunch of people who don't want this story to come out and they're going to try to keep a lid on it. My outfit is not immune to political pressure, but we're probably less vulnerable than a civilian line agency like, say, DFO."

"You've got that right." I put my hand on her shoulder and squeezed gently. "I want you to know that my career means less than nothing to me if it interferes with getting at the truth of this."

"That's good to know." She put her hand on my knee. "We'll settle this affair and then think about other affairs."

"Let's go see Mark."

"One brilliant idea after another. I'm going to have to keep you around for awhile."

Rush hour was starting to build so it took us a while to get to the Canadian Fishing Company dock at the foot of Gore Street. The *Coastal Provider* was floating high and empty, like a duck on a pond. Six other boats were tied ahead of her but they were low in the water, scuppers awash, obviously still full of herring. A seventh boat was alongside the pump float, heeled way over as her starboard tank was emptied with her port tank still full. Louise removed the *Jessie Isle*'s plotter from the trunk and we set off down the ramp to the floats. Mark came out on to the deck to greet us, and Louise handed him the plotter before clambering over the rail.

"Afternoon, all," Mark hailed us. "How has your day been?"

"Progress is being made," I said as we followed Mark into the wheelhouse. "I'll fill you in while you hook up this little baby." He plugged the plotter into a twelve-volt outlet and turned it on.

"This is a much older model," he said. "It doesn't have automatic track record. It might not tell us much."

"I just want to compare it to the trips recorded in the logbook. I'm guessing Alistair wouldn't lie to his logbook, but you never know. Let's start six months back." I took out my copy of the logbook. "November 3, 2003, Alistair took the boat out to Idol Point. Does the plotter show that?"

"You know what? This thing doesn't even display by date. It does show a trip to Idol Point but it won't tell you when."

"Okay, let's just flip through all the trip records just to see if there's any trips that Alistair didn't record in the log." I looked over Mark's shoulder while he put the plotter through various displays. Fifteen minutes later, we had seen tracks of every trip that had been recorded on the plotter. None of them had not been recorded in the log, although there were trips in the log that weren't recorded on the plotter, presumably because they were straightforward trips for which Crowley had not needed the navigational aid of the plotter. "So the logbook is accurate. That's pretty much what I expected. Still, we had to check."

"It doesn't appear to tell us much, but we don't really know what's relevant," Louise said. "The Crown might need it to demonstrate some point during the trial." She paused and looked at her watch. "Jeez, it's five-thirty. Why don't I take you two gentlemen to dinner?"

Mark raised his hand. "Because A, we're not gentlemen, and B, I'm buying. I'm a rich herring fisherman and I want to celebrate. What shall it be? Chinese, Japanese, Thai, French, Italian, German?"

We both looked at Louise. "You know what? Since I moved to the coast, I've become a sushi addict. But I need to change my clothes. Maybe I can meet you guys at the restaurant."

Mark suggested Kanata's, and I agreed. "It's on the same street as your hotel, two blocks west. We might as well all go in your car and you can leave it in the hotel parking lot."

Mark unplugged the plotter and handed it to Louise. He locked the boat after us and we walked up the dock. Back at the Hotel Georgia, I offered to come up and help Louise change, but she demurred. As

Mark and I ambled toward the restaurant, he observed that Louise and I "seemed sort of close."

"Yeah, there's definitely an attraction between us, and maybe more than that. But we're taking it slow and careful."

"Well, I hope it works out, Danny. You deserve somebody to be close to." I showed my appreciation for Mark's empathy and support with an affirming silence.

It was Wednesday night so Kanata's wasn't completely full. The waitress showed us to a table, and I explained that we were waiting for a third but that alcohol would reduce our separation anxiety. I ordered the usual vodka and grapefruit juice and Mark had a pint of draft Granville Island Ale. I updated Mark on the day's work while he sipped his beer.

"The Telus records could provide a lead," Mark said, "but I'm cynical enough to doubt it. However, I've realized that we did get one break. If Alistair hadn't lent me his journals, the murderer would have got them and we'd have nothing. We have to decipher that first journal, the undated one, as well as all that stuff on his computer. This Bette Connelly, can we trust her?"

The thought hadn't even occurred to me. "Absolutely. She had the dubious judgement to turn me down when I offered myself to her, but in spite of that she's an intelligent woman."

"She's climbed the ladder pretty fast. Does she owe anyone anything?"

"You're cynical beyond your years. It is possible to advance within DFO just by being smart. It's a rare occurrence, but it happens."

Mark contemplated this and I gazed idly around the room. I glanced over at the reception area and saw our waitress gesture in our direction, and then my attention was seized by a vision of feminine grace that emptied my mind of all else. It was the first time I'd seen Louise in a dress. Her tanned arms were bare and glowed in the subdued lighting. The dress was, I guessed, patterned silk, and I thought she looked almost as good in it as she would in nothing.

She moved toward us and I rose to embrace her gently. "You look lovely. Words fail me."

"My, there's a first time for everything."

I held her chair as she sat and smiled at Mark. The waitress hovered. Louise ordered a white wine and looked around the room. "Almost as nice as Alexa's."

"The clientele is not the same caliber."

When the waitress came back, we were ready to order: the West Coast combination plate for three. The plate featured some exotic varieties of sushi that Louise hadn't tried yet. Her anticipation was contagious. We avoided talk of the case and murmured platitudes about the weather and traffic. When the waitress brought our food and a bottle of good BC merlot, all talk ceased.

Plates were passed, wasabi was mixed, wine was poured, and chopsticks were deployed. Sensations of bursting seahorse roe were overlaid with the moist oiliness of raw fish. These culinary notes were mixed with the crispness of chives and peppers to perform a veritable symphony of flavors. Another bottle of wine arrived and we continued with the second movement. Flavors sweet and flavors salty stated a theme over the swelling accompaniment of Japanese horseradish. Minor notes of vegetableness harmonized with the tones of rice and seaweed. The third movement overwhelmed us,, whimpering to a premature conclusion.

"Ohmigod." Louise leaned back in her chair. "I'm so full and there's still lots of food left. I hate to feel like I'm wasting it."

"Don't worry. A waste is a terrible thing to mind. Besides, we can get a doggy bag and Mark can take it back to the boat." I waved the waitress over. "Would you mind bagging the leftovers? And would you bring a coffee with Baileys on the side? Anyone else?"

Mark and Louise acquiesced to my dessert suggestion and soon we were sipping rich black coffee mixed with creamy Baileys. After a moment of reflective silence, Mark spoke up.

"What's the plan for tomorrow?"

"We need to talk to Bette at the West Van lab. She'll be able to give us personnel records from 1996, and maybe give us more info on what was going on back then. Plus, I'm hoping she can translate the files off Crowley's computer, as well as that non-language journal. I think Louise and I should go, but I'd like half an hour alone with her first. She might want to divulge a few things off the record."

"Danny, in a murder investigation, nothing is really off the record. Still, I trust your judgement. Why don't you set it up? Tell her I want to interview her at eleven tomorrow morning. No, wait, it's better if I do it. I don't want you looking like my secretary. You can precede me by half an hour or so. But remember, we're getting information from her, not the other way round."

I nodded. "Mark, what are you up to tomorrow? Are you going back to your place in White Rock?"

"I'll stay on the boat tonight. There's nothing in White Rock worth rushing home to."

He recovered his credit card from the waitress, collected his doggie bag, and walked out alone. I felt a twinge of sadness, and then guilt at how soon it left, and then happiness as I realized why it left.

I looked across the table at Louise and she was looking at me. This state of affairs continued for a while. "C'mon. I'll walk you back to your palatial taxpayer-subsidized abode." She collected her coat, and when we were out on the sidewalk, I put my arm around her waist. She leaned into me and we walked very slowly back to the Hotel Georgia. Just outside the entrance, we clung together for awhile, ignoring the suits going in and out.

"I'd really like to come up to your room. It would be way better if we didn't have to say good-bye all the time."

"I'm not sure that's a good enough foundation for a relationship. I think we have to work on the bits in between the good-byes."

"But if we eliminate the good-byes, technically there won't be any in-between bits."

"There will always be good-byes. And hellos. They're sort of like the brackets around important bits of our life. Without them, things would be all muddled."

"How do you get time to philosophize in the middle of solving a murder case?

"Time management. You've just run out. Kiss me and go away."

I did, enjoying the former more than the latter. As I walked away, feelings of regret were offset somewhat by the excitement of what the morrow would bring. Here in this city where nobody was born, but so many were born again, was the answer to an eight-year-old mystery. All we had to do was find it.

Sixteen

When I got Bette on the phone the following morning, she sounded glad to hear from me and told me how proud she was of how well I'd run the herring fishery. "You're a field guy, Danny. You should stay out of offices." Maybe, but offices were where all the important decisions were made. That should be number four on the list of "Reasons Our Bureaucracy Keeps Screwing Things Up." Field people should control things in the field. Office people should control the copy machine. I said I'd drop in around ten-thirty and she said fine.

At nine, I was at Police HQ looking forward to seeing Louise. A constable took me back to the meeting room where she and Tommy were conferring. I sat down and looked at the clutter on the table. "Hey, that's the same doughnut that was here yesterday."

"It'll probably be here tomorrow, too, unless you feel really adventurous."

"Tommy has just finished reviewing all of Crowley's e-mail. Every name on the list is a real person, no code names, and as far as we can see not one of them is connected to the case."

"And I talked to Crowley's sister. His only relative and they were semi-estranged. But, on a positive note, Telus gave us the number that Crowley called right after he found out about your colleague going missing. It's the main switchboard number of the West Van lab. However, the call was at twelve-thirty in the morning, so there was no receptionist there to take it."

I perked up when I heard that. "That reinforces my opinion that the lab is tied into all this. I'm sure there are answers to be found there. We need to know if someone took that call or if it was recorded on voicemail."

"I can do that when I meet Bette Connelly at eleven," Louise said. "I'm going to be the bad cop after Danny plays the good cop. Danny, how do you want to handle it? Are you going to tell her you're assisting us with our inquiries, or shall we pretend we don't know each other?"

I thought that over. "I'm not very good at playing games. I'll tell her we've been working together since we met at Crowley's float house. The truth is always easier to remember. Should I stick around when you talk to her?"

It was Louise's turn to think. She looked at Tommy for support. "I think you should. She could bullshit me about DFO internal matters but she can't bullshit you. And you probably have a better handle on the key information gaps."

I felt a twinge of unease at this glimpse of the cop Louise. Her default position obviously was that all civilians were not to be trusted. Tommy had the same view.

"Bette is potentially a very valuable resource," I pointed out. "You need to convince yourselves that we can trust her. What do we know that would provide a litmus test for her?"

"One of the few concrete facts we have is the call that Crowley placed to the lab. I'll ask her about incoming calls on the morning of April 9. If she doesn't respond straight up on that, we'll know we can't trust her. If she does respond straight up, we can maybe trust her."

My unease deepened. They were talking about a person I knew and liked and had faith in, a person who had done nothing that would make her suspect. Yet suspect she was, until she proved herself reliable. A cop's world was a strange and scary place. I took a deep breath. "All right, I'm going to head over there. My first question, or request, is going to be the personnel records from 1996. I want to know who was working there then who might have been involved in Project Chimera. Second question, what else can you tell us about the lab's projects during that period? If you guys feel comfortable about her after that, and after Louise talks to her, we'll get into decoding the journal and the computer files. And there's no reason why you should feel uncomfortable about her. She's a good person." I took the very stale doughnut and nibbled a crumb. "I hate to take the last one. Any chance of fresh ones this month?"

"Next Monday is budget day. We'll know then if we can afford doughnuts and coffee for the troops. In the meantime, we like to keep our guests happy. Fill your boots."

"I would but I don't want to lacerate my feet. I did my penance in Ottawa." I threw the doughnut in the tin waste bucket and it rang like a solid Little League hit. "Will you guys lend me a cop car or do I have to call a taxi?"

Thirty seconds later, I was in the reception area waiting for a cab that Louise had been kind enough to call for me. Twenty minutes later, I was being chauffeured through the incongruous rain-forest-in-a-city that is Stanley Park. And then I was passing over the incongruous ribbon-above-the-ocean that is the Lions Gate Bridge. The passage over a quarter-mile-long bridge suspended by a couple of cables is impressive: Strait of Georgia to the west, the skyscrapers of Vancouver to the east, and churning ocean directly beneath. The bridge is one of man's supreme accomplishments, and yet it barely merits mention with one of God's trivialities: the narrow strait that it spans.

When the cab dropped me at the West Vancouver lab, I stood for a moment and looked around. This place, this building, and its surroundings, were the scene, I was convinced, of a murder that had led to two other murders. And the first of those killings had taken away a friend of mine, sucked him into oblivion, and left only pain as a marker of his life.

I circled the building, noting the dock at the rear and two outbuildings that were not sufficient to contain decades' worth of project gear—floats, tanks, ropes, anchors, and assorted aluminum assemblages. When I returned to the front of the building, I looked up at the imposing edifice, symbol of knowledgeable authority and commitment to responsible management. I felt sad we'd never lived up to that, angry at the idiots who had prevented it, and a bit scared that some of those idiots might be feeling threatened. A cornered idiot was at least as dangerous as a cornered weasel. And what if they weren't idiots?

When I walked into Bette's office on the second floor, she rose from her desk to hug me. "Wow, you're all tanned and healthy-looking. Office people always look so pale and sick compared to field people. I'm jealous."

I held her at arm's length and gave her an exaggerated up-and-down. "You look okay to me, kiddo."

"Why thank you, Danny. Flattery is a girl's best friend. Or a guy's. I forget."

Bette didn't do coquettishness very well and I couldn't flirt sober, so I went for the direct approach.

"The last time we talked, I asked you some pretty general questions about possibly illegal research that was going on here in the 1980s. Since then, I've come across information that indicates a friend of mine was killed because of that dodgy research. Two more people, one of whom was Alistair Crowley, were killed to cover up that initial murder. This is beyond supposition. It's now a police investigation. We, that is the police and I, need to know as much as possible about what was going on here back then. The fact that you are now operations manager should facilitate that. We hope."

Bette would feel some pressure to protect the department, but I hoped her considerable bureaucratic intelligence would align with her basic morality and tell her to cooperate with us unreservedly.

"Jesus, Danny. Thanks for complicating my new job. Murder? Here? We do science here. We don't kill people. But you know that. Our whole rationale is about discovering the truth, and I won't be part of any cover-up."

"I knew you'd say that. Complication. Some higher level people might be involved, people like Fleming Griffith. At this point it's better if they don't know about the investigation. That puts pressure on you, but you're protected if you can say you were dealing with a simple police investigation. So forget the background I gave you."

She stared straight ahead as she computed the ramifications of this. "I can play dumb for awhile, but I didn't get this job by being dumb and people know that. At some point, I'm going to have to take responsibility for the fallout, even if it's fallout from ancient history. Good management practitioners are supposed to contain bad news. Or at least put the right spin on it."

Good management practitioners? Contain? Spin? Bette was speaking a language I hadn't heard her use before. It was a language, to be fair, that was commensurate with her new position. But did it signal a fundamental change in her thinking? I tried to reassure her.

"I'll do everything I can to spin it as 'valiant DFO staff do everything they can to help solve old mystery.'" I told her. "Beleaguered heroes don't get fired."

"I didn't sign up to be a beleaguered hero," she said, "but you play the cards you're dealt, I guess."

I got specific. "Okay, the first thing I need is the personnel files for 1996. Somebody was here working with Crowley and that somebody is a murderer. Oh yeah, and that person is probably still working here, so we need your current staff list as well."

Bette picked up her phone and dialed a four-digit number I took to be an internal extension. "Hi Bernice, it's Bette. We've got a pain-in-the-ass query from Revenue Canada. Something about pension deductions from staff. Can you dig up our payroll files from 1996 to now?"

"Wow, that's good cover," I said after she'd hung up. "I'm raising both eyebrows in admiration. When did you learn to obfuscate so effectively?"

"An abundance of career models."

"So, here's the big question. What research was being conducted here in the eighties, and up to '96? You told me a little bit about Project Chimera, and how you were asked to delete a bunch of those files. Can you add anything to that? You must have looked at some of those files. Did you see anything that in today's world would be a career wrecker?"

"God, let me think. There was lots of growth data on various salmon species under differing treatment regimes. I saw a couple of project proposals for transgenic work on salmonids, but nothing to indicate those projects were approved and carried out."

"Who wrote those proposals?"

"Alistair Crowley, definitely. He was the senior scientist. I can't remember anyone else."

"Fleming Griffith?"

"Not that I remember."

"But you would remember if you had seen Fleming's name? He's not exactly an unknown."

"You're right. If I'd seen his name, it would have stood out."

"Any names of other people working on Project Chimera?"

"No."

"Project description? Budget? Reports?"

"I remember a memo from Crowley asking for more money. They'd gone way over budget on supplies from some company, like triple. I'll try to remember the company's name."

At five minutes before eleven Bette's phone rang and she answered.

"All right," she said. "I'll come down and get her."

I knew Louise had arrived.

Bette stood up to leave and then paused a minute. "Whose side are you on here, Danny?"

"The side of trying to find a murderer. You're on the same side." She left me alone to stare out the window at the gently rolling waters of Burrard Inlet. I could see a few shrimpers heading out to the Strait of Georgia, their single poles cocked forward like jouster's lances. I wondered if one of them was Cousin Ollie on the *Ryu II*.

Bette led Louise into the room and I stood and imagined embracing her. We all sat and the two unpolice deferred to la policerina.

"Thanks for taking the time to see me," Louise began. "I know you've just taken over this position and I understand how busy you must be." She paused, but Bette only nodded in acquiescence. "I assume Mr. Swanson has given you the background, and you must appreciate the seriousness of the situation. We're going to solve this crime and nothing can be allowed to interfere with the investigation. Having said that, we will make an effort to avoid, for lack of a better word, collateral damage." She crossed her legs and waited.

Bette didn't rush her reply. She leaned forward, elbows on her desk, and rested her chin on her interlaced fingers. "I would obviously prefer that this investigation wasn't happening, at least not now. But I'm not going to snivel in the face of reality. You will have our full cooperation, and let the chips fall, hopefully, not into the delicate machinery of my worn and damaged department."

I felt like a spectator as two skilled heavyweights jabbed and circled.

Louise smiled. "That's very encouraging. Mr. Swanson assured me you'd be helpful, but I needed to hear it from you." Hook to the ribs.

"At DFO, we like to think our work is important. But we realize other agencies have other priorities." Right uppercut.

"Justifiable priorities . . ." I had to interrupt before bureaucratic blood was spilled.

"There's a key question we need help with." I waited for Louise to jump in. She didn't so much as flex her knees. "Early on the morning of April 9, Alistair Crowley placed a call to the main switchboard here. We need to know if someone took that call, or if it was routed to voicemail or an extension number."

"I'll find out and let you know ASAP."

"It would be preferable," Louise said, "from the evidential point of view, if you told us who to talk to and we made the enquiries."

"Of course. Our main desk receptionist's name is, uh, Tina, no . . . Tanya Something-ova. Tanya Screnkova. I'll tell her you want to talk to her. Please don't tell her more than you need to. But of course you won't." She stood a fraction before Louise did and extended her hand.

"Thank you again, Ms Connelly. If Ms Serenkova is on duty now, I'd like to talk to her immediately."

"I'll inform her that you're on your way down and wish to speak with her."

"I appreciate your time. I'm sure we'll talk again."

Louise left Bette's office, and I made a point of lingering for a minute. I did my best to hide my discomfiture. There was figurative blood on the floor, but who cared? We weren't figurines. "Thanks, pal. I'll be back. There's more stuff we need help with." She stared at me expressionlessly and I forced a grin.

Downstairs in the lobby, Louise was speaking to a competent-looking woman at the main desk. I left them to it and wandered outside to stand in the weak spring sunshine. I looked around and tried to imagine the scene eight years earlier when my friend Billy had pulled into the parking lot in his battered Camaro. He'd arrived here just after four-thirty. We knew that because we knew he'd caught the three o'clock ferry from Departure Bay. So the building would have been officially closed, but not long. There might have been people a bit late in leaving, some keeners. Someone must have seen Billy. Actually, we knew someone had. But had any innocents seen him?

Louise strode toward me, a frown on her face. "Another dead end. We played the voicemail files for April 9. Nothing from Crowley. So someone must have answered the call in person."

"At twelve-thirty in the morning? Maybe, but let's say Crowley left a message knowing that our bad guy would hear it before anyone else. Because he always gets in early. So the bad guy hears the message and deletes it. So that's a dead end."

Louise patted my shoulder. "Don't worry. Investigations are mostly dead ends. But one of these leads, it could be anything, will be the key to solving the puzzle."

I gave her a cheerful grin. "It's okay. I've just about got this case solved. As soon as we get the personnel records, we look for someone who's been employed from 1996 until now, and who gets to work early. I'll let you make the arrest."

"That's great, Danny. Let's take the rest of the day off."

"On the slight chance that doesn't work, we'll have to give Crowley's computer and his notebook to Bette." There ensued an uneasy silence.

"I'd really feel more comfortable if we could get someone else to look at it. Bette is involved in this case, if only peripherally, and it's not good procedure to hand potentially key evidence to someone who's not guaranteed stone-cold neutral."

I sighed and rolled my eyes. And stared off into the distance, just so she'd be in no doubt that I was upset. Somehow she missed all the signs. Women could be so insensitive.

"Let's head back inside. They should have pulled those personnel records together by now." The receptionist handed Louise a large, three-inch-thick manila envelope. We walked back to the car and headed for HQ. In the car, I gave her the silent treatment until she must have been quivering inside. Then, not wanting to be cruel, I let her off the hook. "I can understand your reluctance to give evidence to Bette, but really, she's the only one I know who can decipher that stuff."

"I'll take it under advisement." She squeezed my thigh and I was glad I'd let her off the hook.

When we walked by Tommy Yamada's open door, Louise rapped on the doorjamb and kept going toward the meeting room we'd commandeered as our war room. She was opening the envelope as Tommy walked in. "Crowley's call may have gone to voicemail and been deleted by the bad guy." She held up a sheaf of accordion-folded paper. "Personnel records. Mr. Swanson here, in a stroke of genius that leaves me trembling with admiration, has suggested that our suspect worked in the lab in 1996 and still works there. So all we do is compare the names from 1996 with the names on the latest record. If they only have one name in common, bingo: that's our guy." She ripped off the last four sheets and handed them to Tommy. "Two thousand and four. I'll start reading from 1996. You watch us Danny, and make sure we're doing this right. Charlie Allworth."

"Got 'im."

"Susan Anthony."

"Got 'er."

"Samuel Aston."

"Got 'im."

Police work sure was exciting.

"Paul Avignon."

"Got 'im."

And so on and so forth. Alistair Crowley was on the 1996 list. Only eleven names appeared on both lists. Two worked in the payroll department and four were cleaning staff. I doubted if they were involved in a murder plot. "These five names," I said circling the remainder, "they need to be checked out."

"I'm on it," Tommy said, nodding.

I thought of something else. "Can I use your phone?"

I dialed the lab, and then Bette's extension. She answered on the first ring.

"Hi," I said, "it's me. The personnel records aren't telling us much. Did you remember anything more about Crowley's memo from Project Chimera, asking for more money?"

"No. But I remember it was weird for some reason. It'll come to me."

"Thanks. I'll keep you posted." I hung up. "Bette had a vague memory of seeing a note from Crowley, asking for a lot more money for something for Project Chimera. She's trying to remember what it was. Other than that, our best clue is the stuff in Crowley's computer and his notebook."

"Danny wants to give that stuff to Bette Connelly to decipher; I'm reluctant. What do you think, Tommy?"

He chewed on that for awhile. "Connelly might be the only person in Canada who can decipher that stuff. But she must have a counterpart somewhere, maybe the States, who's got the same knowledge base. Let's take a bit of time and ask around."

"To decipher those files, you need someone with a corporate memory. Bette's got that. No one else does."

Tommy rubbed the back of his neck. "Danny, she's DFO. She's

spent fifteen years in the belly of the beast. The only reason I trust you is because Louise says you're not normal: normal DFO that is."

I shrugged and stood up. Louise followed suit. "I'll walk you out."

In the hall, Louise grasped my hand. "We need to be careful here, Danny. Ask Bette about her relationship with Griffith. Did he give her the job at the lab? See how she reacts. If it looks like she's playing her cards straight up, maybe we can come to an arrangement."

"Okay. Can we come to an arrangement for dinner tonight?"

"I need an early night, Danny. I'll see you tomorrow."

On my lonely cab ride back to my lonely hotel room, I tried to ac-cent-uate the positive, e-lim-inate the negative, and so on and so forth. My "relationship" was progressing about as well as my murder investigation. Regarding the latter, there was something teasing me, some connection I should be making but wasn't. Whatever it was, it hovered maddeningly out of reach. I tried not to think about it too hard but failed. Tomorrow, I would work on thinking less hard. Ah, a positive note to end the day.

Seventeen

The next morning, I called Bette first thing. Her assistant told me she was in a meeting at DFO HQ until ten-thirty and I could see her there at elevenish. I went out for a wander and a wonder, and idly perused the fashionably dressed crowd. It wasn't Montreal but it was several rungs up the fashion ladder from Bella Bella . . . or Ottawa, for that matter.

I bought a *Globe and Mail* and decided to treat myself to brunch. I looked for one of the Bavarian joints that used to line Robson Street but they were all gone. Replacing them was a series of upscale eateries of no particular brand. I entered one at random, and while waiting to be seated, I glanced at the front page of the *Globe*. The dollar was down, which was bad, but last week it had been up, which was bad. Economics wasn't just the dismal science, it was positively abysmal. While I wondered at the concept of a Nobel Prize for economics when there was no prize for the equally valid study of porridge, the hostess appeared and led me to a table.

They had organic lager on tap so I ordered a mug while I perused the menu. Pasta seemed like a good choice, since it was about all they offered. While I waited for my meal, I progressed to the editorial page of the *Globe*. The third editorial, wavering stylistically between self-importance and omnipotence, deigned to congratulate DFO on their latest licensing policy. I felt a frisson of anticipation as I read on. DFO was to be commended on their new abalone licensing plan, which would do much to conserve the species while definitely not conserving anyone who hoped to fish them. Area licensing was called for as was fishing with traps. They weren't sure, however, that they could endorse thirty traps per boat. Perhaps the fleet could share thirty traps, the *Globe* suggested. And the traps had to be of sufficient size so the abalone didn't feel unnecessarily confined.

I felt proud that we had formulated a policy worthy of DFO and that the *Globe and Mail* editorial board had seen fit to endorse. By the time, I finished my breakfast I had composed a letter to the editor that called for farming of abalone. All they had to do was add salt to the Rideau Canal.

It was a beautiful spring day in Vancouver, so I decided to walk the fourteen blocks to the DFO building. As I ambled north, toward the mountains, which I could occasionally glimpse between the concrete trees of our 21st-century forest, I pondered the state of play.

We were no closer to catching our bad guy, and even if we did, we probably didn't have enough evidence to bring him to trial, much less get a conviction. Crowley's computer files and that odd journal had to contain answers, if only we could decipher them. I was positive Bette was the only person who could do that. I had to convince Tommy and Louise to trust her.

At DFO HQ, I showed my picture ID to the security guard and he phoned Bette to warn her I was coming. These elaborate and useless security measures had been put into effect after the building had been occupied by some angry fishermen. I still hadn't adjusted to the idea of security people and locked doors being used to keep taxpayers out of public buildings. Perhaps this should be number five on my list of "Reasons Our Bureaucracy Keeps Screwing Things Up." When the general public becomes angry enough to blockade a building, perhaps it is time to re-examine policy rather than hiring armed guards.

Upon being instructed to proceed to the twelfth floor, I decided to use the elevator. When the door opened after an exhilarating ascent, I stepped out and saw Bette striding toward me accompanied by a pretty young thing in an expensive blue suit. Bette introduced him as Floyd Granger, Public Relations.

"There's no public here," I pointed out. "Just us."

"I know, Danny, but Griffith is worried this is going to blow up on us. He wants you to work with Floyd here to minimize the fallout."

"How did Griffith get involved?"

"He's the assistant deputy minister. Involvement is what he does."

This wasn't going well. Fleming Griffith was suspicious and obviously worried. I was damned if I was going to tell Pretty Boy Floyd anything. But maybe I could get some information from them. I smiled charmingly. "I'm certainly onside with damage control. Let's sit down somewhere and examine the options."

Granger radiated friendly concern and teammate-like bonhomie as he took my arm. "Care for a latte? I have the technology in my office."

I couldn't help looking at Bette, but couldn't read her expression. We followed Granger into a large, well-appointed office where he busied himself with latte production while I sank into a low armchair that had obviously been designed to put people at a psychological disadvantage. Bette folded her arms and leaned against the wall. When he had served us, Granger perched pertly on the edge of his desk and sipped at his latte while I tried not to spill mine.

"I'm afraid we're going to have to suck it up and tough it out here. Fleming wants to minimize the collateral damage, so we're going to play hardball. Crowley was no longer a DFO employee and his death probably had nothing to do with us."

"I feel like a bit of a wuss next to you guys," I lied. "Stuff like this scares me. How can we deny what was going on in the West Vancouver lab?"

"We don't need to deny anything if it doesn't become public. And we don't want the police snooping through our files. You seem to be in with them, Danny. Can you sort of steer them away, at least from anything sensitive?"

They didn't have a clue. DFO was about to get Nagasakied and they were worrying about "managing the fallout." I wanted to warn Bette but I couldn't afford anything getting back to Griffith .

"Um, well sure, I guess. I'll do my best. But I have to be sure there was no continuing link between Crowley and the lab. Bette, last time we talked, we hashed over some invoices you'd seen for the unauthorized project. You were trying to remember what they were for."

She looked at Granger and he nodded imperceptibly. "Miniaturized transceivers. A hundred grand's worth. We had to get them from the US military."

"And that obviously had nothing to do with Crowley's death. If it wasn't suicide, it was probably some sordid feud with another fisherman."

"I'm sure you're right. It's good that we're all on the same page now. Well, I'll take my leave and we'll stay in touch." I shook hands with Granger and Bette, made gestures of appreciation, smiled cooperatively and left.

I exited the building, one foot forward and then the other, shuffling off to nowhere in a miasma of depression. My cell rang. It was Bette. "I finally got rid of the PR guy. How bad is it?"

"What do you mean?"

"I've never in my life seen you so polite and agreeable. You're sitting on something and I just know it's bad."

"Bette, there's a bit of a trust issue developing between the cops and DFO. You need to trust us and vice versa."

"Us? I thought *we* were *us*."

"Bette, there's some serious shit going on here. Murder is only part of it. Departmental loyalty is not a card that trumps much in this game."

There was a loud sigh. "What do I need to do?"

"How did you get that job?"

"Excuse me?"

"Some people are worried you owe Griffith."

"For Christ's sake! I had to fight him tooth and nail to get the job. He was pushing Reginald Sanderson."

"So how'd you get it?"

"I don't like to admit this," I could hear her sigh. "The Minister's executive assistant is my cousin. That and the fact that my qualifications are impeccable got me the job."

"Okay, we need to confer. Can you meet us at the police HQ?"

"Yeah, okay. After work tomorrow. Say five o'clock."

"And Bette, no one else, and I mean no one bloody else, can know about the meeting or anything that comes out of it."

"Christ, I'm a biologist and a data whiz, not a goddamn spook. I'll see you there."

Feeling much better, I dialed Louise. "It's me."

"How did it go with Ms Connelly?"

"It went well," I told her. "I think I may have brokered a rapprochement between our two agencies."

"DFO is an agency. The RCMP, on the other hand, is a Canadian icon and a stalwart in the fight for all that is good and decent."

"Don't chipmunks store icons for the winter? Hey, have you discovered any clues lately? It seems like we've hit a few dead ends."

"Tommy's still checking the names from the personnel files, but nobody has 'Psycho Killer' on their résumé."

I tried to keep the disappointment out of my voice. "These are smart people. That's why they scare me."

"We're smarter. And we're tracking them, not them tracking us."

"Hopefully."

"Where are you going to be later?"

"I'm going to touch bases with Mark. Why don't we have dinner together? Vi's on Main Street. A cab will get you there."

"Five-thirtyish?"

"Sounds good."

I wondered where I could find Mark. Was he still staying on the boat or would he be at his house in White Rock? I felt the need for an accomplice beer drinker. I resorted to my cell phone again. "Hi, where are you?"

"I'm babysitting a dozen frozen sockeye on the boat. If the power goes off, our evidence will get really smelly."

"I'm not ready to hand them over to DFO. Maybe the Mounties can take them, put them in the morgue or something. You wanna go for a beer?"

"Sure. The Princeton in twenty minutes."

The Princeton was a pleasantly dingy bar with a noticeable absence of ferns. There were lots of pictures of fish boats on the walls and cigarette burns on the tables. Mark was sitting at the bar but when he saw me he took his pint to a table in the corner. I procured a pint before following him. "I assume you've been diligently pursuing the murderer. How's it going?"

"We've lost the element of surprise. Griffith knows there's an investigation going on and he's circling the wagons. I don't know to what degree he's involved but I do know he'll try to stonewall us, just as a reflex if nothing else."

There was a long silence while Mark looked helplessly around the room. Two old drunks huddled over a table in the opposite corner, glasses of draft half full and hand-rolled cigarettes smouldering between yellow gnarled fingers. They weren't going to help us. I wasn't sure who was.

Mark obviously shared my mood. "Sometimes I feel shitty about something that's going on in my life. Sometimes I feel shitty just for being a human being. Tell me something good."

I was silent. The waiter glanced at us interrogatively and I nodded. He brought two more pints. We sipped quickly. The two old guys were counting their change, hoping for enough for another round. I waved at the waiter and pointed in their direction. He took them two glasses of draft and pointed at us. They raised their glasses to us and smiled graciously. "That guy on the left? He used to run the *Miss Evelyn.*"

"You're right. One of the last of the Bering Sea highliners. Brought enough halibut into Rupert to keep two shifts going at the plant."

We sat in silence and finished our beer. Mark gestured for another round. "When I was a kid, I was forever banging my head or scraping my knee. I always ran to my Mom and she always made it better. Always. When you're an adult, there's no one to make it better."

"But we can stop the bleeding. That's important."

"The way I feel right now, I'd rather *cause* some bleeding. I know the type of people we're dealing with. They're arrogant and selfish and stupid. They hurt people on purpose or by accident. Either way, they don't give a fuck. I'd like to hang them by the balls with number eight trolling wire."

"Why number eight?"

"Number six wouldn't cinch up and number ten would slice right through under the weight."

This was better. Anger was much more positive than depression. "Louise and I are eating at Vi's. We can cab it in ten minutes. Why don't you join us?"

"Sure. But we can't talk about this. Okay?"

"Good idea. We've got time for one more."

"Good idea."

Two good ideas in a row. Things really were looking up. By the time we got to Vi's, we were thirsty again but wisely switched to vodka. When Louise arrived twenty minutes late, we were confident enough to attempt brain surgery but sensible enough not to try it on each other. "I'm not even going to try to catch up to you two. I suggest we switch to more solid fare. Follow me."

She conferred with the hostess, who led the way to a table by the window. Louise arranged herself in her chair gracefully while Mark and I somehow attained seatedness. "There's nothing new on my end and I need a break from the case. Why don't you tell me some fishing stories?"

I looked at Mark and laughed. "I'll tell you how I first met Mark. It's sort of a fishing story."

"Definitely not a love story," he growled.

"We were up in Rupert. I needed a job because I'd walked off Pete Jacobs' boat. Creek-robbing son of a bitch. I knew Mark needed someone because his crew was always quitting. He wasn't catching much fish in those days. Mark didn't know I needed a job, so when I 'accidentally' ran into him in the bar, I let him know that I knew the top end of the straits pretty good, and my Dad taught me how to fish the North Shore, and Mark got all excited and offered me a job."

Mark snorted but I ignored him. "But I played hard to get. Held out for a signing bonus, just like Gretzky. Told him I wanted a new pair of Helly Hansen gumboots. Eighty bucks, at least. And he gave them to me."

Mark raised a finger. "What the all-star here didn't realize was that the boots were mine but they were way too big. So I got him for a pair of used boots."

"They fit me just fine. Goes to show you never could fill my boots."

Louise laughed. Mark shook his head. I waved for another round.

Our first course arrived: steamed mussels, fish chowder, and crab salad. Mark had had the foresight to order a decent white wine, so we sipped moselle and shared our starters.

Mark tried for revenge. "Remember that time you turned the radar on because you thought it was foggy but it was just Christine boiling crabs and steaming up the window?"

"The visibility was bad. Would you rather I didn't turn on the radar?"

"You could have wiped the inside of the windows."

"Well, that was one option. I preferred to utilize modern technology."

I poured everyone some more wine as the waitress brought our main courses. I examined my bacon-wrapped tuna reverently, "Hey skipper, remember that time you were talking to your wife on the VHF and you forgot to turn the deck speakers off? I had no idea you were such a romantic."

I laughed as Mark cringed. And so the evening passed in banter and bullshit. When it was time to leave, I looked expectantly at Louise and she asked if I was staying with Mark that evening, and I realized I was. I walked her to her car and we allowed ourselves a goodnight kiss, which became something else entirely: a good-to-know-you-tonight-and-for-many-tomorrows kiss. After that, there was nothing to say.

Eighteen

When I woke up, it took me awhile to realize I was on Mark's boat. We came to a mutual decision to skip breakfast, and after a medicinal shower, I left. I phoned Louise from the backseat of a cab. "Good morning."

"It is for me. How about you?"

"I feel like my body is revolting."

"Not as revolting as Jabba the Hut."

"Thank you. I'll be there in ten minutes and I expect to be comforted."

Comfort came in the form of a long, wordless hug. Wordless at least until Louise enquired as to whether or not I looked as bad from my side of my eyeballs as I did from hers.

"I may have over-indulged last night."

"You and Mark needed to blow off some steam. Actually, you were both quite funny. I enjoyed the evening."

I loved this woman more with each passing millisecond. "Is Tommy around? We need to do an update."

We found Tommy in the cafeteria, gazing thoughtfully at a large muffin. I pulled out a chair and straddled it cop-style, resting my forearms on the back. Tommy looked impressed.

"I assume Louise told you that I was going to meet with Bette Connelly yesterday."

"Yeah, how'd that go? How much did you tell her?"

"Nothing. She was with some PR twerp who's trying to do damage control. He's been sicced onto us by Griffith and he wants me to guide you guys away from trouble: trouble for DFO, that is. But Bette did volunteer one piece of information. There was an invoice she'd seen from the early days of the sockeye project. It was for a lot of money, which is why she remembered it, but she couldn't remember what it was for. It finally came to her: one hundred thousand dollars' worth of miniaturized radio transmitters."

"That fits," Louise said.

"Bette phoned me later, and I hinted that there was serious shit happening and we needed to overcome some trust issues. Bette's smart. She can read between punctuation marks. She opened up about how she got that job. It was old-fashioned nepotism. Griffith was pushing a different candidate. She doesn't owe him anything. So she'll be here at five o'clock, at which time I'd like to fill her in and give her Crowley's files to decipher. But whatever happens here, she's sworn to secrecy."

Louise and Tommy stared at each other for at least a minute. Tommy pursed his lips, Louise shrugged slightly, and Tommy nodded imperceptibly. "You handled that well, Danny. You didn't give out any info and you picked some up. Good investigative instincts. And that's what a lot of this is about. Instinct. I want to meet this Connelly woman and we'll go from there. Next item: those five names from the personnel list that I was supposed to check out? No joy. Everyone's got a solid alibi. One's in hospital, a couple were at conferences, dinner with friends, etcetera. Pretty rock-solid stuff."

"Shit!" I was disappointed and frustrated. "I was sure that was a hot trail. I think . . ." My phone rang. It was Cecil Brown in Bella Bella.

"Hey, Danny. What's shaking?"

"A procedure involved in gillnetting herring. What's up?"

"I've been reading over Crowley's logbook. There's nothing unusual except for one little thing, and it's really bugging me. Last year, according to the log, he was fishing prawns on May 6. But the prawn season didn't open until May 8. I double-checked. So either Alistair didn't know the correct opening date, unlikely, or as an ex-DFO guy, he chose to fish before the opening. Even more unlikely."

"You're right. That *is* weird. I don't have my copy with me. What does that May 6 entry say?"

"The usual sort of thing. Left Yeo Cove 0600. Arrived Duck Rock 1300. Set one string. Picked up 1700. That sort of thing. Nothing suspicious except it's two days before the opening."

"I'll get my copy and look it over. It must mean something. Okay, thanks Cecil. If you hear anything else, give me a call."

"Roger on that. By the way, Rose Wilson is wondering if there's anything new on Crowley's death. I don't think she ever bought the suicide theory."

"We haven't got anything definite yet. We're working on it."

I hung up and relayed Cecil's information to my colleagues. Tommy said he'd leave us to it and went over to confer with a uniformed cop who'd just come in.

Back in Louise's office, she opened the evidence locker and handed me the log. We sat down side by side, and I opened it to May 6, 1993. It was laid out as Cecil had said and as I remembered: basically dates, times, geographical locations, and catch numbers. Each daily entry followed the same basic format.

May 6
0607: left base
1312: set one string, Duck Rock
1718: picked up, 20 lbs large, 6 lbs jumbo
1802: set two strings, 80 fm hole
2214: picked 1st string—55 lbs large
2321: picked 2nd string—52 lbs large, 15 jumbo
2317: dropped hook, Turner Bay

We stared at the page for a long time. "See anything weird, Danny?"

"No. Those catch numbers are realistic. Have you got Nobeltec on your computer? I'll check Duck Rock and Turner Bay."

"What's Nobeltec? Map software? I don't have it but one of the techs will. Let's go see Gunther."

Gunther indeed had Nobeltec on his computer. We flashed it up and I found Duck Rock and Turner Bay. Nothing unusual. There was nothing left to do but wait for Bette to show up.

Bette arrived five minutes late, looking competently corporate in a navy blue suit. Louise and I greeted her in the lobby and led her to a conference room where Tommy waited. After introducing Tommy, Louise gestured to the chairs and we all sat down. Tommy led off. "Thanks for coming, Ms Connelly. I know you understand the seriousness of this situation and we value your cooperation."

Bette folded her hands in her lap and looked squarely at Tommy. "I understand that you're investigating a murder, or murders, and that takes priority over DFO departmental concerns. I also understand that there's reason to believe that certain elements within DFO may be involved in various activities that impinge on the case. Nevertheless, I'll help in whatever way I can."

"We understand that you're exposing yourself and we appreciate what you've done." Louise paused. I stared at her. She looked at Tommy. Things hung in the balance.

A decision was made. "There is something else you could assist us with, information that could be highly sensitive, and of course we must request confidentiality."

Louise and Tommy didn't know Bette, didn't know the normal mobility of her face and gestures. She sat rigid now and I could read her tension. "Danny alluded to the fact that the situation had deteriorated, that there were aspects other than the murders, God help us. I presume it's all to do with Crowley's work at the lab. I need to know the worst. Not want to know, but *need* to know."

"Of course. Danny?"

I exhibited the classic startle response. "Yeah, okay, well, here's the deal, Bette. Crowley and his colleagues produced a race of sockeye that spends its entire life cycle in the waters around Bella Bella. That includes saltwater spawning. We caught some. They all carry radio tags that transmitted to a collecting facility in Codville Lagoon. Our bad guy burnt it, but there's lots of evidence left. The environmental risks are profound, not to mention that it violates international law."

There was silence. I felt sorry for Bette. She'd worked her entire adult life for DFO, worked hard and climbed the ladder, taken pride in the good things she'd been part of and shrugged off the crap. She'd just found out Santa Claus was a pedophile and Lassie had torn Bambi's guts out. She hunched a bit, one hand over her mouth and the other arm across her stomach. "They were so smart," she said once she'd collected herself. "People called Crowley a genius. Maybe he was. But he was arrogant and, in a way, callous. They were like a whole team of idiot savants who had no concept of consequences. And maybe there was just too much testosterone. They saw it as a big competition and that makes for bad research, at best." She looked down again, spoke quietly, sounding tired. "What do you need from me?"

"I found Crowley's computer. I guess he'd hidden it so the bad guy couldn't get it. It's got lots of files on it, I'm sure they're all to do with the experiment. But they're gobbledygook, created in some program that won't read normally. We need you to decipher them."

She looked at me and I looked helplessly back. "I really don't want anything to do with it. I want to pretend none of this happened." She wiped her hands on her skirt though they weren't dirty . . . yet. "But I suppose I have to pay for my sins—or DFO's. Where's the computer?"

"We have it here, and unfortunately, because it may be primary evidence, we can't release it. It's asking a lot but could you work on it here? Evenings, perhaps?" Louise was showing some sympathy for Bette and that buoyed me somewhat.

"It's Friday tomorrow. Can I come in on the weekend?"

"Absolutely, and thank you for doing this. I know it's tough when the organization you work for screws up. My bunch has stumbled pretty badly on occasion. An organization often becomes more like your clan or tribe, or extended family. When they fail, you take it personally. But you shouldn't. You can't always be your brother's keeper." My thoughts exactly, and I was grateful to Louise for allowing her humanity to overcome her professionalism.

Bette stood up and I gave her a half hug, side-on with one arm around her shoulders. She gave an ironic little smile and I squeezed her shoulder gently. "One more favor, Bette. I'd like to organize a wake for Alistair. We'll get all the guys from the science branch who used to work with him. None of them were Crowley's close friends but it's an excuse to drink good scotch. And I guess there's professional respect as well. Can you let everyone know to drop by the lab tomorrow afternoon. Threeish?"

She nodded. Louise and Tommy reached across the table and shook her hand. She left, considerably more burdened than when she'd arrived. Tommy left us alone, and I went over and kissed Louise. "Thanks for being gentle with Bette. She's suffering."

"Well, it's pretty obvious she's a good guy. Your instincts were right, Danny. As they often are."

"They're right about a lot of things," I said, nuzzling her neck. "I plan to be having sex later on. Care to join me?"

"Why don't you practice on your own for awhile? I'm going to get my beauty sleep. We'll make a fresh start in the morning."

"I wish we really could make a fresh start. Unfortunately, I can't resurrect corpses."

The next morning I resolved to scrutinize Crowley's logbook and try to rationalize the two days he had fished before the opening. I allowed Louise to assist me. I took the logbook over to her desk, opened it to the May 6 entry and commenced perusing. Louise sat beside me, massaging the nape of my neck more than perusing, but I was used to carrying the load. I took a sip of coffee and flipped forward a few pages. I took another sip and then flipped back a few pages.

"Go back to May 6." I did. "May 7?" I turned the page. "Flip ahead slowly. Okay, now back to say, April 30." I followed her instructions. "I've noticed something a little odd. Look at the times given for May 6 and 7. They're quite precise, to the minute. But times for all the other entries are given in fifteen-minute increments, like they're just approximations. What's so special about those two days that Crowley decided to note everything more accurately?"

I thought about that very, very hard. "What I'm thinking is this. Those two days don't really exist, at least not in the prawn-fishing sense. They were before the opening. I think Crowley just made them up as a cover for something else, something he was trying to tell us. Those numbers are a code."

"Where's your magic decoder ring?"

"I gave it to Sandra Delaney in Grade 6."

"See where your romantic impulses get you?"

"I'm hoping they'll get us into a more clothes-free situation."

"That's not romance, that's lust."

"There's a difference? I just said that because you're so cute when you roll your eyes. You did it again. The RCMP or Van City police must have some top-notch code guys, or are they all in CSIS?"

"Ha ha ha. There must be someone who specializes in codes. I'll ask around."

"This afternoon, I'll be skulking around Crowley's wake. Partly because I enjoy a good skulk, but mainly because all those guys knew Crowley, worked at the lab, and must have some knowledge of what was going on."

"Our bad guy may be there. Be careful!"

"I'll just look for someone pallid. Mind you, they're probably all pallid."

Later on, I took a taxi to the West Vancouver lab. I got out and stood for a minute in the lukewarm spring sun. A burst of laughter came from behind the main building and I directed my steps along the asphalt pathway that circled it.

Behind the grey concrete offices, a green lawn bordered the blue water of Burrard Inlet. Two card tables had been set up to hold a collection of bottles and paper cups, and perhaps sixty people stood in small groups, laughing and talking. The vibe was three o'clock Friday afternoon, definitely *school's out* but not quite *yay, summer holidays*.

I helped myself to a paper cup and decided it needed something in it. Scotch is the drink of choice for DFO scientists and there was an assortment of very respectable single malts. I poured three fingers of someone's Glenfiddich and added a few drops of water. It burned pleasurably down my gullet and I surveyed the scene. Pete Van Allen was talking to a couple of bearded types, so I wandered over.

"Danny! Good to see you. Do you know Sam here? He's invertebrates, and Markus is cetaceans."

"Hi, guys. It's nice to see everyone remembering Alistair in the proper spirit, and with the proper spirits." They laughed, and one of them, Markus I think, asked if I knew Alistair. "By reputation only. But I was working out of Shearwater when they found his body."

"What in heaven's name was he doing there?"

"Good question, and some might ask what, in heaven's name was he doing here?" They looked uncomfortable and sipped their drinks defensively.

Pete gestured to the upper floors of the building. "You'll notice none of the brass are here. They don't like to acknowledge that Alistair even existed, much less worked here."

"Well, chickens come home to roost like salmon come home to spawn, or at least like they used to." Sam and Markus looked even more uncomfortable and drifted unobtrusively away.

"Better put the stabilizers out," Pete laughed. "Danny's rocking the boat again. What's bothering you now?"

"Pete, it looks like Alistair was murdered and whoever did it has some connection to the work they were doing here back in the 1980s. Is there anyone here who was part of all that?"

"Jesus, that was never my scene. I only stopped in here once in a while to check something in the library. But Gary Masters, that guy in the Tilley hat over there, he's a geneticist. He'd know something about it."

I looked in the direction Pete had indicated and saw a tall, slightly stooped man listening to someone who looked vaguely familiar.

"Take me over there and introduce me, Pete. Tell them I was the one who recovered Alistair's effects. We'll see how popular it makes me."

"Why don't I tell them you're a loyal and dedicated DFO employee who has nothing but the best interests of the organization at heart?"

"I don't want you to go to hell for lying," I replied.

He grimaced. "Better that than for wasting an entire life in the service of a dysfunctional bureaucracy."

"Bitterness is the first sign of insufficient alcohol consumption." I tried to cheer him up. "Once the ice is broken, and they've decided to like me, you might want to wander away."

"I'll keep my eye on you from afar."

"I'll be okay," I demurred.

"Presumably, Alistair thought the same thing."

We followed the game plan and were soon exchanging pleasantries with Tall Tilley Hat and the guy I was still trying to place. His name was tantalizingly close to recall but hovered just out of reach. Then I remembered: Reginald Sanderson. He'd been at my going-away party in Ottawa, the guy Bette had warned me was Griffith's weasel.

I addressed myself to Tilley Hat. "Genetics. Fascinating field. Wish I'd picked it myself, but I don't know DNA from RSPs. Huge potential, though. Did you work with Alistair when he was here?"

There was a pause while he tried hard not to look at Sanderson. "I was here at the same time as Alistair, but we were not colleagues. My work is more theoretical."

He was about to explain the class distinction between the lab rats like Alistair and the formula floggers like himself when Sanderson intervened. Placing a hand in proximity to my shoulder, but without exactly touching me, which would have forced me to not recoil, he led me out of earshot range. Tall Tilley Hat was left standing like a lonesome pine on a desert mesa. He appeared to be comfortable with that.

Sanderson leaned close enough so that I had to make an effort not to step back. "So, Danny, you got to see all Alistair's stuff after the, uh, after his death. Did he have like a whole library full of records and data?"

I managed to conceal my distaste for his proximity. "Oh yeah, he had stacks of journals, logbooks and there was a computer found under the floorboards of his shack." And then the devil made me do a bad thing. "The cops didn't want any of it, so I've been hanging on to everything. It's bound to be really interesting when I get a chance to go through it all." I'm sure he was dying to ask where I was keeping everything, but he was much too subtle for that. But I knew the message would get back to Griffith and then, if there was a link, our bad guy and then . . . I hadn't thought that far ahead, but I was sure something would happen. And I was right.

I circulated a bit more, sipping scotch and seeking someone who would 'fess up to working with Crowley on Project Chimera, but no one would admit to as much as having heard of it. At about five o'clock, with the sun low over the water, Bette put in an appearance. She spoke to a few of the more senior-looking people, ignored me, and left after about twenty minutes.

I gave it five minutes and then walked around the building to the parking lot. Bette was just getting into her car so I slipped into the passenger seat. I looked behind us but the sun was glaring in my eyes. Hoping no one had seen us, I slid down in the seat and gestured to Bette to drive.

Heading east on Marine Drive, Bette looked down at me. Not, hopefully, down *on* me. "Danny 007. This is so exciting. When do we get to blow something up?"

"I didn't want Reginald Sanderson to see us together."

"He's harmless," Bette replied. "He's just going around leaning on people to keep their mouths shut about anything that happened in the eighties."

"Including Spandex?" Bette looked, no doubt about it, down on me. I forged ahead. "Sanderson may be harmless but he's a conduit to Griffith, and *he* is highly toxic."

She considered this. "Fleming is a backstabber and an assassin, but that's in the world of bureaucracy. I can't see him killing anyone in real life."

"I don't think he recognizes the difference. And he doesn't have to get real blood on his hands. He just has to set things in motion."

She braked for a light.

"Do you live around here?" I asked.

"Back in Ambleside. But I'm on my way to see your Staff Sergeant Karavchuk and take a look at Alistair's computer."

"Hey, I'm going there too. It's a good thing I jumped in with you."

She gave me a quick glance. "You're working very closely with Ms Karavchuk. Just how closely?"

"We're quite fond of one another."

"Fond of one another? I'm fond of my cat. Do you tickle her tummy?"

"Only if she doesn't scratch the furniture."

"Congratulations, Danny. She's a very intelligent woman. I hope everything goes well."

"Thanks, Bette. We need to nail the bastards who're responsible for this mess and then we can concentrate on our relationship."

"Good luck. When the war is over, we can all go home."

The police building hadn't moved. I took Bette inside and Louise met us in the lobby.

"Thanks for coming, Ms Connelly. We've set up a room where you can work."

"Thank you. And please call me Bette."

"All right, Bette. And I'm Louise."

Louise led Bette down the hall and I headed for her office. I was deep in thought when Louise came in and shut the door behind her. "How was the wake?"

"Good scotch. Griffith's right-hand man was there. Reginald Sanderson. He was warning everyone not to talk about Alistair and Project Chimera. But I had a brilliant idea." She looked at me anxiously. "I told Sanderson I had all Crowley's stuff, journals, computer, and everything. I've set a trap and baited it with me."

"For Christ's sake, Danny," she said, groaning unappreciatively.

"You need to discuss stuff like this with me before you do it. You've put yourself in danger and we're going to have to expend a lot of resources to protect you."

"The idea just popped into my head and I acted on it. We were dead in the water, so I had to do something. Anyway, I'm worth it."

"Tommy's going to freak. We better go consult."

But Tommy didn't freak. He was enough of a strategist to see that we had been facing a stalemate and he was prepared to sacrifice a valuable piece (I was at least a Bishop if not a Queen) in order to make progress. And I assumed that the use of the word "sacrifice" was purely figurative.

"At the very least, Danny," he said, "this will clarify some of the relationships. You've always assumed there was a connection from Griffith to our bad guy, maybe through Sanderson. Depending how this plays out, we may be able to confirm that link."

"So, what?" Louise said anxiously. "We stash Danny somewhere, and then let our bad guy know where he is and that he's got Crowley's stuff with him. I don't really like this. We're making a target out of a civilian."

"I'm not the target, Crowley's stuff is. How about this? I'll rent an apartment, get established, maybe invite a few people over for a party, and then pass the word that I have to go to Rupert for a few days. If we're subtle enough, the bad guy will take the bait and make a move while I'm gone."

"We have to okay the apartment," Tommy warned. "It would be better if it was a house, neighbors not too close. We don't want to expose the general public. But I like it. It could be our only shot."

"Our bad guy knows we're gunning for him," Louise said. "You really think he's going to come and knock on Danny's door?"

"It's our best shot, Louise," I said, realizing with a start that I'd almost called her "sweetie." "What is there to lose?"

Quite a lot, actually, as we were to become painfully aware. Some more painfully than others.

We kicked around different scenarios and discussed details. It was close to nine when Bette walked into the office. We looked at her expectantly.

"I made a little progress," she said. "Those files won't open properly because the computer doesn't know the right program, or it probably knows but doesn't know it knows. It was fashionable for the lab guys in the eighties to use an in-house modification of the data-filing system. I think Alistair modified it even further, so only he could read the files. I'm going to have to get in there and examine the code, line by line. It'll take time, but I can do it."

"I'd do it, Bette, but I've got to go house hunting in the morning." She gave me a yeah-right look, waved to the others, and left.

I gave a thumbs-up to Tommy and Louise. "I knew Bette could penetrate Crowley's computer defenses. That's essentially his mind she's looking into."

Tommy stood up and yawned. "You don't need a computer whiz to decipher my mind. Food. Sleep. Repeat as needed." He shrugged on his jacket. "Get some rest, you guys," he said as he left.

Louise and I just sat there for awhile. I put my foot on top of hers and tapped out a message. She replied verbally. "No, I'm not hungry. I'm tired." There ensued a silence. "Your security detail isn't on until tomorrow. I'm a little worried about you tonight."

I almost scoffed bravely but decided that neither valor nor discretion was in order. "You're right. I don't feel safe. Who can I turn to for protection?"

Louise gave me a you're-not-as-dumb-as-you-look look. "We are sworn to serve and protect."

"Protection. Just what I need. And service?"

She gave me a don't-push-your-luck look. "Let's go."

In Louise's hotel room, we noticed that one of the beds was not level. We were forced, therefore, to occupy the same bed, and it should be to the surprise of no one that the evening passed not without a certain degree of what some would refer to, should they be disinclined toward delicacy and prone to displaying the lack of couth which is the unfortunate condition of those disposed to consider such matters, a condition of what may necessarily be portrayed as, for lack of a better word, and one hopes with no fear of contradiction, intimacy.

In fact, we reveled in the warmth and the scent and the touch and the closeness of each other for quite some time. We fell asleep with our naked bodies still seeking each other, mindlessly establishing the maximum area of contact possible.

I woke the next morning and felt good and remembered why. Louise snuffled quietly on the pillow beside me and I kissed her bare shoulder. Carefully sliding out from under the covers, I tiptoed to the window and surveyed the wonders of a beautiful world.

"You know, I think you've got a really cute ass."

I turned. "Gee, that gives us something in common."

"Why, do you think I've got a cute ass?"

"No, I mean we both think I've got a cute ass."

I dodged the pillow and headed for the shower where Louise soon joined me.

Nineteen

In the morning, we found Tommy in his office along with four very young, very fit, very serious uniformed officers. "Hi, Danny. Meet your bodyguards." They all squeezed my hand painfully as they introduced themselves, but because their stereotypical good looks were almost indistinguishable, they blended into an amalgamated character I could only remember as Jerome.

"One of them will accompany you at all times," Tommy said, "except when you're in this building."

"Won't they be a little conspicuous?"

"They'll be in plain clothes, and they've been trained to blend in. They never talk into their armpits."

"Ah."

Jerome left, and Louise, Tommy, and I planned the day's activities. I wanted to spend a little more time trying to decode the May 6 and 7 entries in Alistair's logbook. Then Jerome and I would go house hunting.

Louise had copied the two relevant entries from the log and we spread them out on her desk and sat and looked at them. Louise had already noticed that the times given were to the minute rather than in fifteen-minute increments like all the other entries. As we pondered them anew, I noticed something else.

"Look, the times are given in twenty-four-hour format where the first two digits designate the hour and the second two digits designate the minutes *after* the hour. So 2317 designates seventeen minutes after 11:00 PM. The May 6 entry gives times for seven different activities, the May 7 entry notes ten different times. Of the seventeen times, none of the minute designations is higher than twenty-six."

Louise twigged immediately. "That's because they refer to letters of the alphabet?"

"You're as smart as I am."

Converting the seventeen numbers to letters gave us this:

GLRINUQWKSHVCIRKX

"Case solved. I'll tell Tommy," Louis commented with a hint of sarcasm.

I scrambled to recover. "It's obviously incorrect to convert based on the standard alphabet sequence. There's a key somewhere. All we have to do is find it."

"If you say so."

"I'm positive," I said with as much certainty as I could muster. "Have your cipher guys looked at this?"

"You were right. All our cipher guys did get assigned to CSIS. They're decoding the prime minister's last speech."

I sighed. "I'll look through Crowley's stuff again. Somewhere there's a key sequence that will unlock this."

"Either that or our bad guy's parents couldn't afford too many vowels."

I switched to action mode. "Okay, I'm going house hunting. How many Jeromes do I need to take?"

"What?"

"The bodyguards. They're all Jeromes to me."

"Interesting. They refer to you as 'Meat.'" She gave her head a slight shake. "You need two. They'll follow you in an unmarked car. You can continue to use taxis so you're not changing your behavior."

She left and came back a minute later with two Jeromes. They had changed out of their uniforms, sort of. They were now dressed in jeans and T-shirts, with almost identical bomber jackets. But they had differentiated themselves through footwear. One wore low-cut runners endorsed by someone much taller than me, and the other wore Converse All-Star high-tops in the standard black.

We discussed a game plan. There were five rental houses I wanted to look at. The nearest was not far from Commercial Drive, so that was destination number one, followed by four others in an agreed upon sequence. We exchanged cell numbers and set them to speed dial. I was warned that cell communications could be monitored if the bad guys were technologically savvy. I was sure they were, so messages would have to be cryptic.

This was no big deal to me. Cryptic messages were standard operating procedure in the fishing industry. VHF radio conversations had to convey detailed information over open channels in such a way that only the intended recipient would understand.

"How's it lookin'? Do you see any fish?"

"Remember last year behind the house?" Fish abundance is roughly equivalent to this time last year on the north shore of Malcolm Island.

"You got that new chart yet?" Are you where you said you were going to be in the bar?

"No, we're lost in the Heart of Darkness." No, we're at Uganda Point in Fitz Hugh Sound.

So, confident that my obfuscation skills were equal to undercover standards, we set out. I inspected all the possibilities. The rentals were all nice, featuring several rooms that had floors and ceilings and an assortment of walls. I completed my house-inspection agenda, only occasionally spotting High-Top Jerome and Low-Top Jerome hovering protectively, and was back at the police building by four. Tommy, Louise, Jerome, and I debriefed. Jerome preferred the house on West Sixth Avenue. It was not a busy area, primarily residential, and parking was difficult. Intruders would be easy to spot. And it was furnished. The other pros concurred, so I phoned the real estate agent and offered to sign a three-month lease, the minimum I could get away with. I could pick up a key and move in tomorrow. My friends Jerome offered to help me with my stuff, but I said I could carry my duffle bag all by myself.

I called Bette and asked her to put a notice on the bulletin board at the lab that I was having a housewarming party on Friday. I arranged for the same notice to be displayed on the bulletin board at DFO HQ. And just to be sure it was a fun party, I phoned Mark, Christine, and Fergie.

That night, I spent a pleasant evening with Rugby Pants Jerome in my room at the Ritz. His trouser-type apparel had never been worn on a rugby field, in a rugby clubhouse, or by, as far as I knew although I'd have to check with Tommy, an actual rugby player. But I didn't hold that against him.

I excused myself for a quick phone consultation with Staff Sergeant Karavchuk, which was not as amiable as I'd hoped. In fact, the meeting fell well short of our previous standard of amiability. When I returned to the room, Rugby Pants Jerome was flicking through the channels. It was that awkward time of year, post-hockey but pre-football. Baseball had started but games in May were like men in drag, occasionally spectacular but lacking the fundamentals. The NBA play-offs were in session, but I wasn't comfortable with any game where two digits weren't adequate for scoring. This eliminated cricket as well. He settled on something called the Palm Springs Chevy Invitational Open.

"No sports on?"

"You don't like golf?"

"It's not a sport. It's a fashion opportunity for repressed white guys."

"It takes a lot of skill."

"So does origami. Look, you've got guys standing around with clubs in their hands, there are other people well within reach, but what do they do? They hit a defenseless little ball. It's un-Canadian."

He looked at me oddly. I plopped myself onto the couch and started going through Crowley's journals. RPJ, probably ashamed of himself, flicked past the golf and managed to find *CSI: Peoria*. With a grunt of approval, he settled in to watch, and I settled in to ignore him.

The next morning, we moved into the rental house and the three following days were a fun-filled blur of Jerome-mediated activity. I adjusted to being more the center of attention than I really cared for, and they adjusted to my unconventional nomenclature. I hadn't felt this oppressed since my teenage years, and then I'd been burdened with only two parents. Friday night couldn't come too soon.

I'd moved my bag and briefcase into one bedroom of the house and Jerome, newly designated as my friend from New Brunswick, had appropriated the other.

I'd gone shopping for some essential items: a stereo with hundred-watt speakers, and two extra speakers for the deck.

Friday afternoon was warm so three o'clock found Jerome Number Four and me relaxing with a beer on said deck. I found out later that Jerome was cheating, drinking near-beer out of bottles with phony labels.

The small backyard was heavily hedged, which, I hoped, would muffle enough of the party sounds that I wouldn't have to meet my new neighbors prematurely. Pete Johnson and Albert Ammons were boogying the hell out of "St. Louis Woman" and Jerome Number Four was twitching in a syncopated fashion. I felt validated by my decision to go with Pete and Albert rather than Glen Gould and the Goldberg Variations: better party music.

The front door was unlocked so Christine appeared unannounced with a grin on her face and a case of beer under her arm. I pointed at the plastic laundry tub full of ice, and she added the former to the latter. She removed an already cold one from the tub and sashayed over to us. "Jerome, this is an old friend of mine, Christine. Christine, meet Jerome. You wouldn't know it but he's with the Surveillance Squad, assigned to my ass, the protection thereof."

Christine raised her bottle to him. "You must be a rookie, Jerome. Starting at the bottom, Danny's."

Jerome Number Four blushed and I intervened mercifully. "Christine, Jerome is not a rookie. He served four months as the replacement for the Inuit carving at 24 Sussex Drive."

"And his present client is almost as important." Fergie had joined us. "As the sculpture, that is."

I performed further introductions and then went into the kitchen to set out some snacks. Pretzels in one bowl, salt and vinegar chips in another, and cheese and crackers arranged randomly on a plate. I admired my inbred sense of style. I was sure that Martha Stewart was referred to by many as the Danny Swanson of America. While I was contemplating whether I had time to do a TV show, High-Top Jerome came in and informed me the front door was unlocked.

"Yes, I'm having a party. If I'm forever locking and unlocking the door, people will feel inhibited."

He was mumbling about security procedures when Mark walked in bearing smoked salmon. More introductions. I felt like a first-year text-book: *Introduction to Danny's Friends*. Maybe I should write *Danny's Friends for Dummies*. Maybe not.

I'd asked all three of my shipmates to come early so we could talk about what I was starting to think of, for lack of a better word, as The Case. When we were all comfortably settled on the deck, with beer in hand and food close by and I'd changed the tape to *Let It Bleed*, I inaugurated the discussion.

"Jerome, you probably don't know much of the background to this, or why I need protection." I brought everyone up to date, includ-ing the setting of the trap and the composition of the bait, and then threw open the floor. One of the Jeromes went and stood by the door so our chat wouldn't be interrupted by unauthorized ears, and the discussion began.

"What I don't understand," Mark said, "and what I've never under-stood, is why Billy was killed. He showed up on DFO's doorstep with a mutant fish. So what? All they had to do was say Igor was a new species, *Pacificus uglicus*. Something happened that afternoon at the lab, Billy found out something that made it necessary to kill him. Everything else is sort of a logical progression from that, and until we know why he was killed, we won't solve the case."

I had to force my shipmates to dredge through some painful memo-ries. "We were all in a haze when Billy disappeared. We never really talked it through. We need to try to remember all the little details about when he left."

Christine spoke sadly. "The thing that sticks in my mind is that Billy's cat died the same day he disappeared."

"Christ! I'd forgotten that."

Christine continued. "It was so weird, like there was a connection somehow, although obviously there wasn't. And I felt guilty because I was minding the cat and grossed out about how it died. It was like it had an epileptic seizure."

"And you tried to phone Billy, right? I asked.

"Yeah, but all I got was his voicemail."

"And what time did you leave the message?"

She thought for a minute. "I don't know, early afternoon. It was just after lunch when I went to check on the cat."

"So Billy would have been between Sayward and Campbell River, out of cell range and gumbooting it for the ferry in Nanaimo," I said. "He gets on the ferry, runs into Smug and Snuffy, and settles in for some beer and bullshit. I wonder what time he checked his messages. It might have put him in a bad mood when he got to the lab."

"Except DFO says he never showed up at the lab," Mark pointed out.

"And we never would have known otherwise if I hadn't stumbled across the picture of Igor in the DFO database," I said.

We all contemplated this reconstructed timeline. Something, some little detail, niggled at me. I almost had it and then it escaped.

"The big question," Mark pointed out, "is how Griffith is connected to all of this. He was in charge of the lab back then, but that doesn't mean anything; Crowley could have been running his own show."

"Griffith had to be involved," I argued. "He's too much of a blackheart not to have been. The problem is he's a delegator. His hands will be relatively clean and we'll have a hard time pinning anything on him."

"Unless we get a confession." Fergie gestured with a beer bottle. "If we find the bad guy, I could get a full confession out of him."

Christine leapt in hurriedly. "Jerome, you understand that some of this is off the record." They nodded. "Fergie, you're not wearing a parrot so keelhauling is out, verboten, forbidden, not allowed, severely discouraged."

"Let's not limit our options," Mark chimed in. "The *Coastal Provider* has a lot of barnacles and I can't afford a bottom scraping."

I intervened. "You can't afford a bottom scraping like Christine can't afford a manicure."

There was a minute of silence before High-Top Jerome asked hesitantly, "Why does Mark need his bottom scraped and how does that help us get a confession? The force won't go for any kinky stuff. That all got delegated to CSIS."

Before we had a chance to make him feel really stupid, Jerome Number Four hissed, "Incoming."

All eyes turned to the doorway and I was immensely pleased to see Pete Van Allen. "Look who I brought with me." Behind him appeared George Kelly, the skipper of the *James Sinclair*. He presented a bottle of rum like a Marine presenting arms. It is from that moment that I date the beginning of the party.

People arrived in a steady stream, mostly young field types, but older age classes were also well represented. A bunch of Prince Rupert assessment staff were down for a conference and they added a decidedly looser tone. People were hanging out in the kitchen and on the deck and a small contingent was wandering around the backyard. The conversation was getting louder so I was forced to turn up the music, which made people talk even louder.

The lights were on in the kitchen and reflected off a variety of foreheads. It was a warm evening and the room would have been stuffy were it not for the open door to the deck. Outside, the light was fading and the figures on the lawn appeared slightly undefined and unreal. I pined briefly for Louise but I knew she wouldn't be coming.

The party was, I reckoned, in phase two. The transition to phase three could be tricky. The choice of music was critical. A bronzed and blond young woman approached me and handed me a CD. "Happy housewarming. I think you'll like this."

I looked at the cover. Buddy Holly had been cloned twice. The album title proclaimed *The Proclaimers*. I put it on, turned up the outside speakers and soon everyone was bouncing in place to "Five Hundred Miles." I grabbed another beer. By the time "Saturday Night" came on, sporadic dancing had broken out. "Oh Jean" precipitated full-scale gyrating and I congratulated myself. We had achieved phase three.

Provisioning myself with a fresh beer, I stepped off the deck onto the back lawn. The Prince Rupert contingent had abandoned themselves to the music. They were rocking and rolling like six-beer sex, and I had no choice but to leap into the fray. I attained proximity to someone I could reasonably be seen to be dancing with and commenced to trip the light fantastic. I had progressed to my James Brown spinarama move when Jerome Number Four approached me. He looked serious and I hoped he wasn't carrying the cape. I wasn't ready for the cape. "Danny, your next-door neighbor is at the door. He's complaining about the noise."

This triggered an internal chorus of complaint. *Christ, it's nine-thirty on a Friday night. What the hell's the problem? We're not even at phase four yet. I knew I should have invited them over.* I followed Jerome onto the porch, through the kitchen, into the living room full of people I hadn't met yet, to the open front door.

An unknown figure awaited me. The porch light shone from above, but his baseball hat kept his face in shadow. As I approached him, the pleasant euphoria of the party dissipated like evening warmth when the sun goes down. When he raised his right hand, and I saw the gun, I thought, "He's taking this way too seriously."

Later, I'd be very thankful to Louise and Tommy for saddling me with Jerome. It's doubtful if I reacted at all to the sight of the gun, but Jerome Number Four did. He pushed me sideways just enough so that the first bullet hit the outer ring rather than the bull's-eye. I prefer that metaphor rather than the literal truth: that the bullet smashed into the left side of my ribcage and came close to exploding my heart into so much tomato paste.

With his other hand, Jerome grabbed the gun and pushed it down so that the second shot caught him in the thigh. This didn't impede his forward motion, and he and the shooter tumbled down the front steps in a tangle of limbs. By the time they sprawled onto the lawn, Jerome had both hands on the gun and the shooter had no choice but to run. High-Top Jerome had reacted quickly to the sound of the shots, but he chose first aid over pursuit. That may have saved my life for the second time as I was bleeding badly. And as my body did not consider my brain a vital organ, it shut it down.

Twenty

I drifted through the kelp fronds. It was silent and peaceful under the water. Sunlight filtered down in shifting patterns of light and shade. Brightly colored rockfish scooted and paused, scooted and paused, regarding me with warily surprised eyes. But I wasn't a threat, I wanted to tell them, I wasn't the threat, the threat was . . . behind me!

I drifted again, effortlessly and aimlessly over bright sand. Crabs scuttled from my shadow. Everything was below me, everything available to me. The flat white bottom fell away to an abyss. There was no bottom, just greenness fading to black. I started down, falling slowly toward nothingness. It grew cold. I felt uneasy. There was something wrong. I could feel something behind me, something large and dangerous. I tried to turn my head. I couldn't move. I struggled against paralysis. I tried to scream.

I floated in a vast mothering ocean. Warm water caressed my skin. There was nothing I wanted or needed. All was as it should be. A gentle pleasure suffused my body and brain. Something tickled at the base of my spine. I smiled. The tickle grew stronger, persistent and aggressive. I wished it to stop. It began to hurt. Something was hurting me. I tried to twist away. It was trying to penetrate my skin, to enter me, to harm me. Black malignance. I couldn't breath.

The pain was bad. It wasn't fair. Louise was looking at me. I tried to tell her I didn't deserve this. Someone was moaning. She leaned forward and touched my face, then went away. A nurse came and then I felt better.

Louise was talking to someone. They didn't know I was there. I tried to tell them, but they ignored me. I was irritated. I tried to touch her shoulder. The pain punished me and I cried out. Louise and Christine looked at me, worry and concern written on their faces. A nurse came again and easeful warmth blanketed the pain. Nurse come. Pain go. I felt as though I should remember that.

When I first awoke to full consciousness, it was dark and I was alone. I had no idea where I was, and only a rudimentary sense of *who* I was. The pain was my starting point and I worked backwards from that. Gunshot, man at door, party. Jerome.

After an undefined period of mental fetching and carrying, I had most of the pieces in place. I sighed loudly, and a dark blob materialized by my side. A lamp was turned on and I recognized Rugby Pants Jerome. He peered down at me. "Danny, you awake?" Evidently I gave some kind of affirmative response. "How're you feeling? You've been out for almost twenty-four hours. Hang on, I'll call the nurse."

He must have buzzed because soon a nurse was bending over me. I waited for the euphoric rush, but this time it didn't come. After shining a light in my eyes, she pinched me. Damn, a perfectly good Pavlovian response, one of my best, down the drain.

"Mr. Swanson, if you can hear me, nod your head."

Not wanting to be pinched again, I nodded eagerly.

"Do you know where you are?"

I rasped out a grunt, moistened my mouth, and tried again. I managed a hoarse whisper. "Please don't pinch me."

She looked pleased. "Conscious and aware. Some signs of intelligence. The doctors will be pleased." She patted my arm and left.

I looked at Jerome and grunted. "Time?"

"It's 8:00 AM, Saturday."

I'd had a tough five minutes and fatigue washed over me. Back to sleep.

The next time I woke up, it was light in the room and Mark was in the chair beside my bed, leafing through a magazine. I tried to say "Good morning," but someone's parrot squawked instead.

Mark smiled at me. "Welcome back, Danny Swanson. How was your little sojourn?"

I needed moisture and cast my eyes around until Mark guessed what I needed and held a glass of water to my mouth. I slurped and dribbled until my mouth and throat felt less like sandpaper. Mark wiped my chin and chest.

"They said you'd be dehydrated. But dehydrated is way better than dead. You remember what happened?"

I think I nodded.

"The guy used a .38 Special, not exactly a peashooter. Bullet entered two inches to the left of your heart, smashed a rib and did a lot of tissue damage. You'll hurt for a while."

"Jerome?"

"Took one in the upper thigh. Bled like hell but, like they say, it was only a flesh wound. He's home now, getting ready to receive his medal."

"Deserves it."

"Yeah, but you gave him his big chance. I'd say he owes you."

"Big time."

The aching in my chest had subsided to a dull throb. If I moved carefully, even the sharp jolts of pain were bearable. I made vague sitting-up motions. Mark gestured to hold still, and pressed a button on the side of the bed. There was a comfortable whir and the bed sat me up. I had a better view of the room and nodded to High-Top Jerome in a chair by the door.

"I didn't realize I was so popular. Is it my personality or my quintessentially Canadian good looks?"

"You're my best chance of getting a medal. The shooter probably wants a mulligan, and if I can limit the damage to one slug in you, non-vital location, I'll be tied with Jerome."

"Any chance of getting Louise, Staff Sergeant Karavchuk, over here? We need to figure out what went wrong."

"Something went wrong? Jerome got a medal, I'm getting overtime, there's lots of beer leftover at the house. Life is good."

Louise swept into the room and Jerome pulled off a credible sitting salute that Louise didn't see.

"Danny, you're awake." She took my hand and squeezed it. "You're looking better than the last time I saw you."

"Even with the egg on my face? I'm assuming I didn't get shot by a party-pooping neighbor. Our bad guy was supposed to go after Crowley's files and the computer, not try to whack me."

"We all miscalculated. They thought we didn't care about the files and the only person who might be able to make sense out of them was you. So, eliminate you and eliminate the threat. I don't think the bad guy would show his face in public, so I'm guessing they hired a pro, some kid trained in the drug wars. Jerome spent two days going over mug shots. Nada."

"I'm worried about Bette."

"Theoretically, they don't know she's working on the files. Just in case, though, we've got her wrapped up like a mummy. She took a leave of absence and she's working on Crowley's computer full-time. And Jerome and Heidi provide her companionship."

"Heidi?"

"The bodyguard division also strives for gender equity. If Jerome keeps getting shot, we'll beat our target date."

"He didn't have a lot of time to negotiate. Consensus might not have been achievable."

"Yeah, I know. He did good. Preserved a prime asset."

"Prime asset?" Mark coughed. "There's an extra syllable there. I'll let Christine and Fergie know you're awake."

He ambled out the door, and Louise looked at Jerome. "Can we have a minute?"

"I'll be by the elevator."

He closed the door behind him, and Louise leaned over and kissed me. Her fingers ran over my face, like she was trying to see me through her fingertips. She kissed me again, gently but not casually. I responded as best I could, but she pressed me back against the pillows.

"I was really worried, Danny. You're going to have to stop getting shot."

"Okay, it's not all it's cracked up to be anyway." She nestled her head lightly against my shoulder. I managed to raise one hand to the back of her neck. The pain was worth it. After not long enough of this activity, the door was flung open and Dr. Blissfully Infallible graced us with his presence.

"Ah, Mr. Swanson." Louise could have been a prosthesis for all the notice he took of her. She stood slowly, gave me a wry smile, nodded at the doctor, and left. He glanced at my charts. "How are we feeling this morning?"

"I don't know about you, but I'm feeling kind of shitty. I can't move without causing major pain, and in about half an hour I'm going to be really really bored. How long do I have to stay here?"

"Hmmmm." He felt carefully around the dressing on my chest, then slid his hand between the pillow and my back. "Any pain here? Here?"

He used his stethoscope to eavesdrop on various organs, and then straightened up. "You're fairly simple. You're also lucky that I was available. We had to cauterize two large arteries, and we'll need to monitor them for bleeding. We'll also need to watch for fluid buildup in the trauma cavity. But if there are no complications, and if you make satisfactory progress, I'll release you in three days."

He made some final notes on my chart and strode from the room.

I resolved to make satisfactory progress and was immediately rewarded. A nurse came in and showed me how to use the remote switch to raise and lower my bed. She also swung a small TV into position and handed me the remote for that. I lowered my bed and turned on the TV. A baseball game was on. The pitcher was leaning in for the sign and the catcher was wiggling his fingers between his legs. I fell asleep before the pitch was delivered.

It would be difficult to describe the boredom of the next three days. No-Neck Jerome replaced High-Top Jerome, and I was able to teach him to play crib. He could not, however, be convinced to play for money, and that took all the excitement out of the game.

Whenever golf came on, I'd call Rugby Pants Jerome to watch.

"Look at those slacks, Jerome. Hound's-tooth! With a plaid shirt. Isn't this exciting? Right after this, we can watch figure skating and see what they're wearing." Jerome would grunt and leave the room and I'd be bored again.

Louise would come by in the evenings and we'd rub noses and cuddle. She refused my requests to import cheeseburgers, saying, "You are what you eat."

"I'd rather be a sizzling all-beef patty than a bean salad."

"Unfortunately, you're not very well done."

"I served nine months in a high-security womb. Any more and I'd be an elephant."

"Your ears seem to have done the extra time."

"Other parts of me as well."

"Certainly not your memory. You've forgotten what happens to people who brag."

"What?"

"Nothing."

She left me alone with my thoughts, facing my last night in hospital. There'd been no progress on the case. Tommy was chasing the gunman, cashing in IOUs from every miscreant and snitch he'd ever known, to no avail. Our hopes and dreams were pinned on Bette, but so far she had produced nothing but frowns and irritated silences.

My thoughts wove in and out through thickets of unanswered questions. More and more, they circled around the West Vancouver lab. Something there called to me, something that was central to everything that had happened. God knew what it was, but I had to find out.

My mobility was limited at the moment. It hurt too much to walk more than a few steps, but that wouldn't last forever. As a last resort, I could dip into the store of major-league painkillers I'd been accumulating.

At noon the next day I was sprung, out, free. Low-Top Jerome drove me back to the place on West Sixth. There were still flats of beer stacked in the kitchen, remnants of my aborted moving-in party, but the place was spotless courtesy of, I guessed, the Jeromes. And, delight of delights, sitting in the breakfast nook was my very own honey bunny bun, Staff Sergeant Karavchuk.

"Staff Sergeant, it's good to be able to see you."

"Good afternoon, Mr. Swanson. I imagine you must be glad to be able to see anybody. You came within a few inches of leaving our mortal company. Tommy is on his way over. We've got to discuss a few policy decisions."

"Coffee?" Low-Top Jerome busied himself with the coffeemaker, and I took a seat beside Louise. Under the table she massaged my knee as I waited for my energy level to come up to the maintain basic functions mark. Jerome gave me a cup of sugary coffee and that helped.

Tommy arrived after a few minutes and was profuse with his apologies. "Danny, I feel so bad about you getting shot. I thought we had all the bases covered. I just never thought they'd try to clip you. However, we're going to have to be super careful from now on, especially with you civilians that are involved in this."

"Relax, Tommy. I set myself up. Remember? And I didn't see it coming either."

"What Tommy is trying to say, Danny, is that you're not responsible for us. We're responsible for you. Tommy's got twenty good years on the force, but if a civilian gets whacked on his watch, he might as well requisition a plastic helmet because he'll be back on bike patrol."

"I don't know if you should even stay in this house, Danny. We might be better off putting you on the shelf somewhere. We've got places that don't even show up on property records."

"Hey, you guys, I'm not ready for witness protection yet. I feel perfectly safe with Jerome. Those guys need a chance to earn their medals."

"Danny! No one else will be getting any medals in relation to anything that happens to you."

"Okay, okay. I'm happy on the shelf, ain't misbehavin', saving all my love for you. But you've also got to think about Bette, Mark, Christine, and Fergie."

"Louise probably told you that we've got Bette locked up. We're thinking about your crew, but I can't see how they're any threat to the killer. I'm going to get Jerome to run them through self-protection one-oh-one, but they should be okay. What do you think?"

"I think you're right. But we thought *I* was going to be safe. And some people would be cruel enough to call that a miscalculation. It's hard to figure what the bad guy perceives as a threat. I guess the decider is that the crew wouldn't sit still for any elaborate babysitting. They're a pretty self-confident bunch. All we can do is warn them, and like you say, give them a few lessons in what to watch for and how to conduct themselves."

"And on a positive note," Tommy said, raising one finger to make his point, "the bad guy, or guys, have exposed themselves a bit. Sanderson was the only one you told about Crowley's stuff, so that confirms to me that he's involved in the hit on you, and therefore the other killings."

"And if DFO gossip is right," I replied quickly, "and it usually is, Sanderson is Fleming Griffith's creature. And I've always thought Griffith was up to his scrawny pallid neck in this."

"So, back to you, Danny," Louise said, squeezing my knee again. "At the very least, we're going to pull you out of this house and hide you somewhere. It'll be comfortable and you'll have some freedom of movement, but we've got to take the bull's-eye off your back."

So it was that Jerome and I and my new stereo were exiled to Main Street, about three blocks from the train station.

But first, because there was an outside chance I could ID the shooter, I spent two hours looking at pictures of unpleasant individuals who would very likely not ever be salesman of the year. After that predictable lack of success, Jerome drove a fatigued Danny Swanson to our new digs.

We had one of two apartments on the second floor above an industrial laundry. The other apartment was not occupied by F. Wang, who was "visiting relatives in Hong Kong."

The place was alarmed well enough for a *Globe and Mail* editorial. Starting on the ground floor and up the stairs, along the hall, and obviously in the apartment proper, there were sound, motion and infrared heat detectors. The panel that armed and disarmed them all was partly manual and partly on a timer system. I tried real hard to absorb Jerome's explanation.

By the time we'd set up the stereo and listened to *James Brown Live at the Apollo Theatre* while eating the combination dinner number four from the Golden Palace, I was yawning rudely. I took the bedroom farthest from the fire escape and, after swallowing a single painkiller, crawled gratefully into bed.

As I drifted toward sleep, my thoughts returned to the West Vancouver lab. I saw it from above, a large building, secluded, on the shore of an ocean. It was dusk and then dark. Now I was inside, in a windowless room. I couldn't find the light switch but there was something, something . . .

I woke to the smell of coffee brewing. By the time I'd showered, I also smelled bacon frying. I was thinking seriously of dumping Louise for High-Top Jerome when he appeared at my bedroom door. Clad only in dingy briefs and waving a spatula, he invited me to breakfast. As he turned away, I was interested to note that his back was hairier than my chest. I decided to remain heterosexual. Lucky Louise.

But breakfast was good. Jerome was not in my immediate line of sight, and even if he occasionally hove into view, freshly squeezed orange juice will excuse a multitude of sins, if not go so far as to influence gender preference.

My phone rang, so I answered it. "How's life in the nursery?" It was Bette.

"I don't mind being coddled. It's like having four wives to look after you," I replied.

"But you've got no freedom," she said impatiently. "They control your every move."

"Like I said . . ."

"I'm afraid I'm going to lose it and tell Heidi to go mind her fucking goats."

I tried to calm her down. "You're a step up for the girl. What's new?"

"Bad news. Griffith's in town. He's been trying to contact me."

I felt a rush of fear. "For Christ's sake, whatever you do, don't talk to the guy. You're supposed to be on holiday. You're out of cell-phone range and not monitoring your e-mail."

"That's not like me. He'll get suspicious."

"Let him get suspicious."

"The thing is, Danny, he scares me. I've pulled out bits and pieces from Crowley's computer, and I see Griffith in a whole new light. He's not just another ambitious, amoral bureaucrat. He's a digestive system. I don't know if he has goals or aspirations. He just feeds on people for no other reason than that's what he does."

"He's like a shark and sharks have blind spots." I felt like a Little League coach giving a pep talk. "Griffith is obviously worried if he's left his comfortable office in Ottawa, but there's more damage here than he can deal with. He's bleeding and he doesn't even know it."

"Better him than us," Bette replied. "Anyway, I told Louise that I'll have all the info off the computer by this afternoon. I'll talk to you later."

I took a moment to consider the state of play. Griffith was worried about me. I was sure he'd passed that on to our bad guy and that had led to my near death experience. They weren't sure how much I knew, but they feared what I might find out by going through Crowley's journals and his computer. It was unclear if they knew what Bette was up to, although they were probably suspicious. And they were abandoning the operation. Why else would the bad guy have burned the monitoring station in Codville Lagoon?

I wondered if Griffith might be a little bit upset with his henchman. The attempted hit on me, aside from being botched and drawing extra heat, was not well thought out. The killer was exhibiting symptoms of panic, and maybe that was why Griffith had come back to the West Coast, to assert proper command and control over the operation.

I needed to talk to my sweetie. "You feel like driving me over to HQ?" I said to my breakfast companion, who was now, mercifully, dressed.

"Sure, I'll tell central we're on the move." He made a quick phone call, did something to the alarm panel, and we left. We exited by the private door at the side of the building, Jerome in the lead and me swivel-necking in his wake. It was only about one hundred feet to the car and there were no pedestrians in sight, but the hairs on the back of my neck were quivering the whole way.

As we pulled out of the parking lot, a dark Chevy two-door left the curb and fell in behind us. Jerome's eyes met mine in the rearview mirror. "Friendly." I relaxed a little but my pulse rate didn't go down to normal until we were inside the police building. Louise met me in the lobby and waved at Jerome to take five.

Safely in her office, we embraced until I winced and she drew back in alarm. "It's okay, I'm all right. Just a touchy nerve."

She looked at me with concern in her eyes. "I don't like it when you're in pain."

"Neither do I. But it keeps me focused."

The door swung open and Tommy regarded me anxiously. "How you feeling?"

"Better by the hour. What have you guys been up to?"

"I've been doing paperwork," he said. "And Louise has been pretending not to pine."

"Tommy! I was deep in thought."

"Bette called this morning," I informed them. "Evidently Griffith has slithered onto the scene."

"The Dark Lord himself," Tommy said. "I think he's worried. When they tried to whack you, it was like coming out into the open. Everything they've done up 'til now has been surreptitious. Now it's like they don't care anymore."

"We need to hear what Bette has to say," I said. "What time's she supposed to be here? Two? Let's assemble then and plan our next move based on what she's got off Crowley's computer."

The meeting actually took place in Tommy's office because it was bigger. Present were Louise and me, Tommy, Bette, and High-Top Jerome. Tommy emceed.

"Afternoon, everyone. Everything that's said here is highly confidential, of course, need-to-know-only, etcetera. Ms Connelly, we've been waiting anxiously for your report. The floor is yours."

She seemed hesitant, as if unsure of how to broach an unpleasant topic. She shook her head, looking as haggard as an attractive thirty-two-year-old woman can. But in spite of her grim mouth and tired eyes, I detected a sort of triumphant energy.

"This was by far the toughest job I've ever done," she began hesitantly. "I have the impression that Crowley knew that someday someone like me would need to read his files. He deliberately made it difficult because, in his eyes, only the truly worthy would be able to pass the test. But it was almost too difficult."

She had us spellbound. Was this the missing piece of the puzzle, the information we needed to solve the mystery of three, and almost four, deaths? She continued with growing confidence. "In this binder is a complete printout of Crowley's computer files. Much of it wouldn't be of interest to anyone but a fish scientist. But I'll summarize the high points, or the low points. We know the results of their operation, but Crowley lays out the genesis, that's a good word for it, and the early days of the setup."

She paused to organize her thoughts.

"Griffith organized it, of course, and initially he had a simple goal in mind: salmon farming was metastasizing all over the coast and anyone who could invent a fish that grew really big really fast would be a hero. He didn't have the scientific credentials to pull it off, even though he liked to hang around in the lab. So he recruited guys who did. We know Crowley was arrogant, but the other two guys on the team, who he refers to as 'The Farmers,' made Crowley look like a Buddhist monk."

Tommy made as if to reach for a glass of water but decided to remain still.

"So this unholy trinity," Bette continued, "set out to create a big sockeye, and the methodology of choice was gene splicing. Back in the early eighties, there was a worldwide moratorium on gene splicing, but that didn't bother our guys. Factor in the competitive aspect—don't forget other teams were working on the same problem—and our guys threw caution out the window. The concept of scientific responsibility, of the safety of the public, was treated with as much respect as, in Crowley's words, a cheap date on the morning after."

I leaned across the table. "So they're cutting corners like a blind jaywalker. And they did something stupid?"

Bette shrugged. "So stupid only a genius would have done it. They'd taken genes out of cancer cells, three genes that cause rapid cell division, and they inserted them into the DNA of an Adam's River sockeye. The cells multiplied like crazy but they figured out a way to eliminate mutagenesis, so the cells developed properly as gills and scales and muscle, and they introduced a limiting gene that would stop growth at about fifty pounds."

I couldn't help interrupting. "Jesus Christ, Bette! A fifty-pound sockeye!" Seven, maybe eight pounds was the biggest I'd ever seen. Or heard about. Well, that wasn't quite true, fishermen's stories being what they are. But no reputable source had ever claimed to have seen a sockeye salmon more than about eight pounds. "They actually produced these things?"

"Oh yeah. There are pictures. But here's where things get really interesting. Griffith came back to his team with a second mandate, and Crowley is vague on exactly where this came from. But Griffith told the team that step two, which had been authorized by 'the highest sources' was . . ." Bette hesitated and looked at me. I couldn't read her expression, but it was like she wanted something from me. Absolution?

My thoughts swirled formlessly and the shape of something hideous coalesced out of the darkness. They had produced sockeye that stayed in one area, that spawned in the ocean, that weren't anadromous. Why? And then I saw it.

"They wanted salmon out of the Fraser River!"

"You've got it, Danny. The fifty-pound sockeye would end up being raised in pens by fish farmers. But the Fraser River would still be full of those pesky wild salmon, which the general public are very fond of. How could you dam the Fraser and sell the water to Americans if once a year millions of wild salmon swim up it?"

I was stunned. In my wildest nightmares I'd never foreseen a plan to kill the Fraser River. But that's what it was. I forced my attention back to what Bette was saying.

"I figure this would have been even more exciting for Crowley and his crew. Behavioral changes are more cutting edge than changing phenotypes. Griffith knew they were playing for huge stakes, so he raised the security level and told them to be very, very careful. Problem was, Griffith couldn't really micromanage the project because he was spending a lot of time brownnosing in Ottawa. To whom I don't know, and I don't know if I want to know."

I felt sick. The deliberate destruction of the biggest salmon run in Canada, food for millions, and then one of the great rivers of the world—to choke it to death it with dams . . . This was beyond criminality—it was evil incarnate. Premeditated ecocide. For money. I pulled myself back to the moment. Louise was looking at me anxiously.

I tried to ignore the nausea and encroaching fatigue. Pieces were falling into place like bodies from a burning skyscraper. "We know they partially succeeded; they produced a prototype with a few flaws. How the hell did these things end up in the ocean?"

Bette looked at me dispiritedly. "They started growing the man-made mutants in tanks in the basement lab and everything seemed to be going well. They spawned in saltwater and exhibited spatial preferences, became non-migratory. And then, whomever Griffith was taking orders from decided they needed to demonstrate 'viability in competitive conditions.'"

I couldn't believe it, even though I'd seen the results. "The stupid bastards released a bunch of bioengineered mutants into the wild! How the hell did they manage that?"

"Well, they saw an opportunity. The lab had a contract with the provincial government to produce half a million coho to be released in time for Expo '86. Enhance the image, Supernatural BC, and all that. All the fish were tagged, which is very labor-intensive. So our three basement boys figured they'd just throw some of their experimental sockeye juveniles in with the coho juveniles and the hatchery crew would do the tagging and release work for them. They didn't utilize the radio tags until later."

"My God, they were idiots."

"They were geniuses, which is sort of similar, I guess." She shrugged.

"Later on, they set up the ocean-monitoring system at Codville Lagoon." I was able to supply this part. "Alistair resigned from DFO to live up there and monitor the experiment, right after he saw Billy at the West Van lab."

"At least one of them stayed at the lab and Alistair would send him updates. The other? Who knows?"

I continued putting the pieces together. "So Crowley found out from Mark that Billy had been killed. Presumably because when Billy visited the lab with Igor he saw something that tipped him off to the scheme. Plus, Crowley might have been having a morality attack about introducing mutant fish into the wild. He contacts the guy at the lab, threatens to end the experiment, and our bad guy goes up there and kills him."

"That's an almost credible hypothesis," Bette said, "but I can't see people getting killed because other people were worried they'd get mentioned in memos for breaking in-house regulations."

"Well, don't forget, careers were at stake."

"Were they? You know our bureaucracy is specifically designed to avoid accountability. No one would have been too worried about being outed for doing experiments without the necessary permits."

Bette was right. The accountability thing should be number six on the list of "Reasons Our Bureaucracy Keeps Screwing Things Up." The currency of accountability is praise and blame. No one gets a credit card.

"Did Griffith authorize Crowley's killing," Louise asked, "or was the killer playing Lone Ranger?"

"Don't know," I replied. "Could've been either way. The important thing is we know most of what happened, and Griffith doesn't know we know. So how do we play this? What I'd like to do is feed him some misinformation. If we could plant something in his brain, something that would make him panic, he might do something stupid and expose himself."

"Danny, we haven't done well in setting traps for these guys. They are smart and cautious." Louise's expression was serious to the point of being grim. "We can't afford any more collateral damage, to you or to Tommy's career."

"Louise, I'm a ten-year detective who's never gonna make Superintendent. Let's not worry about my career. You at least have a shot at the big time."

"You mean escorting the PM at the Calgary Stampede?"

"You know what I mean."

"Okay, we're not going to be distracted by career planning, but I don't think Mr. Swanson is ready to take another bullet. We need to be very careful."

Their concern flattered me, but I was still thinking about ways to crack open the case. "I still think we can run a little misdirection play on these guys without leaving ourselves open. I need to think about it. I'm going to have another crack at the code in Crowley's log. Is there somewhere I can work?"

Louise looked at me solicitously. "You're not tired? You need to take it easy."

"I'll be okay until I'm not. Then I'll take a rest." I must have sounded irritated because there was a bit of a pause before Tommy responded.

"You can use interview room number four," Tommy said and winked. "I'll tell them to clean the blood off the floor." The meeting adjourned and I followed Tommy down the hall to my new workplace.

Twenty-one

Interview room number four was not the least bit claustrophobic, unless you happened to be a human being. I sat at a battered table on which I had placed Bette's printout of Crowley's computer files plus Crowley's journals and my copy of his ship's log. I felt like I was stuck with an overdue homework assignment.

I started by quickly leafing through the three hundred and forty-seven pages of Bette's printout. She had summarized the material pretty accurately. The first section was simply the experimental data from the attempt to grow large sockeye. There were even photographs.

The team consisted of Crowley and the two others he called The Farmers. Fleming Griffith would drop in occasionally to monitor progress and "play with the fish." Crowley was pretty caustic in his comments about the abilities of Griffith and The Farmers.

"The Farmers are adept at following Fleming's orders and not much else. Their academic qualifications must have been obtained by filling out the back of a matchbox and their reasoning abilities are just superior to their subject's. Fleming is smarter than the farmers and he seems to revel in it. It is not evident why, as it's the same as being smarter than fish."

Go Alistair!

The second, larger section recorded the experiment from the "second mandate." This was a much more complex endeavour because it entailed manipulating multiple behavioral characteristics rather than a single physical characteristic. There were a number of false starts and discarded hypotheses before the first breakthrough. In 1982, they succeeded in designing a fish that exhibited preference for a slightly lower than normal salinity. They were on their way.

I didn't want to think about who had authorized the second mandate. Griffith wouldn't take orders from anyone below ministerial level and no Fisheries Minister would expose himself to this sort of potential scandal. I pictured a shadowy power broker murmuring in Griffith's ear. Who? Representing what interests? And how would we ever find out?

I turned my attention to the log of the *Jessie Isle* that contained what we had surmised were false entries for May 6 and 7. I was sure that the minutes given in the time entries were actually coded for letters of the alphabet. But the code didn't work if you used the standard alphabet sequence, so there must be a key somewhere. I looked carefully through the rest of the logbook but couldn't find anything that might be a key.

That left only Crowley's journals to examine and it was there that I found it. There were twenty-seven journals, as I've previously recounted, and twenty-six of them consisted of daily observations of his life in Yeo Cove. The twenty-seventh was different. It was undated, and consisted of pasted-in printouts from various databases rather than a linear narrative.

Many of the printouts were in standard spreadsheet layout: rows numbered down the left-hand side and columns headed by letters across the top of the page. On one of the pages, the letters heading the columns were not in alphabetical order. This was unusual and, I thought, worthy of investigation. From left to right, the letters were:

C, E, R, F, D, J, B, G, W, K, I, O, L, H, Y, P, S, M, N, R, A, U, T, X

The numbers given from the time sequences were:

07, 12, 18, 02, 14, 21, 17, 23, 11, 19, 08, 17, 03, 11, 09, 05, 11, 24.

Taking the seventh letter from the sequence, then the twelfth, eighteenth, and so on, I derived a message. BOMEHASTINGSRWDIX. I didn't have to be an MI6 codebreaker to figure that out. I leapt up to get Louise just as she opened the door. Fortunately, the door opened outwards so I escaped injury.

"Look at this. We need to get a court order or something."

I showed her my hasty jottings and basked in what must have been her unbounded admiration. "Who needs CSIS? We'll show this to Tommy. He'll know which judge to grovel to."

Tommy did indeed know which judge to seek permission from and undertook to do so. "The Bank of Montreal at East Hastings. Account in the name of R.W. Dix. I can get a court order to look at it, but it won't be before tomorrow afternoon at the earliest."

I retain a mental image of the three of us at that moment. Tommy hunched forward in his chair, forearms on his thighs, staring intently at Louise. Louise, very still in her chair, arms folded, eyes straight ahead. I was the third point of the triangle, joined to the others by almost palpable lines of force. The net was closing on the killer, but we couldn't afford any mistakes. Three minds in unison were calculating probabilities and running various scenarios. Nervous energy finally overcame my static state. "I need some fresh air," I said." I'll call you guys later."

I collected my Jerome and he accompanied me on a walk across the parking lot. Deciding that was enough exercise for one day, I got in the car and Jerome drove us back to our hideout on Main Street. Jerome navigated us through the alarm system and I was soon resting on my bed while TV noises came from the living room.

I was drifting comfortably toward sleep when my phone canceled the voyage. Fumbling frantically through my pockets, I was thinking only of silencing the damn thing, but when I located it on the bedside table, I thought I might as well find out who to blame for interrupting my nap.

"Hello," I said, likely sounding less awake than I intended.

"Is that Danny Swanson?"

"Yes, who's this?" The phone number was blocked.

"A friend."

"Always nice to have friends. What can I do for you?"

"Maybe I can do something for you. I understand you're having difficulty with Mr. Griffith. I have information that could be useful to you."

"And the price?" I'd read enough detective novels to know that information is never free.

"There's something I need. You could help me get it."

High-Top Jerome appeared in the doorway, No-Neck Jerome lurking behind him. "Shift change. I'm outta here. Don't let this guy cook for you."

My innate instinct for concealment kicked in and I mumbled a good-bye into the phone. Trying not to look guilty, I waved at the new Jerome and slid the phone into my pocket. They wandered away and I was left to wonder what the hell had just happened. Who was the caller and why had I hung up on him? Was it our bad guy that I had talked to? Was he preparing to dump Griffith? Would he phone back? I had better tell Tommy and Louise. On the other hand, I didn't want to admit that I'd tried to hide the call and had maybe bungled a potential contact. I'd wait until he called back, get more information, and then tell the others.

Having dealt with that contretemps, I was now free to resume my rest period.

However, sleep is not always restful. I had become a surgeon. The patient, whose face was hidden, was someone important to me, someone I cared about, someone I was desperate to save. The nurse, whose face was also hidden, or perhaps who didn't have a face, kept clamping off blood vessels. I told her to stop, this procedure was irregular. But as fast as I removed the clamps, the nurse added more. The patient was slipping away. I yelled at the nurse to stop and her answer came out of a cold black fax machine. *Policy. It's the new policy. Approved at the last meeting.*

I wasn't there, I screamed. *I didn't approve this. I never approved it.*

But the patient's blood stopped and stagnated. Then they auctioned her off to an unseen audience, a limb here and a limb there. I knew I'd never see her again. I wept and everyone laughed at me. *Memo to follow,* the fax machine spat out. *New directive, highest authority, prime mandate, consensus report, departmental approval. Memo to follow.* But the memo never came. And wakefulness, mercifully, did.

By noon the next day, the mysterious caller hadn't phoned back. I was torn between feelings of guilt and stupidity. My Jerome du jour looked at me curiously as I paced around ignoring the Jays game on TV. Jerome's phone rang. He listened awhile, snapped an affirmation and hung up. "Tommy got the court order," he said. "He and Louise will meet us at the bank."

The Bank of Montreal on East Hastings was much closer to our hideout than to Police HQ. It seemed as though Low-Top Jerome and I waited in the car for a very, very long time. We got out when Tommy and Louise pulled in, and the four of us walked toward the bank's entrance.

The sidewalk was fairly crowded and an assortment of people passed by us, no one making eye contact or acknowledging our existence: except for one person. An older guy, white hair and beard, glasses, dressed casually but well, looked straight at me as we passed. He said nothing and gave no sign of recognition, but I was sure that if I had been alone he would have said something to me. Casually, so as not to alert Jerome, I turned my head to keep the guy in view. He turned down a side street without looking back.

Was I imagining things? Had that been a meaningful look he gave me, or did I just have something on my face? The incident slipped from my mind as we entered the bank. Louise went to the service counter and asked for the manager. When he appeared, Louise discreetly showed him the court order. He scanned it with a managerial eye and disdain gave way to anxiety. Indicating that we should follow him, he led the way to his office.

Out of the public eye, he relaxed visibly and apologized for the lack of chairs. Evidently loan supplicants didn't travel in packs. "If I understand this document correctly, you are seeking all information relating to any accounts or deposits of a Mr. R.W. Dix and access to said accounts or deposits."

Louise smiled her agreement. "It could be a Mrs. R.W. Dix."

"Yes. If you give me a few minutes, I'll examine our files."

He left us alone to admire the pictures on the walls, Governors of the Bank of Canada, if I wasn't mistaken. One of them was inscribed, "Fiscally yours, James Coyne." A collector's item. We fidgeted en masse until the manager returned and reclaimed his position behind the desk.

"Mr. Dix opened a deposit account in 1985. The initial—in fact, the *only* deposit—was eight thousand dollars. The only withdrawals from the account have been monthly rental fees for a safety deposit box, which he rented at the same time. The current balance is two hundred and fifty-seven dollars and six cents."

Louise held out her hand. "The key?" The manager handed her an ordinary-looking brass key.

"If you'll follow me, I'll take you to the vault." We all trooped after him as he led us to the rear of the bank. The massive door of the vault stood open and I imagined it closing on my finger. Disguising a serious wince, I peered into the vault. It was a surprisingly large room. Separate aisles held locked drawers of assorted sizes. The manager stood aside and waved us in. "Number 481 is right at the back, on the left, third row from the top."

Louise went straight to number 481 and opened it. All of us behind her, including the bank manager, jostled for a view. There were no injuries, although I believe the manager's dignity was bruised. Louise donned a rubber glove on her right hand and removed the only item in the safety deposit box—a videocassette.

"If we could go back to your office, I'll ask you to sign a discovery form and a release form."

I rode with Louise on the way back to the cop shop. She drove and I speculated. I hadn't been this excited since the treasure hunt at my tenth birthday party. I must have been visibly vibrating. "Calm down, Danny. We can't watch it until the techs check it over. It might have prints. It might be defective, or it might not even be a videotape."

But it didn't, it wasn't, and it was.

Tommy, Louise, and I watched it after Gunther inspected it briefly. The video had been shot by a single stationary camera, mounted fairly high, maybe ten feet up on a wall. The lighting was not great but it was good enough to recognize faces.

The scene we viewed, three of us hunched avidly in front of the monitor, like hockey fans for a Stanley Cup seventh game, was of a mundane room roughly twenty feet by thirty, with cages along the three walls that we could see. Each cage held a rabbit and they all appeared to be sleeping, drugged, or both. Fleming Griffith entered the frame and began removing the unconcious rabbits and replacing them with more active specimens. When he had placed new rabbits in all the cages, the video ended. It had played for about five minutes before lapsing into grainy nothingness.

Louise used the remote to fast-forward a bit, check for footage, fast-forward again, check again for footage, and so on, until the end of the tape. There appeared to be only the five minutes of footage we had seen at the start of the tape. We sat in silence until Louise spoke. "What the hell was that all about? I was hoping to see something that would lead us to a multiple killer and all we see is Griffith playing with bunnies."

"I don't think Griffith even knows about the video." I waved at the monitor in a what-the-hell-was-that sort of motion. "It's obvious he didn't know the camera was there. But Crowley considered that footage extremely important, maybe incriminating. He went to a lot of trouble to hide it."

Tommy shook his head, bemused. "Well, look. Let's call up Griffith, tell him about the video. Threaten to give it to the SPCA. That ought to scare the shit out of him."

We all sat there and thought this over. Then we watched the video again, and still couldn't make any sense of it. Dispiritedly, I looked at Louise. She shrugged. "We need a Plan B. Can you work on that, Danny?"

"I did Plan A. Can't someone else take some responsibility?"

On that less than positive note, I left to do something. Anything.

Twenty-two

Back at the hideout, I engaged myself in the development of Plan B. I liked the title. It summed up our organizational focus, in that we had a plan, and it referenced our flexibility, in that we had responded to events to formulate a second plan, which we styled B. Yes, it was a good title.

No-Neck Jerome prepared takeout pizza for supper, and from the wine list I selected Granville Island lager. After we had dinner and I had offered to do the dishes, No-Neck was relieved by Rugby Pants Jerome. I'd just informed him that Tiger Woods had taken up darts because it was a more challenging game than golf when my phone rang.

"Hello."

"What did you think of the video?" It was my caller of the previous evening. Thank God, he'd called back. For a moment, I couldn't figure out what he was talking about, but I knew I needed some privacy. I walked casually into my bedroom.

"What video?"

"I saw you outside the bank, Danny. You're a clever boy. I didn't know if anyone would be able to figure out my clues. Congratulations."

"Who is this?"

"Surprised? Of course you are. Better check my picture on the DFO website. It's still there. Under 'C.' I checked it when I checked yours. I'll call you back tomorrow. And Danny, your friends don't need to know about this yet. You can tell them when we've finished our business."

I quickly fired up my laptop and went to the DFO internal website. I clicked on personnel, bio clips, and down the alphabetical names to

"C." There he was, the guy I'd seen outside the bank, the guy that had stared at me. The picture showed a slightly younger man than the bearded person I'd seen, but it was undoubtedly him. The name at the top of the file was Alistair Crowley.

My mind reeled. Christ, it performed seven jigs and danced the hokeypokey.

The question that crowded to the front of my mental bedlam, elbowed the other questions to the ground, kicked them in the teeth, and stood on their inert bodies, was—who was the dead guy in Yeo Cove? After five minutes of intense thought, examining initial propositions and logical flows, rethinking the conclusion several times, and whacking myself on the forehead more than once, the answer was obvious. It was our bad guy. He had gone up there to kill Crowley, but Crowley had killed him. This put, as they say, a different spin on things.

It also put Louise in a bad light. The constables that had identified the body had been handicapped by the fact that said body didn't have a face, and they had jumped to the conclusion that because it was in Crowley's float house it must be Crowley. That was fairly reasonable, but it was a big mistake, and Louise had bought into it. So had I, for that matter, but I wasn't the investigating officer.

As to whether I should share this development, I needed to think about it and find out what Crowley was up to. But, I brightened, this could be the beginnings of Plan B. Danny Swanson might once again be able to save the day and ride off into the sunset—or buy a float house and live in Echo Bay.

The next day was awkward. Louise phoned and asked what I was doing. I said I was thinking. She said don't hurt yourself and hung up.

I phoned back and asked what she was doing. She said she and Tommy were chasing down leads on my shooter. I said I'd join them but the South West Ford Dealers' Pro Am was on.

That was a lie and I was forced to manipulate No-Neck Jerome into playing professional crib. We didn't play for a lot of money. It wouldn't have been fair as I was the reigning Johnstone Strait champion. To the tunes of Joe Cocker and Ze Mad Dogs and Ze Englishmen, as intro-duced by the anomalous French guy on the record, we fifteen-twoed through the morning.

By the time I'd won enough for a case of beer, it was sufficiently late to drink one guilt-free. We flicked through the cable channels and discovered an Aussie Rules football game. Jerome made grilled cheese sandwiches, and I had my third beer. What an exciting day.

By suppertime, I was as tightly strung as a cheap mandolin. I let Jerome order food and I let him do the dishes and I let him grumble about doing all the housework. My magnanimity was limited just enough to point out that he was the highest paid dishwasher in the universe. After absorbing a significantly smaller portion of dried spare-ribs than Jerome, I retired to my bedroom.

I lay on the bed and stared at the ceiling, waiting for Crowley's phone call. Unconsciously I nodded to the rhythm of the music coming from the living room. Otis Span. "Ain't Nobody's Business." The best blues piano player of all time finished a chorus and Luther Georgia Boy Snake Johnson took over on harmonica. My phone rang.

"Did you look up my picture?"

"You're supposed to be dead."

"That stupid farmer couldn't outsmart day-old sperm, much less Alistair Crowley. As soon as he said he was coming up to talk things over, I knew they were going to try to kill me."

"So you killed him instead."

"Self-defense."

"You said you needed my help with something. What?"

"My recent death is going to be somewhat of a hindrance to my career. In this country, at least. But there are other places that have a more mature attitude toward fish science. I'll be welcomed."

"How does that involve me?"

"I'll need to demonstrate my professional qualifications. My résumé, so to speak, is locked away in the West Vancouver lab."

"What are you talking about?"

"The DNA from all our experiments. It's frozen in room twelve at the lab. If I get it, Griffith won't. And it'll be my passport to a new job and a new identity. But I don't have keys."

"And that's where I come in? Okay, if I agree to help, your part of the bargain is information. I need enough to nail Griffith and The Farmers."

"There's only one now," he said. "He's stupider than the other one, and consequently more dangerous. But I guess you know that."

"How do you know so much about the case? How did you even find out I was involved?"

"So many questions, Danny. We'll have a long talk. At the lab. Tomorrow night."

"Wait a minute." I felt suddenly unsure of things. Scared. I had developed an extreme aversion to getting shot again. "I don't have the keys. I might be able to get them but I'm not sure. Phone me tomorrow at noon, and we'll go from there."

"All right. But remember, Danny, the police can't be involved. They'll want to talk to me and that would spoil my new career. You want Griffith? Then you have to help me disappear. Again."

The line went dead.

I was lost in the slithering dithers. Should I go? Should I tell anyone? Could I trust Crowley? Was I even sure it *was* Crowley?

As dispassionately as possible, I retraced the steps of my reasoning. It had to be Crowley on the phone because he knew about the video, and the guy I'd seen outside the bank had matched Crowley's picture. Did Crowley have any reason to harm me? If he wanted to disappear, he wouldn't want any links to his past. But he probably wanted revenge on Griffith and I was his best chance for that. Add the fact that I was a personable and charming young man, and the balance tipped in favor of him not killing me.

I could tell Louise and get the police to cover my back, but this was probably our last chance to nail Griffith. I couldn't do anything to screw things up. And, anyway, the force's record in protecting me was somewhat blemished. I would have to suck it up and fly solo. But my skin prickled and the hairs on the back of my neck stood up as I succumbed to a quintessential cringe.

I dialed Bette's number. "Hi, it's me," I said when she answered. "How's life with Heidi?"

"Hell is living with someone who exists on seven calories a day and does aerobics without sweating."

"Listen, I need to look around the lab and I don't have keys. Can I borrow yours?"

"I'm sure that violates some rule. I hope you won't report me."

"I've lost my memo pad. How about I come by tomorrow evening and grab them?"

"Sounds good."

With that settled, all I had to do was figure out a way to dump Jerome. I mulled that over for the rest of the evening and much of the next day. Crowley phoned promptly at noon and I told him we were on. After an afternoon of pacing nervously, it was time to order supper. I insisted it was my turn to choose and phoned in an order to a sushi place right next to Waterfront Station. High-Top Jerome bitched that there were closer places, but I told him this was the only place you could get ragfish roe.

When he pulled up in front of the place there was, as I had hoped, no parking places. "I'll run in and grab it. Extra soy sauce, right?" I was out the door before he could object. I walked quickly into Sayonara Sushi, and just as quickly out the side door and into Waterfront Station. I already had the correct change in my hand when I got to the ticket machine. Glancing at my watch, I punched the appropriate buttons and, thirty seconds later, I was dashing down the steps to the SeaBus. My timing was good but not perfect, and I had to wait an anxious two minutes before the next departure. Finally we pulled out, and I was on my way across Burrard Inlet to North Vancouver.

I felt a little guilty about Jerome. There weren't many medals awarded for letting your charge skip out. I hoped he wouldn't put things together quickly enough to have me picked up on the other side. He didn't, and soon I was in a cab headed for Bette's place.

Bette had moved into an older house just above the decommissioned railroad tracks in Ambleside Village. She had a beautiful view of the harbor and enough foliage around to make it seem rural. When I knocked on the door, it was answered by a Heidi, who scrutinized me closely. "And you are?"

Bette appeared behind her. "It's okay. He's an old friend of mine." She threw me the keys and I made a nice catch, which didn't seem to impress Heidi.

"Thanks, Bette." I left, which did seem to impress Heidi. I'd arranged to meet Crowley on neutral ground, the White Spot in Park Royal, so that's where I had the taxi drop me. I ordered coffee to drink and nachos to nibble on and settled in to wait for the man who would deliver up Billy's killer.

He walked in just before eight. He looked left and right, saw me, and indicated to the waitress that he would join me. As he strode toward the table, I studied him closely. He was deeply tanned, with a weather-beaten face and gnarled hands, unlike his academic colleagues, but he carried himself with authority, and behind the glasses, his eyes were hard and unblinking.

He sat down and his mouth tightened in what may have been a smile. "Congratulations again, Mr. Swanson. You had to solve a number of puzzles in order to be here tonight."

"You must have suspected your colleagues couldn't be trusted. So you archived the whole story in code and hoped that someone could find it if necessary." He nodded. "How did you know I was involved?"

"Basic hacking. I know the e-mail passwords of a couple of my old colleagues. After you showed up at my wake, which was very decent of you, e-mails positively flew around about you having my journals and computer. If anyone was going to get to the video, it was you.

"What the hell was the video about? I thought we were dealing with mutant fish, not cute little bunnies."

He looked at me like a prize pupil who's screwed up an exam. Finally, he answered. "When the directive came to release our engineered fish into the wild, it occurred to me to do a toxicity test on them. After all, someone might catch and eat one."

"Oh God." I hung my head. "The rabbits weren't sleeping. They were dead."

"And Griffith replaced the dead ones with live rabbits and informed us that feeding the engineered fish pellets to the rabbits had no toxic effect whatsoever."

"When was the video shot?"

"Nineteen eighty-five. We'd installed a camera so we didn't have to waste time monitoring them. Mammals bore me. Fleming didn't know about the camera because he'd been on the east coast for three weeks. He showed up on a Friday and volunteered to check the test subjects. I said fine, and left him to it. He left a report on my desk saying that there were no toxic effects. When I came in on Monday, I had to check the tape for something, and I saw that Griffith had covered up the fact that these fish could be lethal. It was fortunate that I was the first one to see the tape. I knew valuable ammunition when it was handed to me. It was also my first concrete evidence that Griffith couldn't be trusted."

"Billy Bradley, our shipmate, what happened to him?"

"It was late one afternoon. I was just leaving. Just about everyone else was already gone. I ran into him in the parking lot. He smelled of beer and he had something smelly in a black plastic garbage bag. He insisted I look at it, and I realized it was one of our failures. I wanted time to examine it and your friend was ranting about prize money, so I took him back inside."

"Who else was around? Was Fleming there?"

"I'd seen him strutting around earlier, but I assumed he'd left. As far as I knew, no one else was there. I told your friend to wait in the lunchroom and I took the specimen into one of the workrooms. I photographed it, took physical data and a tissue sample, and then discarded it with the rest of the morts. I went back to the lunchroom prepared to give your friend a scientific-sounding brush-off, but he was gone. So I left too. A week later, I resigned in order to do the transition to field monitoring. I never knew your friend went missing until Mark mentioned it that day in my float house."

"Did you check the videotape the next morning?"

"I had no reason to. And if I didn't remove the tape by noon, it would just start taping over the previous day's record."

"Who were The Farmers?"

"They were two aquaculture biologists, glorified lab assistants really, who had been seconded from the provincial government. Fleming liked them because they worshipped him and I put up with them because they would follow orders without a lot of petty moralizing. Farmer number one, Jerry Mathias, stayed at the lab as my contact. I would phone the main switchboard after hours and leave a message. Jerry would go in early in the morning, check for messages, and if I had left one, he'd erase it."

"So after your conversation with Mark, when you found out Billy had probably been killed, you left a message that, what? Threatened to go to the police?"

"Of course not. I would never jeopardize the experiment. But for some time, I'd wanted more control. It was my project, after all. The others were no more than useful assistants. And if they'd screwed things up by killing your friend, that gave me leverage to demand the final say in decisions. So I left a message that I was not happy and I was thinking about taking our product elsewhere, and we needed to discuss things. The *Kelp* was already late for a scheduled maintenance trip. When it showed up, Jerry told me he'd been delayed by fog at the Port Hardy airport. And he acted strangely, asking all kinds of questions about my files and data systems. He poked around my float house, showing a curiosity he never had before. He picked up my shotgun, checked that it was unloaded, and made some crack about gun safety. After thoroughly arousing my suspicions, he left to run up to Morehouse Bay to check things there, then he was going to come back for me and we'd go down to Lagoon Bay to check batteries and transmitters."

"And, of course, he saw your desktop computer, but not the hidden one."

"Yes. It was easy to keep one step ahead of these clowns. I loaded my shotgun and put it back on the rack. When Jerry returned, he demanded all my files and data. When I refused to hand them over, he pulled out a pistol and threatened me. When I walked over and picked up my shotgun, he laughed. I can hear him now."

"'It's not loaded, Alistair. Did you forget?'"

"It was the last thing he ever said. I pressed the muzzle against his ignorant mouth and blew his stupid head off. Self-defense. He was more useful as maggot food. And it gave me the opportunity to disassociate myself from Fleming and his master plan."

"Why? Because the mutant fish were breeding in the wild? Someone would have found out eventually. Your career prospects would be about as healthy as the east coast cod stocks."

"We were satisfied with our risk-management protocols. We had deniability. It would have been regrettable if the experiment was exposed prematurely, but the data was robust. The real problem was that Fleming regarded the project as his creation and was preparing to take all the credit. And I had done all the work. The key insights, the theoretical breakthroughs were all mine. When the paper was written, it would appear under my name only."

"I guess you can't write the paper now."

"Unfortunately not in the form I'd envisioned. But when I get my DNA samples, I'll be able to set up somewhere else and carry on the work. I have some ideas that will stun the scientific community."

I decided not to comment on this. "Where did you disappear to after the shooting?"

"I took the *Kelp* to Bella Bella. The next morning I hired on as a deckhand on a gillnetter and we left for Stryker Bay. The other deckhand was Mathew Wilson. When the herring fishery was over, we went back to Bella Bella, and I talked him into procuring a boat for me. I went down to Lagoon Bay and burned the place. Then Mathew drove me to Klemtu and I flew back to Vancouver."

"Mathew didn't know who you were?"

"Not a clue. Most of the time he didn't know who *he* was. I paid him enough to buy whatever sort of oblivion he fancied and he'd forgotten me before he pocketed the money."

I gazed out the window at the encroaching dusk. The cars on Marine Drive all had their headlights on and pedestrians were hunching against a wind-driven drizzle.

I looked back at the interior of the restaurant and then at Alistair Crowley, eminent scientist, DFO stalwart, admired mentor, and killer. "It's time to go."

We both stood, I left ten dollars on the table and we walked out, heading straight into the main current of whatever was to be. Crowley was driving a battered old Jeep. When we were settled inside, I turned to him and said I was going to pat him down for a gun. "You don't have to. I've got Jerry's."

"Give it to me."

He looked at me coldly.

"I know I'm not going to kill you," I explained, "but I'm not entirely sure that you're not going to kill me. If you want those DNA samples, this is how the deal works."

"I presume you've got the keys on you. I could shoot you and take the keys."

"You already know I'm not stupid. I don't have the keys on me."

He sighed, leaned over, and pulled a .38 Special out from under his seat. I took it and tucked it into my jeans at the small of my back. "Be right back."

I went back into the White Spot and approached the waitress who'd served us. "I think I must have dropped my keys in here."

She smiled and held up Bette's key ring. "They were right on the cushion where you were sitting."

"Thanks a lot." I attempted a smile, failed, and went out to rejoin Crowley.

In the Jeep, Crowley drove without speaking, our tires swishing on the asphalt the only sound. After a time, he said musingly, "It's a good thing no one did eat those fish. The rabbits didn't die pleasantly. Three to five minutes of convulsions, a final spasm, and death by asphyxiation."

Fifteen minutes later, he pulled into the parking lot of the West Vancouver lab. There were no other cars in the lot. We got out and stood in the darkness and drizzle.

"We'll go in the back. It's the quickest way to the basement and security doesn't have access to the lower labs. Worst comes to worst, just flash your DFO ID."

The drizzle was falling through fog and the streetlights gave off a diffused glow. Raindrops on the foliage sounded like static. We stepped cautiously toward the back of the building. At the door, I fumbled with too many keys while Crowley wiped his glasses with a handkerchief. A hypothesis occurred: main door equals big key. This was experimentally verified and we entered the building.

A hallway led straight ahead and steps went down to our right. Crowley went down the steps and I followed. He led the way through an open area encompassed by closed doors to a room labeled "Wet Lab." This time, a medium-sized key proved successful and we entered a large room, lit just well enough so we could see large fish tanks. I realized it was the room we had seen in the video.

Off to the left was a single door and Crowley gestured to it. This time a small key proved to be the correct choice and we entered the freezer room. The doors of a walk-in freezer took up most of the back wall, but Crowley walked over to a row of standard three-by-six freezers against the room's right side. The third one he opened was apparently the right one. He took a Styrofoam carrying container off a shelf, put two frozen gel-packs in the bottom, and started transferring test tubes from the freezer to the container, talking as he worked. "Thank God, those stupid farmers haven't already taken these. Thinking ahead was never their strong point."

I watched him for a moment and then a thought popped into my head. "I forgot to ask, who was farmer number two?"

I flinched when a voice answered from behind us. "I guess that would be me." I turned and saw Reginald Sanderson pointing a gun at us.

Twenty-three

"I didn't know you referred to us with such disrespect, Alistair."

Crowley looked at Sanderson with contempt. "It's an accurate description. All you were good for was tending the fish, feeding them, and milking sperm. Fish farmers by training and fish farmers by nature."

"Put those samples back."

"No. Leaving them with you would be like leaving a baboon in charge of a cyclotron."

"What did you do with Jerry?"

"I persuaded him to adopt a higher calling. He's maggot food, the finest thing he's ever done."

Crowley gave me a do-something look, but as I inched my right hand toward the gun pressed against the small of my back, Sanderson shot him twice in the chest and then, leaning forward over the inert body, once in the head. The shots crashed and echoed off the concrete walls, and I instinctively pulled my arms in to protect my unhealed chest.

Sanderson straightened up, breathing heavily. "We put the night watchman on leave two weeks ago. Fleming knew someone would show up here trying to cause trouble."

My heart was pounding but somehow the blood had drained from my brain. I felt sick to my stomach and weak in the knees. Switch to automatic pilot. "Good thinking. You guys seem to have covered all the bases."

"We always like to be prepared for eventualities. And now you can help me dispose of that arrogant bastard. But first, put those samples back in the freezer."

As I followed his orders, some primitive, shockproof part of my brain proved capable of basic analysis. He obviously didn't suspect that I had a gun, but he was watching me too closely for me to reach for it. I'd just have to wait for an opportunity. I hoped that opportunity would come soon. It seemed unlikely that Sanderson would wave a cheery good-bye and leave me to write up a report at the end of this.

He tossed a large, heavy-duty nylon hockey bag at me. "Put Mr. Crowley in that."

"You really did come prepared." I held nausea at bay by pretending I was dealing with a life-sized doll. Somehow I managed to arrange Crowley in the bag. With his knees up and his arms across his chest, he barely fit. Studiously avoiding his eyes, I did the zipper up.

"Now drag him outside."

Crowley weighed around one-seventy and it shouldn't have been too difficult to drag the bag along the floor, but I was still missing bits of pectoral muscle on my left side. By the time I dragged him up the stairs and outside, I was bent over and gasping for air. Sanderson realized he had to let me rest a minute. While I recovered my strength, Sanderson placed a call and spoke tersely but triumphantly to, I was sure, Fleming Griffith. "You were right. I've got them both. We'll be in the clear soon." He closed the phone. "Down to the wharf."

I felt a glimmer of something like hope. We were obviously going to take a boat to dispose of Crowley's body. I was at home on boats and I didn't think Sanderson was. Advantage Swanson. The bag slid fairly easily across the wet grass and down the ramp to the float. Sanderson was never more than four feet behind me. There were several boats tied up at the float: Zodiacs, a couple of aluminum skiffs, the huge steel bulk of the *W.E. Ricker*, and the *W 10*, an old wooden pilchard boat that had been converted to a patrol vessel.

"We're taking that one," he said, pointing at the *W 10*. I pulled the bag alongside the gunwale and then straightened up to look at the four-foot height from float to cap rail. Sanderson grabbed one end of the bag with one hand, and carefully pointed the gun at me with the other. Between the two of us, we lifted the bag onto the deck of the boat.

"Climb aboard," he said.

When we were both standing on deck, he motioned to the hatch. "There are some anchors down there. I need you to pass them up."

I didn't like to think what he wanted the anchors for. I grasped one side of the hatch cover, Sanderson took the other side, and we slid the cover back. "A big strong guy like you should be able to manage them." He handed me a flashlight and I climbed down the ladder into the blackness of the hatch.

I switched on the flashlight and looked around. In one corner, there was a pile of halibut anchors. I noted with extreme interest that the lazaret door was open. Not good seamanship, but extremely handy for Danny Swanson in his current circumstances. I stepped through the door, pulled it shut behind me, dogged it, and held the dog handle firmly. Less than a minute later, I could feel Sanderson on the other side trying to unlatch the door. But I only had to hold the handle down whereas he had to lift it up. After a couple of minutes, he gave up and fired four shots at the door. I flinched but I knew I was safe behind three inches of first-growth fir. Five minutes later, the engines started up and I relaxed a bit.

I shone the flashlight around. I could see the steering mechanism and the usual coils of assorted rope. A couple of wooden crates held spare filters, there were three five-gallon buckets of hydraulic oil and one of lube oil, three boxes of large absorbent pads for mopping up nasty spills, plus an assortment of typical boat junk. I took a length of steel pipe, wedged it under the dog handle, sat down on one of the oil buckets, turned off the flashlight, and considered my next move.

The situation obviously called for monitoring so I proceeded without delay to implement an appropriate program. I heard the engine rev and felt the boat pull away from the dock. I flashed the light at my watch. Ten-fifteen. Sitting in the dark, I could hear the foghorn at Point Atkinson, three blasts every sixty seconds. We were leaving Burrard Inlet and heading out into the Strait of Georgia. The foghorn was still a ways ahead of us, but we would soon be in at least one hundred fathoms of water. Then the foghorn was abeam to starboard and I could hear the bell on the can buoy abeam to port. It was ten-thirty. We had to be making about ten knots, which tallied with the scream of the engine at full RPM.

Another fifteen minutes, and we'd be in body-dumping depth, although I hoped there would be too much traffic and he'd have to go farther out. I wondered if he would dare to come down the hatch to get an anchor. I wondered if I had the nerve to open the door to check. No, we could be on autopilot, with him sitting in the hatch waiting to blast me. Besides, he could find something in the engine room to weigh down the body, a deck plate or something.

By eleven o'clock, I figured we had to be roughly off Cape Roger Curtis. There was always lots of traffic in the area: tugs and barges, deep-sea vessels, fish boats, and ferries. I prayed Sanderson would have to steam for at least another half hour to find enough privacy to dispose of Crowley. After some time, the engine revved down to idle. Eleven thirty-five. Perfect. Depending on the heading Sanderson had steered, we had to be within a couple of miles of McCall Bank or Halibut Bank.

I opened my net knife and cut the two rubber hydraulic lines that ran to the steering rams. Because we were now almost dead in the water, it wasn't too hard to manually turn the rudder shaft to hard over and then lash it into position. I figured by then Sanderson had to have dumped Crowley because the engine sped up momentarily. When Sanderson realized he couldn't control the steering, and he was doomed to go around in circles, he cut the engine again. *Your move, pal*, I thought. I wondered what it would be.

I sat for an hour, straining for sounds of Sanderson's movements but hearing little. It was another half hour before I realized the rocking motion of the boat was becoming sluggish. The angle of the deck had changed. We were down at the stern. Sanderson was sinking the boat!

Panic robbed me of thought. For a second there was no me, just a sort of soundless screaming. This was every fisherman's worst nightmare: to be trapped helplessly in a sinking ship. Drowning was a horrible death. Oxygen demand would override every other brain function. Every synapse would be firing with orders to breathe. Just breathe! But there would be no relief, only wide-eyed panic building and building. And then the first trickle of water past the larynx, and then choking, and then more water, and then . . .

I forced myself to think calmly. I removed the brace from the latch but didn't open the door. Sanderson could be waiting out there. This would have to be a last-minute Houdini-like escape.

When I felt water over my shoes, I panicked a bit but realized it was actually a good thing. Water was seeping under the lazaret door, which meant the pressure would be equalized between the lazaret and the hatch and the door wouldn't be forced shut.

I made a couple of rudimentary preparations. Because there was no survival suit handy, I took off my shirt and trousers, wrapped myself with several of the absorbent pads, and put my shirt and trousers back on to hold the pads in place. Insulation. Now for flotation. I emptied two of the oil containers and tied them together with a short piece of rope to form a crude set of water wings. I was as ready as I was ever going to be to abandon ship.

We now had a pronounced list to port and were farther down at the stern. When the water reached my knees, the engine stopped, which meant the engine room was at least half flooded. I'd have to make a move soon. The boat was almost on its side now, and I pushed open the door and looked into the cabin. Dark emptiness. I switched on the flashlight. I was alone, thankfully, and the hatch cover was closed.

Because the boat was heeled over, I had no trouble reaching the hatch cover, but it was dogged shut. I used the only tool I had: the gun I'd taken from Crowley. Two shots at one aluminum lug, bend and twist, and bend and twist, and it was off. Repeat procedure on the other side, push the hatch cover away, and I was out. It was none too soon because water was lapping over the hatch coaming. Any later and the water would have forced the hatch cover shut, sealing me inside.

With nothing to keep it out of the hatch, the water poured in faster and faster, and soon the *W 10* slipped away beneath me.

It was a calm night with a half moon. The water was cold but not January cold. I figured I had three or four hours before losing consciousness. I treaded water as I looked around for Sanderson but he'd obviously abandoned ship much earlier. A mile or so away, I could see two pairs of red and green lights much where I'd expected them to be: shrimp boats working the McCall Bank. I fully expected one of them to be my cousin Ollie because the McCall Bank was his spot.

It wasn't Ollie who picked me up, but he was half a mile behind the guy who did. The skipper phoned the Coast Guard while I climbed into some dirty but dry coveralls, and they announced a search on channel 16. The five shrimpers in the area pulled their gear and were the first to start looking. Every boat in the Strait of Georgia was at least on the lookout, and within forty minutes the Coast Guard hovercraft had joined the search.

Even so, they didn't find Sanderson until the first dim light of morning. The red life jacket was spotted by the *Nootka Girl*, but when they got close enough, they could see Sanderson floating facedown. He had made no preparations for hypothermia, and the ocean had exacted its usual penalty for stupidity. Exposure had robbed Sanderson of strength and consciousness, and the old-fashioned life jacket hadn't held his face out of the water.

Still, I had to ask the medic on board the hovercraft if he was really dead, and when he confirmed it I felt, not relief so much, but that things had been simplified. One more pawn off the board. I jumped on the *Ryu II* with Cousin Ollie, and we headed up the river to his place in Steveston.

The *Ryu II* was well built and well appointed, and I reflected briefly on how well Cousin Ollie had done for himself. He was a comfortable guy leading a comfortable life with a wonderful family, and I envied him greatly.

As we cruised up the river, daylight brought it to life. The gentle red of the sunrise bathed everything in innocence and hope. When the darknesses along the bank had all been erased by light, I could see the way ahead. There was a future.

Ollie sipped coffee for a diplomatic length of time. Finally, he asked the obvious. "What in hell happened last night? I'm guessing you and the dead guy were on the same boat. What went wrong?"

"A lot went wrong, Ollie. All I can say is the dead guy deserves to be. I'll tell you the real story someday, but in the meantime I'm trying to figure out a story to tell the Coast Guard."

Ollie tied up the *Ryu II* at Steveston, and we climbed into his pick-up. We were at his expensive-looking house in time to see his two boys off to school. They gave their Uncle Danny a hug, and set off up the road, skipping and hopping over puddles. Ollie was only four years older than me but already had a wonderful family. I had some catching up to do.

Ollie's wife, the daughter of Second World War Japanese internees, chatted while I sipped coffee and Ollie rummaged through his closet for clothes that would fit me. My own clothes were in the dryer and I'd rescued my credit cards and ID. When I was dressed and had breakfasted, I asked to use their phone. I dialed Louise at her work number.

"Hi, it's me." There was an extremely long two-second silence.

"Just who the hell do you think you are and what the hell do you think gives you the right to put me through what I've just been through and why the hell should I even be talking to you and you better get the hell over here ASAP." Click.

"I'm on my way." I hung up and dialed a cab. When it arrived, I hugged Ollie and Oshie and thanked them profusely. Then I set out to confront a killer.

When we got to the police building, I paid the substantial cab fare with my credit card and hurried into the lobby. Tommy and Louise were waiting for me. "Tommy, do you mind if I have a word with Louise?"

He made a be-my-guest gesture. "I'll be in my office."

As soon as Louise closed the door behind us, I made a pre-emptive strike. I clutched her urgently and pressed my mouth to hers. She did not object greatly. Indeed, she seemed to respond in like manner. I pulled her closer and she moaned quietly as her hands clasped tightly on the back of my neck. The embrace ended with me breathing gently into the curve of her neck.

"I'm sorry, Louise. I didn't have a lot of choices."

She pushed me away gently and sat down behind her desk. "Something changed. What?"

"Four nights ago, I had a call from a dead man. That wasn't Crowley's body in his float house; it was our bad guy, AKA 'The Farmer,' or at least one of them."

Louise groaned and closed her eyes. "Rookie mistake number one. Don't assume anything. But the dead guy's prints were on the gun?"

"He'd handled it two nights before. So those prints matched the body, and all the unknown prints were actually Crowley's. And the reason neither of our bad guys showed up on DFO employment records is that they were officially still BC government employees, on loan to DFO."

I spent the next ten minutes relating everything Crowley had told me and giving a brief rendition of the events of the morning.

"So Crowley actually *is* dead now. I don't think there's any reason to change the initial analysis of the case you made in Bella Bella, if you know what I'm saying."

"Thanks, Danny. But I've got to tell Tommy, at least. He's our partner. After that, we'll see how it plays out. I'm not too worried about looking bad, compared to some of the screwups my colleagues have made." She paused and looked at me intently. "Tell me again how you got out of the bottom of that boat. You said the lid was on?"

I'd glossed over some of the particulars, but now she forced me into a more detailed description. When I finished she leaned back in her chair and breathed deeply. "Danny Swanson. Danny Swanson. Danny bloody Swanson." After a pause she stood up, and said, "Let's go see Tommy."

Tommy's office didn't contain much of interest except him. He was on the phone as we entered, listening intently while scrolling through his e-mail. He gave some instructions to someone he called Wingy and slammed the receiver down. There was a brief pause while he processed whatever had just transpired. Then he turned to us. "Welcome back, Danny. I just know you've got an interesting story for us."

So I went over it again. When I got to the part about the misidentification of the body in Crowley's float house, he gave a sympathetic look to Louise, but made no comment. And then the crucial bit, the part that I hadn't told Louise yet. "And I know why Billy was killed." Tommy looked up, and Louise uncrossed her legs and leaned forward. "Crowley made an offhand comment that didn't register with me right away. When I was bobbing around in the water, my mind went off on its own and made a connection that I've been trying to make for weeks. Crowley casually mentioned that when the rabbits died, they went into convulsions. Christine had reminded me at the party that that's how Billy's cat had died, the day he disappeared."

Louise frowned. "But wasn't the cat back in Sointula? It was nowhere near the West Vancouver lab."

"Yeah, but it had access to one of the mutant fish, Igor. When Igor's picture showed up in the DFO database, I could see that something had chewed on its tail since I had last seen it. I knew that when Billy got home from the pub, the night before he left for Vancouver, he was definitely not sober. I figure, he forgot to put Igor in the freezer. The cat was hungry, chewed off a piece of Igor's tail, and paid the price for it. Billy probably noticed in the morning that the cat had chewed on Igor, but he wouldn't have thought anything of it."

"I'm starting to put this together," Tommy said. "But how did Billy know his cat had died?"

"Christine left him a message," I said. "When Billy found out his cat had died, he put two and two together, and realized that these fish, which DFO had released into the wild, were poisonous. So when he got to the lab, he raised shit."

"But not right away," I said. "Crowley saw him when he first arrived at the lab, but didn't say anything about Billy making wild accusations.

I figure that after Crowley gives him the brush-off, Billy gets in his car and carries on to Vancouver. At some point, he checks his messages, realizes what exactly is going on, and drives back to the lab. Crowley is gone by this time, but Griffith is there. Billy confronts him, and tells him what kind of a DFO asshole he is, and what he's going to do about it. Griffith can see the project, his career, his entire life going up in smoke. So he kills Billy to keep him quiet."

"That's a lot of suppositions, Danny," Louise said thoughtfully. "Logical, yeah. But what kind of physical evidence is there? We're going to need something if we're going to tie this to Griffith."

"That could be difficult," I conceded. "We have a shortage of bodies. I don't think we're going to find Billy after eight years. Les Jameson was the next to die and the Coast Guard couldn't find him after searching for two weeks. Then, supposedly Crowley was killed but it was really one of the Farmers, and then Crowley does get killed a month later, but we don't have either of those bodies. All we've got is Reginald Sanderson, who died of natural causes in a slightly unnatural way."

Tommy and Louise analyzed and debated and reviewed options with considerable energy. I, on the other hand, was fading fast. The adrenaline had burned off long ago and I was forcing myself to concentrate.

"What a fuckin' horror show," Tommy said, drumming his fingers on his desk. "I can't even imagine what the charges should be if we do nail the bastard. Experimenting with undue care and attention? Leaving the scene of an environmental disaster?"

Louise looked at me. "We'll get him, Danny. We've come too far to let him slip off the hook. But right now I've got to get word back to Bella Bella to avoid eating any sockeye. They might have caught some of those normal-looking males. I'll phone Rose Wilson at the health center. She'll pass the word."

"Jesus, you're right." I was jolted out of my fatigue. "Tell them not to eat any sockeye—canned, smoked, frozen, or fresh."

"It'll be tough. Louise said. "Sockeye is such a major part of their diet."

"Well, tell them to feed a bit to a cat first. That's how people used to test clams for red tide."

"It seems a bit hard on cats."

"It's their evolutionary niche."

"Bit of a comedown from being worshipped by the Egyptians." Tommy said. "But let's concentrate on what we're going to do next."

I was drained, physically and mentally, and probably not at my strategic best. But I was clear about one thing: "It's time to take this to Griffith. He's been operating in the shadows for too long, pulling the strings of his various puppets, keeping his hands clean. Now it's him and us, no one to cover for him, and that's a completely different ball game than he's used to."

"So what's your plan?" Louise asked.

"Have you got the resources to put a tail on him? Twenty-four-seven, without him knowing it?"

Louise deferred to Tommy. "I suppose we could pull something together."

"All right. It occurred to me that Griffith might not know Crowley is dead. When Sanderson phoned him from the lab, he just said he'd got both of us: no mention of blasting Crowley. And if he didn't phone again from the boat, then Griffith has no idea Crowley is dead. I'm going to go and see Griffith. Tell him we've got Crowley and he's threatening to roll over on Griffith. Would Mr. Griffith like to be of assistance to us, say, in the death of Billy Bradley?"

"But he's not going to confess to killing Billy," Louise said.

"Yeah, but if he tries to pin it on Crowley, he might let something slip. At the very least, we'll scare him and he might do something stupid." There was not a single cheer of congratulations or shout of acclamation. "Look guys, it's all we've got. Apply a stimulus and observe the results."

Finally, Louise shrugged. "Okay, set up a meeting. You can wear a wire. And Jerome goes with you."

"I'll meet him in his office. He's not going to kill me on DFO premises. It's against policy."

"Jerome goes with you. Two of them." I started to protest, but Louise was adamant. "They can wait outside his office, but they'll be within fifty feet of you. That's the way it's going to be."

And that's the way it was. I phoned DFO and was put through to Griffith's secretary. He was in the building that morning but was unavailable until after lunch. "And who is this please?"

"Torchie LaFlame. Tell him I've had my last operation and now we can be together." I hung up. "I'll see him right after lunch."

"Good timing," Tommy said. "It gives me a chance to organize the surveillance."

I stood up and tried to ignore the concern on Louise's face.

"Are you ready for this, Danny? You've had kind of a rough night."

"I was born ready. However, I do have time for a nap."

Two hours later, we collected an additional Jerome and headed for DFO HQ. I sat in the backseat and practiced deep breathing. I got Jerome to stop and grab a large coffee for me. By the time we got to the DFO building, I'd almost forgotten that I'd spent much of the previous night floundering around in the Strait of Georgia instead of snoozing.

We took the elevator to the twelfth floor and walked down the hall to Griffith's office suite. When we entered, his secretary looked at us from the other side of the counter, and I inquired politely as to whether or not Mr. Griffith was in.

"Yes, he's in, but I'm afraid you don't have an appointment. You can't see him without an appointment. Regulations."

"People are more important than regulations. It's time everyone in this building realized that." I opened the gate in the counter and started down the hall to Fleming's office. The secretary was making alarmed noises but she stopped when Jerome flashed their badges.

I didn't knock. I entered Griffith's office, where he was sitting at his desk, no papers in front of him, just sitting there looking serious and important.

"Mr. Swanson, I'm afraid I can't talk to you now. I'm waiting for a very important call."

"Reginald Sanderson won't be reporting in."

He considered this. "That's unfortunate."

"Especially for him. Fleming, may I call you Flem? I've taken a real interest in your career lately. Why, just last night I was having a chat with your old colleague, Alistair Crowley. You know of course that he survived his encounters, first with Jerry Mathias, and last night with poor Reggie. Crowley was able to fill me in on many of your little secrets. I also have his computer files and an amusing video that he shot of you at the lab, doing deceptive things with dead rabbits. How do you think the Minister will react to your unorthodox experiments?"

"You amuse me, Mr. Swanson. But there are two things that insulate me from your juvenile threats: important friends and a very good pension."

"Fleming, you're just going through the motions. Crowley is ready to deal with us. We already know everything about Project Chimera. But there's one little matter that you could help us with. In 1986, a person named Billy Bradley showed up at the lab with one of your mutant sockeye, and then disappeared. Crowley is hinting that you killed him."

"Crowley is an insubordinate peon! He wasn't there that night." He stopped suddenly.

"And you know that because you were?"

"I need to talk to Crowley."

"That would be difficult." I didn't tell him why.

"If you won't let me talk to Crowley, you need to give him a message. Tell him there's been an administrative change. Operational control has been delegated upwards."

"That sounds to me like you're copping out."

He didn't reply and I didn't relent. "We know you faked the results of the toxicity test. You allowed poisonous sockeye to be released into the wild. I wonder how many people have died from eating them." There was still no response. I tilted my head back and stared at him. He sat motionless with his hands flat on the desk in front of him. He was still staring at them when I left. The two Jeromes followed me out and escorted me back to the car.

I phoned Louise. "You get that?"

"He didn't give much away."

"Yeah, but he's worried. He wants to talk to Crowley."

She replied, "Let him worry. The more the better. Tommy's got him covered like a blanket. If he moves, we'll know where, when, and how."

"So now we wait."

"Right."

"Shall we wait at my place or yours?"

"I don't want to come between you and Jerome," she said. "But I'll meet you for a drink after work. Lounge of the Hotel Georgia." She hung up.

I turned to Jerome. "We've got some time to kill. What do you want to do?"

"Let's not go for sushi," one of them said petulantly.

Before I could make a clever reply, Tommy's voice came over the radio. "He's on the move. In a cab, south on Burrard. I'll get the drop-off."

Twenty-four

I hoped that Griffith had finally cracked. We had scared him out of the office and into the field. Now we'd see how he would handle himself in the real world. Tommy came back on the radio. "He's going to the airport, south terminal."

I grabbed the mike. "He's heading for Bella Bella. We need to beat him there. You guys got air support?"

Louise came on. "The next flight will only get him to Port Hardy this evening. He'll have to overnight and then catch the next Bella Bella flight at eleven tomorrow morning. Our pilot is on standby and we can take off in an hour.

"Okay. I'll see you there. We can wait until Griffith checks in, just to confirm my instinct is right, and then we'll take off and beat him up there."

"Danny, why is he going to Bella Bella?"

I didn't have to think. It was as if Griffith had suddenly lost his cloak of bureaucratic invisibility and I could see him clearly for the first time. "They've destroyed most of the physical evidence from Project Chimera, and most of the human players are dead. There's one last thing that could link him to a crime, not the murders, but the release of poisonous fish into the environment."

There was a pause while Louise engaged in the same logical exercise that I had just completed. She didn't break a sweat. "Crowley had been helping Rose Wilson update and digitize the Heiltsuk health records. Why? He wasn't exactly a public service kind of guy."

"You've got it. Part of Crowley's job, aside from monitoring all the field data, was to see if local consumers were suffering any health effects from the mutant fish. They played this charade in the name of responsibility, even though Griffith and Crowley both knew these fish could kill people."

I could hear the disbelief in her voice. "And Griffith is worried that Crowley found evidence in the Heiltsuk health center records that people were being affected. He's going to destroy those records."

"Yes, and now's our chance to get him. He's out of the big corner office and running around with no protective cover."

"I'm going to phone Rose Wilson and tell her we'll need to meet with her. She'll want to know why we want to poke around in her records."

"Okay. See you at the airport."

The RCMP transportation budget had obviously been cut. I was expecting a sleek and shiny jet but all they had was a single-engine prop job with RCMP markings: sort of a semi-stealth Cessna. However, the pilot wore the approved *Top Gun* shades, which enabled him to get us to Bella Bella without incident.

Louise had arranged to meet Rose Wilson first thing in the morning. There was nothing for us to do except retire to Louise's cozy little house and make love by the light of the fire. In the morning, we sipped coffee and gazed appreciatively at each other. Finally, Louise stood up and moved behind me to nuzzle my neck, which I found extremely pleasant.

"It's time to go and meet Rose."

"She's going to want an explanation of the eat-no-sockeye edict. Also, why Griffith wants access to her records, and why she can't let him anywhere near them. I think we have to tell her pretty much the whole story."

Louise nodded. "You're right. And Rose is well versed in confidentiality concerns, so she won't blab anything she doesn't have to."

We met Rose in her office at the health center. She greeted us warmly, almost like family. I think Rose considered most people to be sort of family. That made her reaction to the story all the more painful to me. She tried to hide her disappointment, but I knew I'd failed her. We all had. Rose had expected me, us, DFO, to protect, 'her people' and we hadn't. Finally, she raised her eyes and spoke quietly. "Eight months ago my nephew, Sammy, died after experiencing convulsions. We thought it was meningitis. I can remember similar cases over the last few years. You're telling me they died because DFO was experimenting with genetically altered sockeye?"

"Crowley and Griffith were operating on their own, Rose. Their work wasn't sanctioned." Somehow that didn't make me feel any better.

"And this Fleming Griffith is coming here? To destroy some of my files?"

Louise answered. "He'll be coming off the eleven-thirty flight. He'll want to meet you."

"And I want to meet him. I definitely want to meet him."

"If you could stall him, it would help," I said. "Tell him the building is closed for cleaning or something. We'll be watching him and he might lead us to other evidence, physical evidence that would tie him to the sockeye experiment."

Rose considered this. "There's a potlatch this weekend. All my staff are involved in the preparations. I'll tell him he can't have access to the files until Monday."

Louise stood and placed her hand on Rose's shoulder. After a while she said, "I'm sorry, Rose. I'm sorry we didn't catch on to this earlier. But we're closing in on Griffith now. He's got four days to stew over this. He'll do something stupid and we'll be there to nail him."

Rose didn't say anything and after a bit we left. I had to stay out of sight so Griffith wouldn't spot me. I went back to Louise's house, while she went to alert her constables and arrange their coordination with Tommy's two surveillance guys who would be on the plane with Griffith.

I sat in Louise's kitchen and stared out over the water. The water taxi came around the corner from Shearwater. A herring skiff ran across to the other side of the bay and stopped. *Checking a crab trap*, I thought.

Two seine boats made a stately transect from south to north and exited out into Seaforth Channel. *Heading home to Rupert,* I thought. *How very normal. There's no way those waters could be harboring mutant sockeye produced by mad scientists working in secret. Poisonous mutant sockeye that kill people.*

When I'd almost convinced myself that it was all a bad dream, I turned my thoughts toward Fleming Griffith. In spite of the confident façade I was displaying for Tommy and Louise, doubts were creeping in about our ability to nail him. Best-case scenario: we'd find evidence in the records that people had died from unexplained causes. Could we link the deaths to eating the sockeye? Probably not. When Griffith got access to the files, he would probably try to destroy them. So what? Shredding files wasn't in the Criminal Code of Canada. We could probably damage his career. He'd be forced to retire and live on his pension. That would show him!

My growing depression was alleviated somewhat when Louise walked in bearing dinner in a box marked "pizza." The labeling was commendably accurate. As we engaged in slice allocation, Louise brought me up to speed. Griffith had pressed Rose for access to the files but had been refused. He was now wandering around town looking angry and out of place.

"What now?" I asked.

"He'll probably go over to Shearwater to stay in the hotel. It occurred to us he might try to take a boat to one of their locations we haven't discovered yet. We left a couple of bait skiffs at the wharf. They've got hidden transmitters so he'll be easy to follow."

"How's Rose?"

"She's hard to read. She spent a long time talking to Griffith, pretending she didn't know why he wanted access to the files. He made up a story about looking for cases of red tide poisoning."

"I hope you're right about her being discreet," I said. "If she told anyone what Griffith had done, he'd probably be dead by morning. We wouldn't want that. Would we?"

"Of course not. I don't want to have to arrest anyone for doing my job."

"Doing your job?"

"Justice, Danny. Bringing Griffith to justice. And that's my job and no one else's." She went to the fridge and pulled out a bottle of Riesling. For the next half hour, we interspersed sips of wine with bouts of serious nuzzling. Then the phone rang. Louise answered it and listened for a second before swearing quietly. She slumped back into her chair.

"That was Rose. Griffith is at her place and he's taken ill. They're moving him to the clinic."

I was shocked. This wasn't part of our game plan. I thought for a moment. "You go to the clinic and check on Griffith. I'm going to talk to Rose. Where's her house?"

Her answer was muffled by her hands covering her face. "Two houses down from the school. Opposite side of the street."

I left in a hurry. When I got to Rose's house, she was sitting placidly on her porch. I took a second chair and sat down beside her. "What happened, Rose?"

"Mr. Griffith is a guest in our village. I did the necessary thing and invited him to supper. I meant to take a spring salmon out of the freezer, but I must have made a mistake and unthawed a sockeye."

I sat for a while, trying to think of the proper words. "Rose . . ." Nothing came to me, so I left. I tried really hard to ignore the dead cat next to the stairs.

I got to the clinic quickly and was shown to Griffith's room. A nurse and a doctor were paying more attention to him than he deserved. Louise observed from a corner by the window. The doctor issued some orders to the nurse, along the lines of "I don't know what the hell he's got but watch him closely," and he left.

Griffith looked awful, which cheered me immensely. His usual pallor had taken on a grayish tinge. He was sweating and panting and on the verge of panic. I waited until the nurse had left. "Flem, buddy, I think I know what's ailing you. I think you know too."

No response.

"Flem, buddy, does the phrase chickens come home to roost have any meaning to you?" No response except for quicker breathing and dilated pupils.

"Flem, buddy-oh, several people, we don't know how many, have died from this and it's entirely and completely and absolutely your fault. Any thoughts on that?"

No response but moans and momentary spasms.

I leaned in over him. "Crowley's got the antidote."

His eyes focused on me. I offered him the deal, which was as honorable as his entire career had been. "Tell me what happened to Billy Bradley, and I'll try to hook you up with Crowley." I didn't care if God wouldn't forgive me. I hoped my Mom would, but she didn't know.

Crowley groaned and grabbed one twitching arm with the other. He spoke with difficulty, jaws and lips not entirely obeying his commands. "Why do you care about him? He was a fisherman. He pushed his way into the lab and ranted and raved about some dead cat. He threatened to disrupt an experiment that would have put us at the cutting edge of genetic manipulation. We could have dedicated the Fraser River to a better use."

"You asshole! Do you think anyone cares about your stupid experiments? Billy Bradley wasn't an experiment. He was part of our lives. What the fuck did you do to him?"

"I was using an electroshocker on some large spring salmon. Your friend lunged at me. The shocker contacted his chest. He was dead. Not my fault. Now tell Crowley to phone me. I need help."

"I'll try to pass on the message. One other thing—who authorized the second mandate?" But it was too late. He had slipped into unconsciousness. I looked at Louise and we walked out together.

"Sweetie," I squeezed her hand. "Rose inadvertently fed one of the mutant salmon to Griffith. Do you think that's a cause for concern?"

She stiffened. I looked away from her. She spoke in a slightly distant voice. "Bit of a species mix-up. Why would the RCMP be concerned?"

"Didn't think so."

Six hours later, Griffith ceased to exist. I waited until the morning and then phoned Mark. He was remarkably unemotional. "I've sort of known for a while what happened to Billy. But it's good to know the details, I guess. I'll tell Christine and Fergie." A pause. "You okay?"

"Better than I've been for a hell of a long time."

"I think we all are. Friday, the Princeton, 6:00 PM. We'll all be there."

"Roger, skip."

Twenty-five

The gathering at the Princeton was quiet at first, but gained volume as everyone became more comfortable with the story.

"How did that cocksucker look at the end?" Fergie wanted to know. "Suffering?"

"He was struggling for breath," I said. "Twitching, starting serious convulsions. And maybe starting to realize the phone call from Crowley wasn't coming." I examined my guilt quotient and discovered it had increased not one bit. "I didn't stay until the end but Griffith was starting to look extremely un-ministerial."

"Poor Billy," Christine said. "He lacked bureaucratese. If he'd had Igor in a proper fish carrying case, and maybe offered to fill out a form, he'd be with us now."

Mark spoke very seriously. "It must be hard on Rose Wilson, knowing that she accidentally poisoned Griffith." He looked at Louise, who responded impassively.

"Rose is coping very well. Obviously there will be no repercussions for what was clearly an accident."

I tried to save Louise from any further obfuscation. "I'm sure we could have nailed Griffith eventually." I paused to see if my nose was growing. "But this outcome saved everyone a lot of trouble. I think Billy would be satisfied."

Fergie asked, "What happened to Billy's body?"

I filled him in on the details. Bodies can be difficult to dispose of, but not if you have access to two thousand pounds of anchors and four thousand feet of water. The circumspect waters of Burrard Inlet, conveniently available from the DFO dock with a DFO workboat, became Billy's final resting place. His beloved Camaro was driven across the Patullo Bridge to the less than genteel district of Queensborough. Abandoned on a back street in the land of not-fully-licensed auto wreckers, it quickly disappeared. Thus ended the not unlamented life of our shipmate and dear friend, William George Bradley.

They all seemed to share my sense of satisfaction at the outcome. It wasn't textbook justice, but it was undeniably justice. After some desultory conversation and promises to get together soon, the crew began to disperse.

Louise and I were left alone. She spoke in a contemplative voice.

"Relationships are strange, aren't they? You can't really plan them, although everybody tries to. But they do need consideration. What do you think, Danny? How much thought should you put into a relationship, as opposed to just letting it develop?"

I looked around nervously. There was going to be some emotional heavy lifting here, and I hadn't had any nourishment for quite some time.

"Well, you certainly can't force a relationship. It's kind of like juggling: if you think about it too much, or try to analyze what you're doing, you'll drop all your balls. I guess a relationship is something that you should, you know, just sort of do."

"Hmm, the running shoe philosophy of human relationships. How interesting. Fortunately, we're not having a relationship. We're just having casual sex. Sort of just doing it, you might say."

"Louise, I don't do casual sex. Anymore. At all. Sex is important, um, meaningful, you know?"

"Danny, I want to get to know you."

"I guess I've always sort of mistrusted anyone silly enough to be interested in me. But you seem to have very good judgement."

She placed her hand over mine. "Trust me."

Louise took me to meet her parents. She'd already met them, of course, but they hadn't yet had the pleasure of my company. Fortunately, for them, they lived in Hope.

My vehicle was in Ottawa and Louise's was in Bella Bella, so we were vehicleless. Vancouver to Hope would have been a hell of a taxi fare, so we took the train.

It felt good to sit on the train. It was going where we wanted to go with absolutely no effort on our part. For the first time in quite a while, I felt free of fraughtness. As the train followed the Fraser River more or less east, I regarded my companion and felt more or less in love.

Louise squeezed my hand and pointed to a bunch of kids angling from the bank of the river. Time-honoured childhood pursuits, fishing for dreams and catching memories.

I thought about the river and the fish. The salmon that pulsed up the Fraser like an annual heartbeat had sustained humans for eons. Native fishermen had fed body and soul. Commercial fishermen had built lives and raised families. Sports fishermen had fed their inexplicable but undeniable need to hook and land fish. But none of them, dream-dazzled child, time-drenched Native elder, commercial pragmatist, or Gore-Tex-clad idealist, had even an inkling that this miraculous gift had almost been stolen. Louise and I and our steadfast friends had defeated the river killers.

Chaos was stayed. The center had held.

I felt good.

Acknowledgments

Many of the sayings in this book I have "borrowed" from friends of mine. The soliloquy on number eight trolling wire came from Laurie Belveal, an old shipmate who has now crossed the bar. The saying about not going ahead too fast but never going backwards came from my longest-serving skipper, Bob Koskela. The dissertation on the sociological similarities between the Scots and the West Coast Native culture came from Yvon Geisinghaus, an old friend from Alert Bay.

Finally, I would like to thank my friend Shane Field, who was the first non-Bruce Burrowsoid to read and comment on the book; Ruth Linka from TouchWood Editions who phoned one day and said she liked the book; and my editor, Linda Richards, who made me work much too hard.

Any errors in the book are obviously mine, although I'll try to pass them off as the literary license of a creative mind.

With years spent working as a fisherman, commercial diver, and most recently, an at-sea observer, **BRUCE BURROWS** is a true man of the sea. During his time as a fisherman, he wrote a weekly column called "Channel 78, Eh" about fishing on the West Coast. His collected column can be found in *Blood on the Decks, Scales on the Rails* (1992). Bruce lives on a small island off the northeast coast of Vancouver Island. *The River Killers* is his first novel.

A detail of one of Kayak Bill's paintings appears on the cover of this book. **BILL DAVIDSON**, known as Kayak Bill, was born in 1948 and grew up in a Calgary orphanage. He found escape in the mountains and cliffs around Banff. Bill became a legendary climber, but gravity sets limits with harsh consequences. Around 1980 he escaped to the inlets and passageways of the British Columbia coast. He became a self sufficient hunter gather and self taught painter. In 2004, while living on the isolated Goose Islands, he escaped altogether and forever. Facebook.com/pages/Kayak-Bill-Prints

REBEKAH PARLEE's drawing of the *Maple Leaf C* appears on page ii. She was born in 1975 and raised in Jennis Bay, hand logging and fishing. She began selling her art at the age of fifteen, and in 1997, began a four-year course at the Emily Carr Institute of Art and Design, supporting herself by skippering a prawn boat for part of the year. In 2001, she moved to Sointula. artifexus.com